"This way," Taj called, turning away from the maddened swarm. Jack followed the man for a few steps before he realized the young Afghani was not with them.

"Taj!" Jack cried.

The man turned, saw the young Afghani. "Borak!" he cried. "Follow us."

But the young man shook his head. "I will stop them."

"No!"

The Afghani turned his back on them, lowered the muzzle of the Uzi he drew from his sash, naively fired. The bullets chewed through the squirming, squealing tide without effect. The brown flow swarmed around the young man even as he emptied the magazine into the panicked horde. The rats nipped at his sandals, clawed at his legs. The young man howled and dropped the useless weapon. Reaching into his loose shirt, he pulled out an old, Soviet-made grenade.

"Not in here!" Taj screamed.

But the boy was too frightened to hear him. As the rats swarmed over him, forcing the boy to the ground, he popped the pin on the grenade.

Without a word, Taj and Jack ran away from the rats, the impending explosion. Jack figured on a ten-second fuse and counted down in his mind.

Eight . . . Seven . . . Six . . .

"Get ready to hit the ground!" Jack cried.

Five . . . Four . . . Three . . .

"Down!"

24 DECLASSIFIED Books

OPERATION HELL GATE

Coming Soon
VETO POWER
TROJAN HORSE

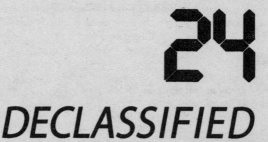

24

DECLASSIFIED

OPERATION
HELL GATE

MARC CERASINI

Based on the series by Joel Surnow & Robert Cochran

HarperEntertainment
An Imprint of HarperCollinsPublishers

This is a work of fiction. Names, characters, places, and incidents are products of the author's imagination or are used fictitiously and are not to be construed as real. Any resemblance to actual events, locales, organizations, or persons, living or dead, is entirely coincidental.

HARPERENTERTAINMENT
An Imprint of HarperCollins*Publishers*
10 East 53rd Street
New York, New York 10022-5299

ISBN-13: 978-0-06-084224-6
ISBN-10: 0-06-084224-5

First HarperEntertainment paperback printing: October 2005

Printed in the United States of America

Visit HarperEntertainment on the World Wide Web at www.harpercollins.com.

10 9 8 7 6 5 4 3 2 1

This novel is dedicated to the men and women on the front lines, at home and abroad, who fight the war against terror every day.

ACKNOWLEDGMENTS

The author would like to thank Hope Innelli and Josh Behar of HarperCollins for their vision, guidance, and support. Thanks also to Virginia King of 20th Century Fox for her continued encouragement.

Very special acknowledgment to the groundbreaking, Emmy Award-winning "24" creators Joel Surnow and Robert Cochran, and to their talented writing team. And especially to Keifer Sutherland for bringing the memorable character of Jack Bauer to life.

Thanks to my literary agent, John Talbot, for his ongoing support. And a very personal thank you to my wife, Alice Alfonsi. A guy couldn't ask for a better partner—in writing or in life.

People who spent their lives in bureaucracies were typically afraid of breaking rules. That was a sure way to get fired, and it cowed people to think of tossing their careers away. But . . . James Greer had given him all the guidance he needed: *Do what you think is right.*

—TOM CLANCY
Clear and Present Danger

Let us therefore animate and encourage each other, and show the whole world that a Freeman, contending for liberty on his own ground, is superior to any slavish mercenary on earth.

—GEORGE WASHINGTON
General Orders, Headquarters,
New York, July 2, 1776

Nothing in life is so exhilarating as to be shot at without result.

—SIR WINSTON CHURCHILL
The Malakand Field Force

24

DECLASSIFIED

OPERATION
HELL GATE

After the 1993 World Trade Center attack, a division of the Central Intelligence Agency established a domestic unit tasked with protecting America from the threat of terrorism. Headquartered in Washington, D.C., the Counter Terrorist Unit established field offices in several American cities. From it inception, CTU faced hostility and skepticism from other Federal law enforcement agencies. Despite bureaucratic resistance, within a few years CTU had become a major force. After the war against terror began, a number of early CTU missions were declassified. The following is one of them . . .

PROLOGUE

A necessary evil.

That's the way Jack Bauer rationalized the debriefing. The mission was over, the field work ended, the split-second, life-and-death decisions made. Now the bureaucratic mind needed its cushion of explanations, its round of second-guessing. The fact that it was Richard Walsh conducting the after-action interview made it significantly more bearable.

Where the typical middle manager was mired in keystrokes, speakerphones, and PDF attachments, hobbled by continual rounds of mind-numbing review meetings, Walsh was ex–Army Special Forces and a former field agent who'd bellied up to a desk but never lost his edge. Governed not by cover-your-ass double-talk but conviction and ethics, he was the sort of rare good man who made Jack feel his efforts were worthy.

"Take a seat, Special Agent Bauer."

Walsh had flown in this morning from D.C. He sat behind the conference table next to a portable tape recorder and two microphones. The square block of monitors in the center of the table were black, which meant that all surveillance and recording equipment in this room had been deactivated. What Jack was about to say was sensitive enough to be deemed highly classified. Walsh and his superiors wanted sole control of any recordings—and, ideally, any interpretations of said recordings.

Jack entered the briefing room and closed the door. Immediately the outer office sounds of computers, phones, voices, fax machines, and footsteps were muted by the soundproof grates on the walls and ceiling. Jack sat at the opposite side of the table from Walsh, but he didn't lean back. He didn't relax.

Walsh slid one of the mikes across to him, then opened a blue plastic folder and rested his arms on the table. Tall and powerfully built, he wore a gray suit that seemed snug at the shoulders, the red striped silk tie knotted too tightly under a prominent Adam's apple. Walsh's manner was remote, calm and professional, his walrus mustache a throwback to ghosts of law enforcers past.

For a long moment, Walsh silently scanned the files with sharp blue eyes that, in Jack's experience, missed nothing. Though he was in his late forties, the man's face appeared older. Creased by age and anxiety, it remained characteristically expressionless under sandy-brown hair sprinkled with gray. Superficially, Walsh had the innocuous look and manner of a government bureaucrat, college professor, or youth counselor more than an operative in America's newest anti-terrorist organization. But the reality was Richard Walsh had been all of those things—and the closest thing to a mentor Jack had ever known.

Walsh had been the one to bring Jack into intelligence work in the first place: first through a third-party invitation to join the Army's elite Delta Force, later as a recruit in this newly created and still controversial Counter Terrorist Unit. Jack had long suspected CTU owed its existence to Richard Walsh's vision, though the origins of the organization, a domestic unit within a division of the Central Intelligence Agency, were highly classified.

There were those at CTU who thought Jack Bauer even physically resembled Walsh—minus the arched eyebrows, bushy mustache, and thirteen extra years of hard-earned experience. The similarities were there. Both had the same sandy-blond hair and unsettling gazes. On the other hand, Richard Walsh lacked Jack Bauer's outlaw tattoos—a few gained in undercover work; most part of Jack's personal roadmap. And Bauer lacked Walsh's practical patience and easy diplomacy.

Though not conspicuously charismatic, Walsh exerted a stalwart moral authority that manifested powerful sway in D.C., where his opinions and expertise were respected on both sides of the political aisle. Walsh was no political animal, but he'd spent enough time inside academia and the Beltway to develop dexterity in greasing the bureaucratic wheels when necessary.

Jack, by contrast, had never read a business book in his life or lay awake at night contemplating personal techniques for managing up. Yet he'd developed a solid reputation as an effective, galvanizing leader who employed the kind of under-fire problem solving that defined a Special Forces officer. Some of Walsh's higher-ups at Division, however, worried that he was a loose cannon—and this latest mission hadn't dissuaded them from that notion.

"Let's go," said Walsh without preamble. He activated the tape recorder. "Special Agent Richard Walsh, Administrative Director, CTU, Los Angeles, debriefing Jack Bauer, Special Agent in Charge of CTU, Los Angeles."

Jack leaned forward, spoke clearly into the microphone. "On June 3, CTU's Los Angeles office received an anonymous tip through a phone call to our public phone line. The caller, a male, warned us of what he believed was an imminent plot to shoot down a cargo plane as it approached Los Angeles International Airport.

"This phone call, a recording and transcript of which is attached to File 1189 in Kernel 19A of CTU's intelligence database, was both detailed and specific, citing the time, date, and location of the attack. I immediately issued an alert—"

"Almeida stated there was a thirty-minute lag between the call and the alert in his debriefing."

"Ryan Chappelle ordered Jamey Farrell to put a recording of the call through a voice stress analyzer in an attempt to determine the veracity of the caller."

"The result of the analysis?"

"Inconclusive at the time. I determined on my own authority that the threat was credible enough and I took appropriate action. A Counter Terrorist Unit Special Assault Team was dispatched to LAX under my command. It appeared we arrived just in time to prevent a potential disaster . . ."

The white airport maintenance van swerved off the pavement, onto the scrub grass that lined the black asphalt. The service road ran parallel to the busy East Imperial Highway, less than half a mile away. Dust billowed behind their vehicle and hung in the arid, Southern California air.

In the passenger seat, Jack Bauer tensed. The brown cloud was large enough to give away their presence to the terrorists, but nothing could be done about that now. If the tipster was correct, time had already run out.

"I see another maintenance van near runway seven," said Jack. "Vehicle identification tag 1178 Charlie-Victor."

Behind the wheel, Tony Almeida squinted against the yellow glare of the morning sun. Tony was Jack's junior by seven years. Latino, originally from Chicago, he was a single ex-Marine with advanced degrees in computer science. Average height, muscular build, black hair worn short, and a soul patch beneath his lower lip. On paper Almeida looked good—Scout-Sniper School and Surveillance and Target Acquisition Platoon School. But Jack hadn't seen the man in the field enough to trust him completely.

"I count two men inside," Almeida said quietly, "both wearing maintenance uniforms."

Jack was also clad in airport maintenance overalls. His black combat chukkas, however, were standard-issue military. As he continued to catalog the flat featureless landscape through binoculars—gray concrete runways, black asphalt service roads, brown grass—Bauer's headset crackled.

"1178 Charlie-Victor is an authorized repair," Agent Costigan announced from the van's cargo bay.

"Roger that," Jack replied.

Gina Costigan waited for Bauer to relay more information. She was in her late twenties and, like Jack, married with one daughter. Former LAPD Special Weapons and Tactics, she'd been recruited by Walsh as well. She was presently squeezed into the windowless space in the back of the van with four large men. She could see nothing. Like her, all were clad in bulky assault gear—black Kevlar helmets and body armor harnesses, response belts, holsters, weapons, and chukkas. But unlike the men, Gina, her face pinched with tension and beaded with perspiration, balanced a laptop computer on her knees. Beneath her straight brown bangs, her green eyes never left the monitor screen. Across its flat surface were displayed the international airport's daily maintenance schedule and flight manifests, including arrival times and departures—even scheduled deliveries by outside vendors. The data scrolled in an array of display boxes. Gina's quick glance scanned each in turn, evaluating every fragment of information.

"I've got another vehicle, two o'clock, near the concrete power shed," said Jack, increasing the magnification on the binoculars. "It's a black Ford Explorer with a valid LAX security sticker on the inside front window." Jack carefully read out the license plate number, already certain they'd located their target.

When she replied, Agent Costigan could not hide the excitement in her voice. "That vehicle was reported stolen from a driveway on Essex Street in Palmdale two nights ago."

Jack dropped the binoculars onto the seat next to him, drew the SigSauer P228 from its shoulder holster under the airport coveralls. He checked the magazine and chambered an extra bullet, bringing the ammo capacity to the maximum thirteen rounds. Then he spoke into the headset.

"Tactical Team Two, are you with us? Over."

From somewhere behind them, a voice responded. "With you, Team One."

"I want you to move in now. Follow our coordinates. What is your estimated time of arrival?"

"EST less than two minutes, sir."

Jack cursed. "Too long."

"If we brought a parade with us, we would have attracted attention," Tony reminded him.

Agent Chet Blackburn, the assault team leader, stuck his helmeted head into the cab. "Maybe we should have used an assault chopper."

Jack glanced at Blackburn, looked away. "We couldn't risk bringing a chopper into the airport. Too much air traffic."

"I see three men on the ground. There's another inside the vehicle." Tony's voice was flat, but his hands were putting the steering wheel in a choke hold.

"Get this van as close as you can without letting them know we're coming," said Jack.

"Too late," said Tony. "One guy definitely sees us."

Tony slowed the truck. "Listen, Jack. All they're really seeing is a maintenance van coming their way. But trucks like this are all over the airport. Why don't we just roll past the target, circle around, and come up behind them using the power shed for cover. Otherwise we're sure to end up in a firefight."

Jack visualized the maneuver, nodded. "Okay. We'll try it."

Gina Costigan's voice crackled in Jack's headset once again. "Special Agent Bauer?"

"Yes."

"We have an aircraft approaching runway seven from the southwest. It's National Express Cargo Flight

111 out of Austin, Texas. General manifest. Crew of three . . . It's less than two minutes away, sir . . ."

Bauer digested the information as the van steadily approached the suspects. For a long time, no one around the black Explorer moved, though at least one of the occupants was monitoring them. Finally, one of the men turned his back on the maintenance van, went down on one knee, and pointed an unfamiliar object at the sky. Even from a distance, the device appeared ominous—two black tubes on a metal handle. The device must have been unwieldy; the man rested it on his shoulder to steady it.

"That's a weapon," said Jack. "Some new kind of surface-to-air missile. Looks like they're locking onto a target."

Tony sounded doubtful. "You sure?"

"We don't have time to be sure. We have to move *now*. Hit it."

Tony smashed the gas pedal, the van shot forward, and Jack was jolted back in his seat by the abrupt acceleration.

"Lock and load," bellowed Agent Blackburn inside the rocking cargo bay.

Gina Costigan slammed the lid of her laptop, drew the Heckler and Koch UMP out of her Velcro back strap. She slid a twenty-five-round magazine into the state-of-the-art submachine gun, switched the fire selector to semi-automatic, and lowered the visor on her helmet.

Ahead, the man remained on his knees beside the black Explorer, seemingly oblivious to their approach. On his shoulder, the device was still pointed at the cloudless sky, where the silhouette of an aircraft had appeared. Suddenly one of the other men pointed toward the maintenance van and drew a weapon.

"Artillery! Get down!" Bauer warned.

The first shot blew out the windshield and roared through the cargo bay. It punched an exit hole in the rear door large enough to shake it off its hinges. Daylight flooded the cargo area as the steel door broke free.

Outside, the shooter aimed the .357 again—this time at Jack Bauer. Almeida swerved the vehicle onto a concrete access plate. When the front wheel struck, the van bounced high enough for the second shot to slam into the engine block instead of the cab. The van began to bellow steam and smoke as the engine locked. Forward momentum carried the stalled vehicle closer to the suspects, who were all scrambling for cover by now. Another shot blasted through the already-shattered window and into the cargo area. This time Jack heard a meaty thwack, a cry of surprise. Someone had been hit.

Finally the white van rolled to a halt, not fifteen yards from the Ford Explorer.

"Out! Move!" Jack shouted. He popped his own door and rolled into brown desert grass. Engulfed by a cloud of dust, he could barely see the black Explorer. From the shouts and sounds in his headset, Jack knew Blackburn and the rest of the tactical team had burst out of the side and rear doors of the crippled van and laid down suppressing fire.

Finally an opening appeared in the brown haze. Jack spied one of the suspects racing toward the concrete power shed. The other two had dived into the black Explorer with the third man. One was obviously wounded, the other clutched the unfamiliar shoulder-mounted weapon.

"Don't let them leave the area!" Jack cried.

Then he was on his feet. P228 in hand, he pursued the lone runner toward the power shed. A few yards away from the concrete block structure, a wave of hot gases washed over him, followed in a microsecond by an earsplitting roar. Jack was blown off his feet as the Explorer detonated in an orange fireball. The three occupants were engulfed. Completely immolated.

Clothing scorched, ears ringing, Jack stumbled to his feet and lunged forward. He slammed his back against the power shed's metal door—still hot from the blast. Fearing an ambush, he glanced to either side of the square hut, weapon clutched in both hands. Finally Jack dropped to the hard ground and rolled to the rear of the shed.

The man was right where Jack thought he'd be. "Freeze! Put your hands up."

He was maybe twenty-five. Thin torso but muscular arms. He wore black jeans and a leather vest, his oily hair long, a prominent gold front tooth. He was on his knees, one boot removed and clutched in his hand. He appeared ready to smash an object on the ground. He grunted something, but Jack's ears were still vibrating and he couldn't make out the words.

"I said freeze."

The man stared at Jack, then raised the boot. Jack lowered his weapon, crossed the space between them with a leap. He slammed against the man, using his shoulder to bring him down. The boot flew off into the scrub grass. The man struggled to rise, but calmed considerably when Jack placed the muzzle of the P228 against his temple.

"Move and I will kill you."

Vaguely, through the ocean's roar in his ears, Jack heard pounding footsteps. Two of Agent Blackburn's men appeared on either side of the power shed. Intimidating in full body armor and helmets, they trained their weapons at the suspect, who threw up his hands.

"Take him," Jack ordered.

One agent grabbed the man by his vest and hauled him off the ground. The other twisted his arms behind him and snapped plastic cuffs over the wrists. Jack rolled onto his hands and knees and searched the ground. He found what he was looking for within thirty seconds—a black plastic device shaped like a handgun's magazine, featureless except for a USB port and a tiny inscription on the side—Asian script, perhaps Japanese.

Jack knew his hearing had returned when he heard the roar of a Boeing 727. Its wheels skidded onto the tarmac of runway seven, on its fuselage the familiar red and gold National Express banner.

Jack stood and showed the prisoner the device. "What is this?"

The captive smirked, and one of the agents cuffed him with an angry backhand. Jack quickly stepped between the two. "Enough," he said simply. He slipped the mysterious object into his overalls and searched the prisoner's pockets. He found a butterfly knife and a wallet, which contained over a thousand dollars in cash, credit cards issued in several names, and a New York State driver's license with a Brooklyn address. Jack held the picture up next to the captive's head for comparison. They matched.

Jack tried to key his headset, only to discover he'd lost it in the explosion, or the fight. "Raise Tony

Almeida on the horn; tell him to get me all the information he can on a Dante Arete out of New York—"

"Can't raise him, sir," said one of the agents.
"Almeida is off the net."

Leaving the two agents with the prisoner, Jack
jogged around to the front of the power shed. Ahead
he saw the hollow shell of the Explorer, burning too
hot to approach. Black rubber flowed like water from
the melted tires; the human occupants were unrecog-
nizable. Farther ahead, the white maintenance van in
which they'd arrived was still smoking, a bullet hole
the size of a baseball had tattooed the grill.

Two CTU tactical assault vehicles were just rolling
up behind the smoldering white van. A five-man assault team bailed out of each vehicle before they came
to a complete stop. Jack glanced at the digital display
on his watch, surprised that less than one hundred
seconds had elapsed since the first shot was fired.

Jack exhaled with relief when he saw Tony standing
next to the open bay of the disabled van. Agent Blackburn was next to him, his helmet off, leathery brown
skin gleaming with perspiration. Only then did Jack
see the figure sprawled halfway out of the van. One of
the agents had been struck by a stray bullet. Jack recalled the meaty sound, saw that a river of blood had
poured out of the van from the agent's shattered helmet. He raced forward until he was close enough to
stare into Gina Costigan's shocked, dead eyes.

"Son of a bitch—"

Tony turned at the sound of Jack's curse.

"Call for a medivac," Jack told him.

"We did. It will be here in less than a minute. But
it's too late, Jack. She's gone . . ."

Bauer leaned against the wrecked van, its stilled engine hissing and popping as it cooled. He sucked in the desert air as the adrenaline that had pumped through his body finally drained away, leaving him weak, thinking of Gina's husband, her daughter . . . then of Teri and Kim.

"What have you got?" Tony was there, in front of his face.

Jack looked up, eyes bleak. "A prisoner named Dante Arete, and a piece of plastic . . ."

Ninety minutes later, the point team for CTU Los Angeles sat around the table in the briefing room. A brunette with a face of sharp angles and a large, expressive mouth, Nina Myers, Jack's wisp-thin Chief of Staff, brought the group up to speed on the man Jack had apprehended at LAX.

Nina was a machine—dependable, efficient, methodical. Single, in her thirties, she had come to CTU with a reputation as a gifted intelligence analyst and a respected authority on domestic and international counter terrorism policy. She was one of the few people Jack had ever met whose level of intensity and commitment appeared to match his own. Unlike Jack, however, who saw the importance of encouraging and protecting underlings, Nina managed staff by being blunt. Jack rationalized this as "directness" born of earnestness. Maybe he cut her some slack because she was so damned good at what she did, maybe because she physically resembled his wife, Teri. One thing about Nina was certain, however; her frosty blue gaze was as penetrating as his own.

"Seven years ago, Dante Arete, under the street name Apache, was a small time crack cocaine dealer in the Red Hook Projects in Brooklyn," Nina began.

"At the age of eighteen he allegedly killed his first man—a rival drug dealer. Since then, Dante Arete has climbed the ladder in the New York City narcotics scene, and recently he went national. It is alleged that Arete is currently involved in drugs and weapons smuggling, primarily across the Mexican border. He is suspected to have played a role in eleven gang murders in the past five years, as well as the killing of an innocent bodega owner who agreed to testify against one of Arete's lieutenants, a member of the gang Dante founded, the Columbia Street Posse . . ."

"Your source for this information?" Jack asked.

Nina brushed back her black bangs before she faced him. "Primarily the New York Police Department and the Metropolitan Anti-Gang Unit. The DEA has also furnished a profile of Arete's alleged activities over the past five years."

"What does the FBI have to offer?"

"Nothing. They have yet to respond to our request for information on any ongoing investigations."

"Standard operating procedure," Tony observed. "The Federal Bureau of Investigation doesn't share their information, and that goes double for CTU."

Milo Pressman—a systems specialist in his mid-twenties with sensitive features, soft eyes, and an earring—tapped the table with a well-gnawed pencil. Jack found Milo to be competent, though frequently naïve.

"Maybe we should raid their database," he suggested.

Almeida rolled his eyes. "We're supposed to be on the same side."

Jamey Farrell, a petite young Hispanic woman, displayed a printout. Jamey was head programmer. A divorced mother of a young son and an LA native, she had been recruited by Walsh out of Microsoft's Seattle office. Jack found her to be a loyal worker and reliable under pressure. "Using the Federal Aviation Administration airline database, I've found Dante Arete's name listed on the passenger manifest of half-dozen flights to France—Marseilles—over the past two years alone."

Milo Pressman scratched his scraggly goatee and unshaven cheek. "A lot of heroin still comes out of Marseilles. Maybe he's got a French connection."

"I'm thinking more about the illegal arms trade," said Jack. "Arete is already involved in gunrunning—which may mean he also has ties to international terrorism and is looking to expand."

"The weapon his men used? Was it recovered from the explosion?" Milo asked.

Jack shook his head. "Just bits and pieces. Nothing specific to any surface-to-air missile system we're familiar with. All we have is the unidentified object Arete was trying to destroy."

"It's a memory stick," said Milo Pressman. "And you could be right. This memory stick might interface with a targeting system of some kind; there's a port for the transference of data, and there's a chip inside that seems to contain a massive amount of information."

"Like what?" Tony asked.

Milo shrugged. "It's blocked by a security code, but the Cyber Unit is working on it now. They'll come up with answers soon."

"What about the Japanese characters inscribed on the outside?"

"They're Korean, Jack," said Nina. "North Korean, specifically."

A moment of perplexed silence followed.

"We need to put this investigation into high gear, ramp it up," said Jack.

Nina stepped forward. "We got lucky. The Marine Corps agreed to send an officer from their Special Weapons Unit to examine the device. Seems they've seen something like it once before . . ."

Milo perked up. "And the embedded software?"

"Division is dispatching a software security expert to extract the data it contains. She's apparently an expert on the intricacies of Korean software."

"What about Dante Arete?"

"He's giving us the silent treatment," Tony replied. "A real tough guy. Acts like we're not even in the room."

Jack activated one of the monitors in the center of the conference table. Dante Arete sat on the only chair in the interrogation room, gazing straight ahead, his arms cuffed tightly behind his back. Jack studied the image onscreen. "I need a hook to get into this guy. We need to find out what he was doing, and who he's working for."

A three-toned ring interrupted his thoughts. Jack answered the briefing room phone, listened for a moment, then slammed down the receiver.

Nina met his eyes. "What's wrong?"

"There's an FBI agent at the security gate with two federal marshals in tow. They're here to claim custody of Dante Arete."

"They can't do that!" Tony threw up his hands. "We haven't even told the other agencies about this operation yet. How the hell did the FBI find out?"

Jack glanced back at the monitor, then rose. "Tony,

Nina. Intercept our visitors, stall for time. I'm going to talk to Arete right now."

Almeida folded his arms and shook his head. "Come on, Jack. Get real. How long do you think we can stall them?"

Jack stared at Tony, his voice soft steel: "As long as you can." He strode to the door, jerked it open. Ryan Chappelle blocked his path. The Regional Director of CTU locked eyes with Jack, who looked away.

"Hello, Jack . . ."

"Ryan, I've got to go—"

"You've got to stay right here, Special Agent Bauer," Chappelle said evenly. "We're going to sit down together and wait for Special Agent Hensley of the FBI to be escorted in." Chappelle looked over Jack's shoulder. "The rest of you can go back to your stations. Now."

As they filed out, Nina gave Jack a sidelong glance, Tony Almeida couldn't hide his disgust.

"That's okay," said Milo Pressman, glancing at his watch. "I'm off duty as of an hour ago."

Jamey Farrell paused at the door, searched Jack's face for some sign of what to do.

"Get back to work, Jamey," Chappelle commanded, impatient with what he saw as the Loyal Staff act. He'd seen it before where Jack's people were concerned, and he didn't like it. When the petite woman was gone, he closed the door behind her. Then Ryan Chappelle turned to find Jack Bauer in his face.

"You can't let the FBI take Arete away from us." Jack's voice was soft but tight. "At least not until we interrogate him."

"It's out of my hands."

"Ryan, I lost an agent today. She was twenty-eight years old—"

"A tragedy." Ryan turned from Jack, brushed his fingertips along the conference table. "The good news for you is I won't hold you accountable, even though I recommended that we hold off on the action you took until further voice tests could be made on the phone tip."

"There was no time, Ryan. You know that. And you know we paid a high price for Arete. We can just give him up without a fight."

Chappelle sat down, leaned back, and opened his arms. "We're all on the same team, Jack. Think of it as a gesture of interagency cooperation."

Almost imperceptibly, Jack winced. "Cooperation's been a one-way street with the Bureau since day one. You know that, Ryan."

"Maybe this gesture will change things."

But Jack knew letting go of Dante Arete would change nothing. The current Administration had intentionally erected an impenetrable wall between the various governmental law enforcement and intelligence agencies. They were not allowed to share intelligence, even if it involved the same suspects, the same crimes. The CIA had allowed CTU to be created as an experiment in getting around those dangerously constraining walls, but they only seemed to grow higher. These days, interagency cooperation was not only rare, it was illegal. While Jack bristled under the limitations of what he saw as an absurd policy, the pragmatic and ambitious Ryan Chappelle chose to adapt.

Chappelle was the new model for a career bureaucrat. A product of Wharton's MBA program, he'd come up through assistant positions in the Agency; no field work, no military or police training, which made him suspect in Bauer's mind. Post–Cold War Washington had already taken the teeth out of its intelligence communities, making the language of *give-and-take* and *compromise* and *political correctness* the terms of survival in the current Federal system. Now it was breeding a special kind of administrator, more political animal than intelligence agent. Jack worried about the sort of man who floated to the surface in such an ocean. There were men like Walsh, thank God. And then there were men like Chappelle, who paused to factor career advancement—or decline—into every critical decision, regardless of whether the security of the nation was in question.

"Excuse me, gentlemen." The door had opened without a knock. Jason Ridley, Chappelle's young, dapper assistant, escorted FBI Special Agent Frank Hensley into the conference room. With a polite nod, Ridley quickly departed. Chappelle rose to shake the man's hand. Bauer was already standing.

"Special Agent Hensley, your fame precedes you," said Ryan Chappelle. "I received a call from Dennis Spain, Chief of Staff to Senator William Cheever of New York. He mentioned you were coming."

"Senator Cheever has been keeping close tabs on the Arete case," Hensley replied.

"This is CTU Special Agent Jack Bauer. He commanded the assault team that apprehended your man."

Frank Hensley gazed at Bauer through close-set eyes that were so dark blue they were nearly black. Under thick brows and a shock of dark, slicked-back hair, Hensley's sneer appeared to be a permanent fixture on his face. The shape of his jaw, his thin lips, and aquiline nose were all slightly twisted, as if to better accommodate the man's perpetual scowl. As tall as Jack, Hensley was thinner, more compact under a perfectly tailored charcoal-gray suit and spotless white Egyptian cotton shirt, a tie of cornflower blue.

"Special Agent Hensley." Jack offered his hand.

Hensley clenched his hands into tight fists and rested them on his hips. "You're the guy who blew two years of sweat, blood, and hard work."

Jack lowered his arm. "I don't understand."

"I mean I put two years of work—nine months of it undercover—to gather enough evidence to indict Dante Arete. The case was almost made. We were ready to grab him in his Red Hook hangout, along with his associates, his cache of weapons, drugs . . ." Bristling now, Hensley slapped his fist into the palm of his hand. "We had that SOB Arete under constant surveillance. We had wiretaps, electronic surveillance. My partner followed him around for six weeks with a goddamned parabolic amplifier!"

Jack didn't blink. "If that's the case, then how did Arete end up in Los Angeles, pointing an anti-aircraft missile at a cargo plane?"

Instead of answering, Hensley looked away, stared at the closed door for a good twenty seconds. "Two days ago Arete slipped through our net," he said at last. "He murdered my partner and got away. Used a stolen credit card and fake ID to fly to California. The next thing we heard was that you had him . . ."

"I'm sorry about your partner," said Jack.

Hensley nodded. "I heard you lost someone today, too, Special Agent Bauer."

Jack changed the subject. "Tell me again how you heard about Arete's apprehension?"

Hensley smirked, then hid the gesture with a

frown. The micro expression lasted just long enough for Bauer to suspect Hensley was lying, and he and Ryan were being manipulated.

"Arete has a lot of associates here in LA. In Chicago and Detroit, too," Hensley said smoothly. "We put out an APB with the other FBI district offices and got lucky this morning when one of our own undercover agents saw him in South Central. We were ready to pounce—"

"When we got in your way," Jack said, forcing a regretful smile.

"And used too much force for the situation," Hensley added.

"His associates were about to launch a surface-to-air missile at an approaching aircraft. We had to act," Jack replied.

Hensley flashed dark. He leveled his gaze at Bauer. "You've recovered this missile launcher?"

Ryan Chappelle stepped between them. "Unfortunately the missile launcher was lost when Dante Arete's associates blew themselves up in their escape vehicle."

Chappelle failed to mention the memory stick they'd recovered. Jack was certain the omission was deliberate, that Ryan suspected Hensley was lying, too.

Hensley frowned. "Then you don't have any proof to back up these absurd assertions, do you?"

"What are you getting at, Agent Hensley?"

"Well, Mr. Chappelle, Dante Arete most certainly smuggled weapons across the United States border in the past two years. But he's very careful to be far, far away when those weapons are used. And the notion of Dante's greasy gang-bangers blowing themselves up to avoid capture . . ." Hensley snorted, shook his head. "They're urban punks, not Japanese kamikaze or Muslim terrorists. Suicide isn't their style."

Ignoring Chappelle, Hensley faced Jack. "Any chance your guys were popping off so many rounds it was you who blew up the van?"

"No," said Jack evenly. "No chance."

Hensley sensed Jack's animosity, pulled back a bit.

"Well, you couldn't have known about the FBI investigation, anyway. And a newly formed unit like yours is bound to stumble a few times before learning to walk."

Hensley fixed his dark blue eyes on Jack, who ignored the slight, glanced away. Jack understood now that Hensley was a master manipulator. It was time for Bauer to rise to the level of play.

"Look," Jack began with the proper tone of contriteness. "The FBI put a lot of hours into this investigation. I understand that. But we put in some sweat and a little blood, too—not to mention the fact that I have to deal with all the paperwork that comes with a casualty situation."

Jack rested his arm on Hensley's shoulder. "Why don't we go in right now and interview Dante Arete together. He's been sitting in that cell for hours. I'll soften him up, you make the deal you need to make with him. I'll even stay out of it. When I have enough information to write up my report, you can take the prisoner back to New York City and we've both covered our asses."

Hensley shook his head, just as Jack knew he would.

"No can do, Bauer. What Arete may or may not say impacts at least half a dozen separate investigations—FBI investigations."

"Let's talk to your superiors, then," said Jack. "Maybe we can work something out."

Again Hensley shook his head. This time he barely bothered to hide his smirk. "They're going to want to sit in on the interrogation too. Arete's a big catch. A lot of folks are going to want to hold the net. But he's not big enough to have half the New York bureau fly out here to CTU just to chat with him—"

"I'll fly to New York," said Jack.

Hensley blinked. Jack pressed: "You came in an FBI jet, right? I'll just hitch a ride with you to the East Coast, fly back on a commercial flight."

Jack glanced at Chappelle for support. Ryan shot warning daggers, but didn't overturn him.

"Jack's proposal has merit," Ryan said. "I think even Senator Cheever will be comfortable with the arrangement. If you have doubts, I'll speak to Mr. Spain about it right now." Chappelle then gave an admirable impression of reaching for the phone.

Jack forced himself to mask a smile. When Chappelle got his priorities right, it was a thing of beauty.

Hensley threw up his hands. "All right, you win. But if this is some ploy to stall for time and talk to Arete by yourself, forget it. He's not cutting any deals with CTU. To make sure of that, I have two Federal marshals outside who are going to be with Dante from now until we arrive in New York City."

Jack folded his arms, met Hensley's gaze. "He's my prisoner, and CTU protocol requires that Dante Arete be in my custody until we reach your jurisdiction. That means he's to be handcuffed to my wrist—just to make sure nobody tries to talk to him when I'm not around."

Hensley nodded. "Fine, Agent Bauer. Play your games. But as soon as we're wheels down in New York, Dante Arete is mine."

1 2 3 4 5 6 7 8 9
10 11 12 13 14 15 16 17
18 19 20 21 22 23 24

• •

**THE FOLLOWING TAKES PLACE
BETWEEN THE HOURS OF
9 P.M. AND 10 P.M.
EASTERN DAYLIGHT TIME**

• •

*9:04:52 P.M. EDT
The sky over Queens, New York*

The steady drone of the jet engines suddenly changed pitch. Jack opened his eyes, instantly alert, surprised he'd slept at all. He sat in an airline seat next to Dante Arete, the fugitive still chained to his arm by a pair of nickel-plated steel bracelets. Two federal marshals sat across the aisle, in another cluster of chairs. The younger marshal's seat was back, he slept mouth open and gently snored. The older man—perhaps forty— was awake, though hardly alert as he sipped bottled water and leafed through a dog-eared copy of *Sports Illustrated*.

As for Special Agent Frank Hensley, there was no

sign. He'd entered a separate compartment shortly after they'd lifted off from LAX and hadn't reappeared
since. Jack suspected there was a bunk in the forward
compartment, and Hensley had taken advantage of
the hours to get some sleep.

Hensley reminded Bauer of an army, safely en-
sconced in a fortified town surrounded by the enemy.
Instead of waiting for the inevitable attack, an aggressive commander would dispatch pickets to prick his
foe into premature action. Hensley's barbs—fired at
Jack, at CTU, even at Ryan Chappelle—seemed to be
timed to divert attention from the psychological de-
fenses Frank Hensley had erected to keep the world
at bay.

Jack sat up and stretched as much as the handcuff
on his wrist would allow. Then he looked around.
The FBI aircraft was not laid out like a commercial
airliner. There were no rows of airline seats, only
clusters—about a dozen in all. Some chairs were set
around affixed tables, others were placed along the
fuselage, near the windows. There were no air stew-
ards, either. They'd been replaced by a stocked refrigerator, a coffeemaker, and a microwave oven.

Jack glanced at his watch, already set to Eastern
Daylight Time. He discovered he'd slept for nearly
thirty-five minutes—the longest interval of rest he'd
had in the last fifteen hours. Bauer leaned forward,
rubbed his face. Then he checked on his prisoner.
Dante Arete had curled up into a ball and had fallen
fast asleep as soon as the FBI aircraft was off the
ground and the "fasten seatbelt" lights went dark.
Jack shook him awake, and Arete immediately demanded to go to the bathroom. Still cuffed together,
Jack escorted the prisoner to the head, then used it

himself. Even in the tight confines of the restroom, the two men did not exchange a word.

When they returned to the cabin, Jack was surprised to find Hensley had reemerged. The FBI agent sat at one of the tables with the two Federal marshals, who had roused themselves into a semblance of vigilance. Hensley looked up when Bauer and his prisoner entered, then went back to punching data into his PDA. The wall, Jack noted, was still in place. Either Hensley was the most professional law enforcement agent he'd ever met—or something else was going on behind his half-lidded eyes.

"Strap in. We're landing in five minutes." Hensley commanded, wand poised over the tiny PDA screen.

Jack pushed Arete into a seat near a window, then strapped his prisoner down. After his own belt was fastened, he gazed out the window. Far below, Jack could see the winking lights of the Borough of Queens spread out before him, a muted golden glow against a purple-black evening sky. Jack's stomach lurched as the aircraft dipped sharply, then leveled off as it began its final approach. A high-pitched whine, then a thump, signaled the deployment of the landing gear. The flaps dropped and the aircraft slowed drastically.

Jack watched out of the corner of his eye as Hensley unsnapped his seatbelt and stood up to stretch. The marshals ignored him, gazing out the window or straight ahead. Hensley turned his back to the others, reached into his jacket to carefully tuck the PDA into his suit pocket. When his hand came out again, it was clutching a Glock 19, the semi-compact version of the standard 9mm recoil-operated composite handgun, undetectable to weapons scanners. In one smooth motion Hensley disengaged the safety, cocked the striker.

Then he turned and pointed the weapon at the larger of the two marshals.

The man saw the Glock, and his mouth opened in surprise. Then the noise of a gunshot reverberated throughout the cabin. The dead marshal jerked spasmodically as the back of his head blew out, but the safety belt kept him erect in the chair. Gore splattered the beige plastic panel behind the corpse, splashed to the floor in thick black drops.

Shocked, the other marshal stared up at Hensley while Jack reached for his P228. Bauer had just slipped his own gun free of its holster when Dante Arete punched him full in the face with his free hand. Jack reeled when he felt the hot sting on his jaw. The SigSauer flew from his hand and bounced across the floor. Bauer felt Arete's hands groping for his throat—ineffectively because of the handcuffs that hobbled his movement. As Arete continued trying to strangle Jack, Bauer released his safety belt, pushed himself out of the seat, and slammed the heel of his hand under Arete's jaw. The man's head snapped backward.

Meanwhile, with a bored expression on his face, Hensley shot the second marshal in the forehead before the young man could even draw his service revolver. Then he swung around to train his weapon on Jack Bauer—only to find the CTU agent hiding behind Dante Arete's body, his arm locked around the helpless prisoner's throat. With a muttered curse, Hensley dropped the Glock on his empty chair, drew his own FBI service revolver, and aimed it at the two men.

"Don't shoot, man," Dante Arete whined, free arm extended to ward off destruction. "Don't fucking shoot me."

"Listen to your prisoner," hissed Jack. "You'll have to put a slug right through Dante to get to me." As he spoke, Jack eyed his gun on the floor, too far away to do him any good.

Hensley's neutral gaze turned poisonous. "You crack me up, Bauer. What makes you think I care about the life of the punk son of a bitch who murdered my partner?"

Jack watched apprehensively as Hensley tightened his grip on the trigger . . .

9:16:07 P.M. EDT
CTU Headquarters, Los Angeles

"I can carry my own luggage, thank you very much!" The young woman charged past the security escort who'd met her at the airport and chauffeured her to CTU headquarters. She also ignored his call as she pushed through the double glass doors.

The young woman was gangly and too thin, her legs lean and muscular under a purple micro-mini and black tights. Her oversized Doc Martens clip-clopped on the unpainted concrete floor as her long, skinny arm hauled a bulky Pullman behind her. Strapped to the back of her "Nasicaä—Valley of the Wind" T-shirt was a pink Hello Kitty pack containing a personal computer, a cell phone, an MP3 player, and a PDA. A large black messenger bag dangled from her small shoulder, swaying with every bold step she took.

Seeing her barreling forward, the guard quickly stepped around the security desk and blocked her path. "Stop right there, miss. You need a pass to go in there."

"I've got time to get a security pass, but no time to

find a place to sleep? Jeez, I mean, what's the rush? At least let me check into a hotel!"

The young woman's head seemed large for her wispy frame. Her pale features and wide mouth were hidden behind a silky curtain of long, straight black hair, parted only by dark-framed glasses too large for her tiny face. Behind the oversized lenses were wide, curious, almond-shaped eyes. Her only makeup was black eyeliner.

The young woman tapped her giant shoe impatiently while the guard verified her CTU identification and administrative transfer from the D.C. office. Finally he snapped her picture with a digital camera mounted on the desktop, then handed her a small plastic ID badge with a magnetic strip that allowed her access to some but not all areas of the CTU facility.

When she was officially checked in, the young woman kicked her American Tourister into a leaning position. Then she yanked it along, rolling it behind her as she marched into the center of CTU's busy command center. Technicians and analysts scurried about, ignoring her as they raced from station to station.

"Hey! I need to speak with the person in charge, please."

Nina Myers heard the cry and left her workstation.

"Can I help you?"

The girl released the Pullman and blew an errant lock of hair away from her face. She offered Nina a bony hand sheathed with smooth, ivory skin. "My name is Dae Soo Min. Someone around here is supposed to know I'm coming."

"You're the software expert?"

The young woman nodded. "If it's made in Korea I can hack it."

Nina could not hide her surprise. She had expected someone older, with more experience. Perhaps an ex-military type, a veteran of the North/South Korean demilitarized zone—or an *adult*, at the very least. Dae Soo Min looked to be about seventeen and was acting much younger.

Nina shook the woman's hand. "Hi. I'm Nina Myers, Ms.—"

"My friends call me Doris."

Nina picked up her bag. "Follow me and I'll introduce you to the rest of the team."

Jamey was at her workstation processing the hourly reports when Milo Pressman appeared at her shoulder. "Hey, check it out."

She followed Milo's gaze. "My God. Is CTU recruiting at elementary schools now?"

"Quick, pretend to be looking at the monitor," whispered Milo. "I think they're headed this way."

By the time Nina and Doris arrived, Milo and Jamey were seemingly swamped in the sea of intelligence data. "Sorry to interrupt your work," Nina said without a trace of irony. "I want you to meet—"

"I'm Doris. Hi."

"Milo is our security systems specialist, Jamey is our head programmer. You'll be working with them for the duration of this assignment."

Milo and Jamey exchanged looks. Nina crossed to the auxiliary workstation and powered it up. "Jamey, could you send all of the encrypted data we've recovered from the memory stick to station six, so Doris can begin her preliminary evaluation?"

Jamey frowned. "Jack put everything that has to do with the Arete case on Level Four security clearance . . ."

"No problem. I'm assigning Doris a Level *Three* security code."

Behind Nina's back, Milo made a face at Jamey.

"You got to be kidding me," Jamey protested. "I didn't get a Level Three clearance code until I worked here for over six months."

Nina rose to her full height, looming over the seated Jamey. "Do you feel threatened? I understand if you do. But not to worry, the situation is only temporary. Just until Doris cracks the code."

Milo watched Doris sit down in front of the keyboard. Inside of a minute she began isolating data, separating the wheat from the chaff. He scratched his sparse goatee. "At the speed she's working, that won't be very long . . ."

9:21:51 P.M. EDT
The sky over Queens, New York

Dante Arete stared down the muzzle of Special Agent Hensley's weapon, eyes wide, lips beaded with sweat. Jack Bauer's grip around his throat tightened.

"What the hell are you doin', man?" Dante croaked, wide eyes staring at Hensley. "This ain't what we talked about. This ain't part of our deal."

Jack dragged Arete against him in a bear hug, spoke in his ear. "What deal? Tell me what deal you made with Hensley."

"Shut up, both of you," said Hensley.

Arete ignored Jack, glared at Hensley. "You kill me and the whole deal's flushed, man."

Bauer moved backward, dragging Arete with him, until his spine touched the walls of the pressurized cabin. He risked a glance out the window. The ground was coming up fast, Jack could see cars on the highway, busy residential streets with people on them.

"Shoot now and you'll puncture the fuselage, depressurize the cabin," Jack warned.

Hensley shrugged. "We're almost on the ground. I'll risk it."

The engine's whine became more pronounced as the aircraft decreased its speed. Turbulence buffeted the airliner, and the motion rocked Hensley on his feet, foiling his aim. Fearfully, Arete struggled against Bauer's tightening grip, but Jack held him firm. A moment later, Hensley steadied himself, his aim true. "Like I said, Bauer. When the wheels touch the pavement, Arete's mine."

From the corner of his eyes, Jack saw a flash outside the window. Hensley saw it, too. A bright orange object rose toward the airplane from a cluster of low, featureless concrete buildings.

Jack threw Arete to the cabin floor as a brilliant yellow ball of fire lit the windows on the starboard side of the airliner. Interior alarms sounded and emergency oxygen masks dropped from their ceiling compartments as the aircraft lurched and the interior lights winked.

Then came the noise of the blast, deafening as the shock wave shattered the windows. The interior of the cabin suddenly mimicked the inside of a dryer running full blast. Papers, cups, cushions, magazines, napkins—anything not nailed down flew about the cabin or was sucked outside.

Jack heard the engines straining to keep the aircraft aloft. Then they cut out and the wheels slammed onto the runway, too hard for the landing gear to support the impact. Tires blew, steel snapped, and the landing gear folded. The burning aircraft teetered to port, then the belly hit the concrete and skidded along, trailing a torrent of hot white sparks.

9:32:18 P.M. EDT
CTU Headquarters, Los Angeles

Tony's land line warbled. He reached across his desk and grabbed the receiver. "Almeida."

"There's a Marine Corps captain checking in at the security desk and asking to see Ms. Myers. But the Chief of Staff is not responding to my call."

"Nina's in the middle of a video conference with Bill Buchanan from the Seattle office," Tony replied. "I'll be right there."

Tony locked down his computer and headed off to the security desk. On the way, he stopped by Jamey's area and picked up the latest printout on the mysterious memory stick, which he stuffed into the folder under his arm. He glanced at it first, disappointed to find they had discovered next to nothing in the past two hours of "expert analysis."

At the security desk, Tony discovered that not all Marines are created equal. This particular captain had blond hair caught in a ponytail, a killer figure in a dress blue uniform, and clear blue eyes to go with her two silver bars.

"Captain," said Tony, offering her a smile with his hand. "I'm Agent Almeida, head of intelligence here at CTU."

Nearly as tall as Tony, the woman met his openly appraising gaze as she took his hand in a firm grip.

"I'm Captain Jessica Schneider. Commander of the Special Weapon Analysis Unit in South Korea."

Her name jarred his memory cells, but the context eluded him. "Welcome to Los Angeles. Come with me and I'll bring you up to speed."

As they moved through the busy command center, Captain Schneider took in the setup while Tony deciphered the ribbons and service pins that adorned her uniform. "First Marine Division," Tony observed. "Looks like you and I ate some of the same dirt."

A half smile crossed her full lips. "You're a jarhead?"

"Ex."

"You're missing all the fun, then."

Tony discerned a slight Texas drawl, another clue he felt was important, but he had yet to make the connection. They arrived at the cyber-analysis section. Tony ran his key card through the lock, opened the door. "We actually have lots of fun here at CTU, too."

Tony offered Captain Schneider a chair, then slid the latest report on the memory stick under her nose. "This is what we've got, so far."

Captain Schneider opened the folder, leafed through it. She lifted two photographs of the object and studied them closely. After a moment, she reached into her pocket and donned delicately framed reading glasses. "And you found this memory stick where?"

"At LAX, this morning," Tony replied. "It was attached to an array of tubes in the hands of a suspected terrorist. The device looked like a shoulder-fired anti-aircraft missile launcher. Unfortunately we lost both the terrorist and the device when the group self-destructed to avoid capture."

Captain Schneider closed the file. "This data stick

you recovered is a component in the most advanced handheld anti-aircraft missile launcher developed to date by the hostile regime in North Korea."

Tony was impressed. "You're sure."

"I've seen one before. The launcher, not the memory stick."

"On the DMZ in Korea?"

Captain Schneider's blond ponytail bobbed when she shook her head. "On the Texas/Mexico border. About eight weeks ago, the DEA grabbed a launcher in a narcotics raid. The system is highly advanced. It has been code named Long Tooth by the Pentagon. The launcher has twin firing tubes and a computer programming system that interfaces with the missiles themselves. Unfortunately no missiles were recovered so we don't know their capabilities as yet . . ."

"How did the Marine Corps find out about it? The DEA isn't known for sharing intelligence with the military."

"I found out through a . . . personal contact. I know someone on the House Intelligence Oversight Committee."

Tony Almeida closed his eyes a nanosecond, stifled a groan. "Your father—he's Congressman Roy Schneider of Texas?"

The Captain nodded. To cover her discomfort, she changed the subject. "Have you retrieved any data from the memory stick?"

"It's encrypted. We have an expert on North Korean software trying to crack it now. No progress to report."

Captain Schneider felt it, just then. The instant chill. One mention of her father and there it was: clipped words, tense posture, guarded look. Amazing how fast he shifted, she thought. While she was not surprised by the CTU agent's reaction, she was more than a little disappointed that he had so easily—and predictably—made the same assumptions as everyone else. No matter how hard she worked, no matter what she accomplished, every time her colleagues discovered the identity of her father, they immediately assumed that she had attained her rank and position through nepotism rather than merit.

Captain Schneider rose, tucked the file under her arm. When she spoke, she added frost to her own voice. "Agent Almeida, I'd like to meet this expert of yours, see for myself how the decryption is progressing."

9:41:24 P.M. EDT
John F. Kennedy International Airport

Jack's first sensation was pain. His ribs felt bruised. Something warm and sticky had trickled from his head to the side of his face. He heard a crackle. Without moving a muscle, Jack slowly opened one eye to find a live wire dangling from a shattered panel near his head. When he glanced down, he saw the steel bracelet was still clamped to his wrist, but on the other end of the chain was a pair of empty cuffs, the key missing from his pocket. Jack took a deep breath and almost gagged on the thick smoke he'd thought for a moment was just his hazy vision.

The aircraft's interior emergency lights were still functioning, the fuselage tilted at an odd angle. Jack realized that he'd been thrown into a corner and the airline seat had broken loose from its mount and covered him. Squinting through his eyelashes, he saw

Arete standing near an emergency exit. He was having trouble opening the door. The impact of the crash probably had jammed the hatch.

Stumbling through the smoke, the pilot emerged from the forward compartment, fumbled for the handgun at his belt. Arete froze, unarmed and helpless. Then a shot boomed loud, followed by another. The pilot was thrown back, into a bulkhead—dead before he hit the ground. Frank Hensley emerged from the shadows, reloading the Glock.

He looked at Arete. "Where's Bauer?"

"Why the hell should I help you, *amigo*? You were gonna shoot right through me."

"Don't be a jackass," Hensley replied. "I was bluffing. Talking tough. You should know all about that. Anyway, I just shot that pilot to cover your ass."

Arete rubbed his wrist where the cuffs had chafed him. Then he kicked the stubborn emergency hatch. "Bauer's over there, man. Under that goddamned chair. It don't matter anyway. We ain't getting out of here alive . . ."

Hensley glanced in Jack's direction, spied Bauer's legs sticking out of a pile of wreckage. He pulled latex gloves and a handkerchief out of his pocket, donned the gloves, and carefully wiped down the Glock with the handkerchief. Then he shifted the Glock to his left hand, drew his service revolver with his right, and approached Bauer.

Through his half-closed eyes, Jack had been watching Hensley. But playing dead in a burning aircraft was no longer an option. He had to act. When Hensley hauled the chair away, Jack grabbed the live wire above him and shoved the still-sparking tip against Hensley's left arm. The FBI agent yowled and jumped backward, simultaneously discharging the revolver and letting go of the Glock. The shot missed Jack, who was already rolling away, snapping up the Glock before diving behind the cover of upended seats.

"Kill him, man!" Arete was frantic. Over the crackling fire and popping steel, they heard the distant sound of sirens. "You better waste him fast. If he starts talking—"

"Shut up!" Hensley spied Jack a moment later and opened fire.

Arete kept clutching his head and moaning. "I don't wanna die here."

Pinned, Jack looked around for an exit, saw one not five feet away—through five feet of open space. He'd have to get there, release the lever, and hope it wouldn't jam before Hensley had time to hit him. Jack figured his chances were less than ten percent, but he had no choice.

Suddenly the broken aircraft lurched again, setting off a series of explosions from somewhere outside. The force of the successive blasts rocked the airplane and bounced its inhabitants around. Two things happened next: Hensley was jerked against a table bolted to the floor. He flipped over it and struck his head, his service revolver tumbling to Dante Arete's feet. And the jammed hatch that wouldn't budge for Dante a few moments before burst open, filling the choking compartment with cool night air.

Arete didn't hesitate. He snatched Hensley's weapon and jumped through the exit. Jack cried out, stumbled to his feet. Still clutching the Glock, he bolted for the same exit, stopping in the doorway to see Arete's heading. Then he turned around and tried to find Hensley, but the smoke had become too thick.

In the choking darkness of the fuselage, he bumped into the corpse of one of the murdered Federal agents. Jack reached into the man's jacket, found a loaded Browning Hi-Power and some extra ammo.

Jack had to make a choice and he knew it. He gave up trying to find Hensley. Instead he climbed out of the shattered aircraft and took off across the tarmac, in pursuit of the fugitive Arete.

9:52:09 P.M. EDT
CTU Headquarters, Los Angeles

Milo Pressman sat at his workstation, located between Jamey Farrell's cubicle and the auxiliary computer station where Doris had set up shop.

Milo had been complaining for hours, to anyone who would listen, about being called back to work and away from his girlfriend. Apparently the whole mess was a relationship wrecker, or so he told Jamey Farrell.

"Look," said Jamey. "Either she understands what you do or she doesn't."

"Tina *used* to understand. Now she *doesn't*."

Milo's pocket sent out ringtones of a Green Day download. Of course it was Tina. The cell phone conversation quickly degenerated into an argument. Jamey and Doris heard every word on Milo's end. He hadn't bothered trying to make the call private.

Jamey decided to fill in some blanks for Doris.

"Of course I'm not with some other woman," Milo told his girlfriend.

"No," whispered Jamey. "But your tongue was sure hanging out when Tony introduced you to Captain Schneider."

Doris pushed up her large glasses with her index finger. "What's a girl like that got that we haven't got?"

Jamey shrugged and smiled. "Blond hair, rich daddy, and a sexy drawl that makes men drool."

Doris smiled back and shook her head. "Barbie in a uniform. Hardly seems fair."

9:55:21 P.M. EDT
John F. Kennedy International Airport

"Agent Hensley! Agent Hensley!"

Sirens wailed, emergency lights flashed. In the distance, a massive aircraft hangar burned, orange flames licking the black night sky. A firefighter cupped blackened hands around his mouth and called out for Hensley one more time.

Others took up the call, their loud voices followed by the stabbing beams from a half-dozen flashlights, columns of light that cut through the smoky darkness. Deep inside the wreckage of the aircraft, someone coughed.

"Over there! He's alive," yelled a firefighter.

A stocky man in a gray pinstriped suit pushed past the emergency workers swathed in asbestos, splashed through the fire-retardant foam that surrounded the shattered fuselage. Feet slipping, he climbed onto the broken wing and crawled through the emergency hatch, into the cabin. "Frank! Is that you? Are you in here?"

"Over here," a voice called weakly.

"You can't go back there," a fireman called. "There still fuel in those wings. It's a miracle this aircraft didn't explode on impact."

Special Agent Ray Goodman ignored the man. "Frank! Talk to me, Frank," he yelled again.

One of the firemen pointed. "I think someone's moving over there."

Minutes later, Goodman and the firefighter carried Frank Hensley out of the wreckage. Hensley hung limply between the two men until they reached an ambulance. Immediately, paramedics placed Hensley on a stretcher, slipped an oxygen mask over his face. The FBI agent swallowed air in great gulps. Agent Goodman loomed over him.

"What the hell happened, Frank?"

Hensley shook his head. "Don't know . . . A missile, I think . . ."

"It was a missile, all right," Goodman interrupted. "What happened to Dante Arete? The marshals, they looked like they'd both been shot."

Hensley nodded. "It was that CTU agent, Jack Bauer. Somehow he . . . he must have smuggled a Glock aboard. As the pilot was making the final approach, Bauer just started shooting. Killed the marshals . . ."

Hensley gasped like a fish out of water. A paramedic steadied him but he pushed the emergency worker away, struggled to rise. "When the plane hit the ground, Bauer shot the pilot, too. Then he helped Arete escape . . ."

"Steady, Frank."

"You don't understand," Hensley moaned behind the oxygen mask. "That man has got to be stopped— caught. Dead or alive. Jack Bauer is a traitor and a murderer and he's got to be stopped . . ."

• •

THE FOLLOWING TAKES PLACE
BETWEEN THE HOURS OF
10 P.M. AND 11 P.M.
EASTERN DAYLIGHT TIME

• •

10:02:02 P.M. EDT
CTU Headquarters, Los Angeles

"The FBI aircraft ferrying Jack Bauer and suspect Dante Arete to New York City crashed upon landing thirty minutes ago."

Shocked, disbelieving voices erupted in the command center. Nina Myers had just descended the metal staircase leading to Jack's glass-enclosed office. She'd gathered personnel to update the Crisis Management Team on their boss's situation. Among the group stood Tony Almeida, Jamey Farrell, and Milo Pressman. Doris and Captain Schneider stood on the sidelines listening.

"As yet," continued Nina Myers over the chatter,

"there has been no official word on what occurred. Unofficially, I believe the airliner was shot down as it landed at JFK, perhaps to prevent Dante Arete from talking to authorities. Firefighters and emergency service personnel have only just reached the crash site. Burning debris started a major fire inside a nearby hangar, which impeded rescuers from reaching the scene—"

Jamey's face turned ashen. "So we don't know if there are any survivors."

"No word yet . . ."

"Jack is carrying that new CDD satellite communicator. I can try to raise him," Jamey offered.

"Let's give it a little time. We're supposed to be observing radio silence. Let's follow protocol. Jack's in the field. Let him contact us."

Jamey chewed her lip. "Maybe I should activate the tracker."

Nina nodded. "Start the protocols, but don't transmit the signal until you get the order. For the rest of us—be advised that the Threat Clock has been pushed ahead three hours to Eastern Daylight Time." She glanced at her watch. "That makes it 10:05:52. Synchronize your chronometers, station clocks, and personal timepieces."

"What do we do until we hear from Jack?" Tony asked.

"*If* we hear from Jack?" whispered Milo.

"For starters, I want everyone to monitor all the communications coming out of New York City," said Nina. "That means emergency radio, police bands, fire and medical services, the traffic bureau, city and county government security frequencies—the works."

The staffers began to return to their stations. Milo

heard his cell go off in his pocket. He checked the caller ID, groaned inwardly. No doubt another tearful voice message from Tina.

"One more thing," called Nina. "CTU is now in an official lockdown. No one leaves this building until the current crisis has been resolved . . . No exceptions."

Milo cursed, opened his cell phone, and began to toggle to Tina's stored number. Jamey Farrell reached out and snapped the lid closed.

"We have a situation on our hands, Milo. Get busy. You and your girlfriend can kiss and make up some other night."

10:28:52 P.M. EDT
Queens, New York

The tavern was called Tatiana's—a seedy dive situated at the end of a dead end street in an industrial section of Queens. A cinder-block building with thick, glass-brick windows, Tatiana's was trimmed with electric-blue neon and topped by a skylight and a satellite dish. Its litter-strewn parking lot was crammed with a mixture of pimped-up SUVs, tricked out high-performance cars, Harley-Davidson hogs, and, oddly, a late-model black Mercedes with New York plates.

Tatiana's was the epicenter of activity in this lonely area of urban blight, and it was Dante Arete's destination after escaping Federal custody. Running from the chaos at the airport, Arete had slipped through JFK's perimeter fence, crossed a busy highway, and passed through a neighborhood of run-down two-story row houses. Finally he entered a forsaken industrial area of concrete, grime, and graffiti—the last of which appeared to be gang tags. Small factories and automotive repair shops lined either side of the potholed street, occasionally interrupted by a long stretch of chain-link fence capped by barbed wire or an abandoned building shuttered tight.

An unseen shadow in the warm, close night, Jack Bauer had stalked the fugitive's every step. Though he wasn't certain where he was in relation to Manhattan, Jack knew he was still close to JFK because, every two minutes or so, airplanes roared low overhead as they made their final approach. Soon Jack would activate the GPS system embedded in his CDD communicator and determine his exact location. But Jack couldn't risk stopping for any reason. Dante Arete was moving fast, and Jack was determined to shadow him until he reached his final destination.

Shells of abandoned cars littered this stretch of road, along with various parts from a variety of models—seats, bumpers, slashed tires, steering columns. Chop shop heaven, he assumed, which explained the clientele when he finally reached Tatiana's. Jack watched his fugitive walk down the middle of the deserted street, toward the neon brilliance of the bustling tavern. Old-school rap music spilled through the door as a young olive skinned man with strong Italian features stumbled outside wearing baggy jeans and a muscle T-shirt, climbed aboard a Harley, and revved it up. In a cloud of dust the chopper roared out of the parking lot, past Dante Arete and up the street.

Jack was forced to duck behind the skeletal remains of a gutted Lexus to avoid the headlights. Next to the automobile shell, a cracked, rusty engine block sprouted weeds. Dante Arete's gaze followed the motorcycle, his eyes lingering on the darkened street long after the chopper was out of sight. Finally, Arete turned when shouts came from the shadows. Out of the mass of parked cars, a group emerged. Jack counted five Hispanic men, all in their early to midtwenties, all clad in baggy denim and loose blue buttoned-down shirts worn open over white muscle Ts. Blue bandanas were worn in various styles—as headbands and kerchiefs. And each had a coil of bloody thorns tattooed around his neck.

The group had all the markings of a street gang—the same style clothing, the same color bandanas and tattoos. Jack's stint with LAPD SWAT had given him enough of a primer on the basics: the hand signals, the postures, the tags, the colors. From his proximity to JFK, Jack knew he was still in Queens. The Latin Kings were known to be the most active gang in that borough. But this crew approaching Dante Arete wasn't sporting the trademark five-pointed crown on their body tattoos or clothing.

Los Angeles had been awash in gang activity for decades. The Bloods and Crips alone had made the city the drive-by shooting capital of the world. Still, those drug-dealing gang-bangers had active "sets" or chapters in almost every state in the country; and although they were predominantly black gangs, many other ethnic groups had adopted their names and colors out of sheer recognition if not direct affiliation.

Jack might have guessed these young men were part of a Crips crew from the blue bandanas, but Crips didn't favor tattoos, and the identical tattoos around their throats looked more like something out of the Mexican Mafia—a group that had begun in the California prison system decades ago and had since claimed members all over the country. That gang also favored the color blue, but its symbols of MM, La Eme, a "13" and three dots, were nowhere in sight.

Four of the group were also wearing long dark blue dusters, unbuttoned and flapping in the night breeze. The coats were out of place on a warm night in late spring, unless one wanted to hide something—like an automatic weapon. Suddenly one of the group, a stocky, powerfully built man with a shaved head, called out to Dante using his gang tag—

"*Apache, mi hermano!*"

He moved forward, catching Dante in a bear hug. The two men slapped each other under the glow of a streetlight as the other young men formed a protective circle around them.

"*Ese, Apache! Ese!*"

"*Hasta la muerte, guerrero!*"

That's when Jack knew. These men were members of the Columbia Street Posse, Dante's nonaligned Brooklyn-based gang. Jack darted across the street, slipped into the parking lot, and dived behind the first car he could reach—a Z28 Camaro Coupe repainted a metallic green with a white racing stripe. Quietly he stepped between vehicles until he was less than a dozen feet away from Arete, near enough to hear their conversation clearly.

"I'm lucky to be here at all, *guerreros*," Arete said. "I thought I was gonna die in that stinking airplane."

Shaved Head laughed. "It wasn't luck, Apache. The Paddies really came through for you tonight."

Cautiously, Jack raised his head to peer through the car's spotless windows. Two men stepped into the light. Respectfully, the Posse parted. The newcomers were impeccably dressed in tailored summer-weight suits. Jack guessed the younger of the two—a fiery redhead with the florid face of a drinker—was in his mid-thirties. The other man was at least a decade older, broad-shouldered, with sharp features and steel-gray hair.

Dante Arete eyed the pair. "You bastards shoot good," he said.

The redhead grinned. When he spoke, his Irish brogue was thick. "Got a present for you, Apache. For all yer troubles."

The redhead popped the trunk of a black Mercedes with an electronic key. The older man reached inside, pulled out an attaché case. Rising cautiously from behind the car, Jack traded the risk of being seen for a better look inside the trunk. In the dull white glow of the boot light, Jack saw a missile launcher, its twin steel launch tubes gleaming dully. Then the trunk closed, and Jack ducked down again, breathing in the humid night air.

"You know what to do," said the silver-haired older man, his brogue less pronounced. "After tonight, don't contact us again."

Arete took the attaché case, turned his back on the pair to confer with his crew. The two men strolled away, to lean against the Mercedes while they observed the discussion. Jack thrust the Glock in his belt, then reached into his charcoal-gray jacket to retrieve his CDD communicator.

The speaker at Nina Myers's workstation crackled. "It's Jamey. I've got Jack Bauer on the line."

"Put Jack through my speakerphone. I want you to listen in, too, and patch Milo in if you can."

Nina waved Tony Almeida and Ryan Chappelle over to her cubicle. "It's Jack."

"Jack? What happened? Are you all right?" Ryan asked with practiced sincerity. In an urgent whisper, Jack summarized the events of the past hour. He told them about Hensley murdering the marshals, the shoot-down of the airliner, Arete's escape, the rendezvous in Tatiana's parking lot, the two Irishmen and the missile launcher inside the trunk of their car.

"That's . . . well, that's quite a story Jack," Ryan said doubtfully. "Can you back any of this up."

"Not yet," Jack replied. "But I intend to secure a vehicle and follow the Mercedes wherever it goes. Once I have the missile launcher and the men in custody, we can sort this out."

"What about your prisoner?" said Ryan. "You can't just let Dante Arete get away."

"I'm sending CTU a positioning signal so Jamey can pinpoint my location."

After a few seconds, Jamey spoke. "Okay, I've got Jack on my monitor. I'm overlaying a grid map of the area now."

"Forget about me, Jamey," said Jack. "I want you to activate the tracker."

"Are you sure you want to do that, Jack?" Tony protested. "The chemical battery is only good for about twelve hours."

"Hopefully that's all the time we'll need. Do it, Jamey. I need to know that the tracker is functioning properly."

A moment passed while Jamey transmitted the signal. Jack risked a peek at the gang revival meeting. It was breaking up. Dante Arete and the tattooed man climbed into a white SUV, lingered for some further conversation. "Hurry, Jamey. I need that tracker now."

"I have him. He's less than twenty meters from your position," said Jamey after too long a pause. "But we have a problem, Jack. The distance between here and New York is causing a twenty-two-second real-time delay in the satellite relay."

"We'll have to live with that," said Jack. Next he read off the license numbers on the Mercedes, then on Dante's SUV to Jamey. "See if you can dig up any useful information from those plate numbers. The SUV is probably stolen. But we might find out something useful about the other vehicle."

Ryan spoke up. "What are *you* going to do, Jack?"

"I'm going after the missile launcher inside that Mercedes."

"Jack! Wait," cried Chappelle. "What about your prisoner? What about the FBI? They're going to be asking a lot of questions soon—"

But the line was dead. Bauer had ended the conversation.

Face flushed, Chappelle turned on Nina. "What the hell is going on here?" he demanded. "If we lose Arete we lose any chance we have of cracking this case."

"We're not going to lose Arete," Nina assured him. "The medical team that examined Dante Arete after capture embedded a sub-epidermal tracker under his flesh. We can trace every move he makes for the next twelve hours."

"That's fine," said Ryan. "But right now Dante Arete is only part of the equation. We need to know more, so I want you to find out everything you can about FBI Special Agent Frank Hensley. And I want that information on my desk in one hour."

10:59:26 P.M. EDT
The parking lot of Tatiana's

Jack ended the call when he saw Arete close the door to the white SUV and the big man with the shaved head climb behind the wheel. A moment later, the white Explorer backed out of its parking spot. The other members of Arete's Posse remained behind, watching as their chief sped away.

Jack slipped a wire from his shoe, worked it into the keyhole near his head. It took less than ten seconds for him to pick the lock, but he paused—worried that the interior light might alert the others to his presence.

Instead, Jack watched as the Columbia Street Posse drew mini Uzi submachine guns with the stocks removed, slid thirty-two-round extended magazines into the breech, then slipped the loaded guns under their long coats. Weapons concealed, the four headed for Tatiana's front door.

The two Irishmen watched them go, then climbed into the black Mercedes—the young one behind the wheel, the older man in the passenger seat. The finely tuned engine purred to life.

Time had run out.

Jack popped the Camaro's door, rolled into the front seat, and quickly closed the door again. Rather than risk being seen, he crawled under the dashboard and worked in the dull glow of the streetlight outside. First he carefully unscrewed the steering wheel cover, revealing the guts of the ignition system. He tore away frayed wires, stripped them to expose enough metal to cause a spark.

Outside, Jack heard the Mercedes engine purr as the vehicle rolled past him. "Come on, come on," he hissed.

Suddenly the car's interior went completely dark as the glow from the streetlight was blocked. Jack looked up.

Surrounding the Camaro, a group of pissed-off punks stared down at Jack. Scruffy, hostile, and more than a little inebriated, they had been bored and looking for action. They had found some. One of the youths grinned and juggled a butterfly knife, another slapped a stout nightstick in the palm of his hand.

"What the fuck are you doing in my coupe?" growled a dark-skinned man with dangling braids and a lightning-shaped tattoo on his right cheek. Cornrows crisscrossed his scalp.

Jack swallowed hard as he watched the black Mercedes speed away.

••

**THE FOLLOWING TAKES PLACE
BETWEEN THE HOURS OF
11 P.M. AND 12 A.M.
EASTERN DAYLIGHT TIME**

••

11:04:12 P.M. EDT
The parking lot of Tatiana's

Jack stared through the windshield at the dozen hostile faces surrounding the car with what he hoped was a neutral, nonthreatening gaze. The black Mercedes was gone, the missile launcher stashed in its trunk still a threat to innocent lives. Yet Jack was compelled to thrust that dilemma aside for the moment.

Rather than challenge the youths and risk a fight he might be able to avoid, Jack placed both hands on the steering wheel to convince the men he was unarmed. "Look, I can explain this. My name is Bauer. I'm a Federal agent—"

"You're a fuckin' Fed?" cried the big man with the

lightning tattoo. He smiled, revealing a gold front tooth. "All the more reason to bust your head for trying to jack my ride."

"Look," Jack continued. "Just let me go and we can work this out—"

Someone ripped the door open. Strong hands moved in on Jack to strike him. He guessed that only two or three men were actually assaulting him. The rest of the group stood back and watched, shouting encouragement and enjoying the show.

The men on Jack slapped at him. Jack stayed in the car, didn't resist—not yet. Instead he tucked his head in his chest and curled up on the seat into a defensive ball, protecting his soft spots—along with the Glock in his belt. His left arm covered the shoulder holster where he'd slipped the dead marshal's gun after he'd lost his own. He would need both weapons soon. Then he felt and heard a crack. Someone had swiped at his head with a bat or stick. It was a glancing blow, or he would have been dead instead of seeing stars.

The men dragged Jack out of the vehicle and dumped him onto the pavement. He rolled, dodging kicks, to their frustration. Finally the big man with the lightning tattoo bent down to pry his arms apart. Jack kicked him in the groin with all his strength. A scream cut the night and Jack lashed out again, seizing a handful of the man's long braids. He used them to drag his head down and strike it against the pavement, stunning him into silence.

Jack backed against the car and rose, Glock in hand. Most of the crowd scattered then, ducking behind cars or fleeing into the street. But five men stood their ground, whipped out guns of their own. If they'd fired just then, Jack would have been a dead man. Instead they began to wave their weapons around in an absurdly threatening manner, hurling insults and threats.

"You want to start shooting, mother—"

"Hey man, go ahead, you pull your trigger and we'll pull ours—"

"You gonna die, asshole, 'cause you don't know who you're messing with—"

They were untrained, unskilled, not particularly bright, but they made a lot of noise. Punks, not professionals, but they had him outgunned five to one. Jack knew from experience standoffs like this never lasted long. Someone always got impatient or scared or stupid or all three. And no matter how the situation ended, someone was bound to end up dead.

Jack had to break the impasse, the only way he knew how. He raised the Glock and aimed.

11:08:36 P.M. EDT
Tatiana's Tavern

Georgi Timko knew the four men were trouble the moment they walked into his tavern.

Up to that time, it had been a quiet night, by Tatiana's standards at least. Some fists were thrown early in the evening, but the tussle was dealt with by Alexi, the bar's three-hundred-pound bouncer and veteran of the failed Soviet invasion of Afghanistan. Both Olga and Beru were making nice tips from eager young men who tucked dollar bills into their skimpy G-strings, whether they were dancing on stage or serving drinks on the floor. The pool tables were both crowded, and the clientele—mostly bikers from a

Queens "motor club"—were generally behaving themselves while consuming copious amounts of beer.

Icing on the cake for Georgi this night—the satellite broadcast had just ended and the Bulgarian soccer team, heavily favored in the match, had lost to the Armenians—which meant a big payoff for Georgi, who almost always bet on the underdog. He'd brewed some tea in his private samovar in celebration.

Then, eight minutes ago, the men in the long blue coats arrived and spoiled Georgi's evening. They'd come through the door silently, not speaking to anyone, not even one another. They ignored old toothless Yuri, who always sat by the entrance nursing his beer, hand extended to anyone who entered in the hope someone would spot him another one.

Without even a glance at Beru, who swayed topless on stage to some mindless hip-hop song, the men sat down together in one of the booths along the wall. With a professional eye, Georgi noted that's exactly the place he would have chosen. From that booth the men could watch the crowd at the pool tables and keep a watchful eye on Alexi near the cash register, and Nicolo drawing beers behind the bar.

Olga sauntered over and tried to engage the men in a little flirtatious banter, but failed to elicit more than a mumbled demand for a pitcher and four mugs—another bad sign.

Now the men had finished their beers and were stirring. They stood when Georgi rose from his chair behind the bar to fill his teacup at the steaming samovar. As the men approached him, Georgi turned his back to them as he sweetened his tea. He could feel their eyes watching him, and the base of his spine tingled—one of the many danger instincts he'd acquired as a juvenile delinquent in his native Ukraine thirty years ago.

In those days the dangers were the police or the KGB—a branch of the Soviet intelligence apparatus directed against Western espionage, but always eager to imprison a fellow member of the Soviet brotherhood for dealing in U.S. dollars, which Georgi and his peers in the mob did on a regular basis—how else was one to grow prosperous in a Soviet state were the national currency was worth less than the paper it was printed on?

Fortunately for Georgi, America was fertile ground for the kind of criminal enterprises he'd practiced in the old Soviet Union. So when the Iron Curtain rose and the KGB files were opened to the public, certain information Georgi had provided to the secret police came to light. That information proved damning to Georgi's rivals in the Ukrainian Mafia, many of whom were sent to Siberia. A few others—particularly nasty sorts, in Georgi's estimation—ended their lives facedown in a filthy prison shower, a KGB officer's bullet placed behind their ear, solely on the evidence he had provided.

Unfortunately, those men had relatives, friends, and criminal associates. When the truth was revealed, many sought revenge—and so Georgi was forced to emigrate in a hurry.

Here in America, he was able to start anew in a less economically repressive world. In America the police were much less of a problem, and a fascist organization like the KGB nonexistent. There were, of course, dangers. But here in America, here in Georgi's adopted country, that danger came courtesy of four young gangsters wearing dusters on a warm summer night.

Georgi shot a glance at Alexi. The bouncer seemed prepared, his beefy hand poised to reach for the bulge in his safari jacket.

Well, I certainly hope he's ready, Georgi mused, *though at times poor Alexi is a little slow.*

Georgi always had a soft spot in his hard heart for veterans of the Afghan war, though he despised Russians in general. Only now, at this tense moment, did it occur to him that his compassion might cause his death this night.

So be it.

With a degree of fatalism, Georgi Timko sniffed the steaming mug of tea as if it were his last. Then he turned to face his assassins.

That's when all hell broke loose—but not the way Georgi expected it.

Suddenly the tavern's thick, glass block windows exploded inward in an avalanche of broken shards. On the ceiling, a light fixture shattered in a shower of hot sparks, plunging much of the bar into darkness. Two spider-webbed bullet holes cracked the smooth surface of the wall-sized mirror behind the bar. A third whizzed by Timko's brow, to punch a hole in the stuffed buffalo head mounted on the wall.

A final shot smashed a gallon jug of Jack Daniel's, and in the silence that followed, Georgi listened to the rich brown elixir drip onto the scuffed hardwood floor.

As the echoes faded, the patrons who'd thrown themselves under tables when the shooting started now stumbled to their feet. With angry shouts they crowded around the single exit as they all tried to escape the building at the same time.

11:09:47 P.M. EDT
The parking lot of Tatiana's

The punks were stunned into paralysis when Jack fired the Glock into the crowded tavern. Jack was careful to keep his shots high, far over the heads of the patrons inside.

Instantly, a dangerous horde of furious customers poured out of Tatiana's. Jack dropped the empty Glock and held up his hands.

From the bar's doorway, a biker with a long oily ponytail pointed at the gun-toting young men. "There they are! There's the bastards shooting at us!"

The punks bolted, vanishing among the parked cars. Jack stood alone, hands raised. The bikers approached, not friendly.

"What the hell are you doin'?" one yelled. He drew a police special from his pocket.

Jack kept his arms raised, but if they searched him, they would find the other gun—and more. Suddenly a sustained barrage of automatic fire discharged inside the darkened tavern. Then the bartender burst through the front door, running full tilt for the street. He only made it a few steps before a stream of 9mm slugs chased him through the doorway, tearing bloody red holes in his back. The bartender staggered for a moment, then pitched headfirst onto the concrete.

When he saw that, the biker with the police special turned tail and ran, too, as yelling men and two screaming women in thongs and high heels stampeded. Engines roared to life all around Jack. Cars, trucks, motorcycles, until the noise drowned out the chattering guns.

Inside the tavern, the shooting continued. The automatic weapons' fire was first met with single shots from a large-caliber handgun. Then Jack heard a familiar sound, easily recognizable from his service with Delta Force in Eastern Europe—the distinctive crack of a Soviet-style AK–47 assault rifle.

Jack found the choice of weapon intriguing. It also occurred to him that Dante Arete had sent the shooters inside that tavern personally. That might mean that the assassins' intended victim was involved in whatever plot was unfolding. This person might even know something about the missile launcher, and the two men who had driven away with it. If Jack was really lucky, he might capture one of Arete's assassins alive, and possibly find out where Dante was holed up.

So while fleeing vehicles sped away from Tatiana's Tavern, Jack drew the Browning Hi-Power from his shoulder holster and moved cautiously toward the building.

11:28:58 P.M. EDT
CTU Headquarters, Los Angeles

Ryan Chappelle caught up with Nina Myers and Tony Almeida at Jamey's workstation. Jamey was watching a map grid on her monitor. Dante Arete's GPS beacon blinked intermittently. Meanwhile Nina was attempting to interface with the DEA's database and Tony was tracing the license plates Jack had read off.

"We've finally heard from the FBI," Ryan announced. "The New York office has issued an arrest warrant for Jack Bauer."

Jamey exploded. "That's crazy. What are the charges?"

"The murder of two federal marshals and the wounding of an FBI pilot. Aiding a fugitive to escape federal custody, one Dante Arete."

"Ryan, that's ridiculous and you know it," Nina said.

"I'll admit it sounds far-fetched," Ryan conceded. "But Special Agent Frank Hensley survived the airline crash; he's talking to his bosses and that's his story."

"Are there any other survivors?" Tony asked.

"Besides Jack and Dante Arete? Just the pilot, and he's not talking."

"The FBI keeping him under wraps?"

Ryan flashed his displeasure. "He's in a coma, Tony."

Almeida bristled at Chappelle's tone. "Hold on a minute, Ryan. You sound like you believe the FBI's version of what happened."

"I don't believe and I don't disbelieve anything. I'm waiting to be convinced—"

"But you heard what Jack said. He's innocent and you know it," Nina argued.

"I don't know anything," Chappelle replied. "Until another witness steps forward, what happened is open to interpretation. What happens next is up to you. You're going to have to convince me that what Jack Bauer said is true—"

"Convince *you*?"

"Yes, Tony. Convince *me*. Because I'll be the one who has to turn around and convince the Secretary of Defense that Jack Bauer hasn't gone off the deep end."

11:34:27 P.M. EDT
Tatiana's Tavern

Georgi Timko cowered under a table; another toppled on its side served as scant protection against the 9mm bullets whizzing around the room. Still clutching the warm cup in his fist, he gulped reflexively, scalding his tongue.

From somewhere inside the shadowy tavern, lit neon blue from the sign outside the shattered window, old Yuri was still plugging away at the remaining assassins. The ancient AK–47 rattled, muzzle flash bright. Georgi could hear spent cartridges bouncing on the floor following each carefully timed burst.

Georgi smiled, remembering the surprise on one assassin's face when the old man who begged for pennies at the door suddenly pulled the assault rifle from its place behind a loose wall panel. Before anyone could react, Yuri stitched a bloody line of holes up the gangster's chest with an opening burst—hey, not so "toothless" after all. The dead man still lay where he fell, head askew, eyes staring blankly. The Uzi he had brought with him lay just out of Georgi's reach.

Another Uzi fired, the burst shattering what remained of the mirror, which came crashing down behind the bar. Georgi hugged the dirty floor, cursing his laxity in not wearing a firearm, or fetching one when the four assassins first stepped into his establishment. Instead he trusted his employees to handle things. Now Nicolo was dead and Yuri was cornered, though the old man was still fighting valiantly. Poor Alexi had not fired a shot in a long time, and Georgi feared the worst.

He shifted his position in an effort to reach the Uzi on the floor. His movement elicited a burst of fire that chewed up the floorboards and shattered a chair near his head. Yuri answered the shots with a burst of his own, drawing the assassins' fire away from his boss with the last of his ammunition.

Georgi Timko cursed. He wanted to protect such loyal men, but feared he'd already cost them their lives. Only luck or a guardian angel could save them all now.

11:41:09 P.M. EDT
Tatiana's Tavern

Jack Bauer had slipped to the back of the tavern and used a metal Dumpster to get a boost to the flat tar roof. He waited until he heard shots. Then he peered through the skylight, into the darkened tavern. By the blue light of the neon exterior, he counted three shooters—someone moving right under him was using the AK–47. Arete's men, the two left standing, fired 9mm Uzis from behind splintered pool tables. Jack saw three other shapes from his vantage point— two on the ground, the third sprawled across a table. A pair of those men were Arete's; Jack recognized them from their dusters. The third was unknown to Jack, and most likely dead.

Jack ducked away from the skylight, leaned against the satellite dish while he contemplated his next move.

He had to capture at least one of Arete's men alive. The only way to get information fast was a rough interrogation of the suspects. He was certain he could quickly break any of Arete's punks—if they had any useful information.

Jack also wanted to speak to the person or persons Dante Arete sent his hit squad to assassinate. Jack didn't always subscribe to the dictum that the enemy of my enemy is my friend, but right about now he could use an ally on this coast to make up for the deficit of CTU support he was facing. And if Arete wanted someone dead, it was probably because he knew something that could hurt the gang leader. Jack wanted a part of that as well.

In the tavern below, a short burst from the AK–47 was followed by a hollow click on an empty magazine—the shooter was out of ammunition. Arete's men knew it, too. Like shadows in the blue neon glow, they slipped out from behind the pool tables and moved to flank the defenseless man.

Jack balanced over the skylight, reloaded his weapon. He shot through the glass and dropped into the middle of the tavern. Jack landed in a crouch in front of a startled gunman. The man raised the Uzi and Jack fired, blowing the top of his head off.

Jack ducked under a broken table and rolled as the other man fired on him. The shots kicked up splinters from the floor.

"Give up and I won't hurt you," Jack cried. He was answered by another burst—which also ended with an empty click.

Jack leaped to his feet and leveled his weapon. The man in the blue duster looked up fearfully, then let the weapon fall from his grip.

"Step forward and I won't—"

Suddenly shots filled the tavern as a long burst tore the man in the long coat to bloody pieces. Jack whirled to find a heavy-set man facing him. The man instantly dropped the Uzi and threw up his arms when his eyes met Jack's.

"You must help me," Georgi Timko pleaded. "That son of a bitch over there shot my friend. I . . . I think he's dying."

1 2 3 4 5 6 7 8 9
10 11 12 13 14 15 16 17
18 19 20 21 22 23 24

··

THE FOLLOWING TAKES PLACE
BETWEEN THE HOURS OF
12 A.M. AND 1 A.M.
EASTERN DAYLIGHT TIME

··

12:01:00 A.M. EDT
CTU Headquarters, Los Angeles

On his way through the command center, Tony
Almeida fell into step beside Captain Jessica Schneider.

"Where are you headed, Captain?"

"The same place as you."

Tony stopped and faced her. Nina had summoned
the CTU Crisis Management Team to Doris's workstation. As far as he was concerned, the CTU team
didn't—and shouldn't—include an entity from the
DOD.

"But you're not part of the Crisis Team," he informed her.

"I am now, Special Agent Almeida. Nina Myers just notified me of the security clearance upgrade."

Tony looked away. "RHIP," he muttered.

Captain Schneider fixed her blue eyes on him. "You are correct. Rank does have its privileges. But is it really my rank that bothers you?"

Tony glanced to his right and left. "It's not your rank," he said quietly enough to keep their conversation private. "It's your relationship to a powerful member of the House Ways and Means Committee."

"A person can't control the situation she was born into. But let me assure you that no strings were ever pulled for me. . . . I earned the rank and responsibilities I hold."

She whirled and stalked away before Tony could make his meaning clear. He didn't give a rat's ass about the woman's career trajectory. It was her direct line to another branch of government that gave him indigestion. If Captain Jessica Schneider decided to pass judgment on what and how they did things at CTU Los Angeles, she could pass that judgment on to her father, who wielded plenty of influence via his position on a Capitol Hill oversight committee. So why didn't Nina *get* that?

Tony continued on alone across the command center floor. He arrived at the Crisis Team meeting to discover a crowd silently watching the young Korean-American woman stretching in her cubicle. Her back turned to the spectators, Doris—head tilted on her long neck—was balanced on the tips of her toes. With balletic grace, she dipped to one side then the other, blithely unaware she had attracted an audience. When she finally stretched her arms high over her head, spun around, and opened her eyes, she found the others watching. Scattered applause followed. Doris, blushing, put her arms to her sides and dropped back down to the soles of her bare feet.

"Sorry. I was sitting so long I kinda needed to stretch . . ."

Nina had watched with arms folded and a look on her face as if she were indulging a child. Now that Tony and Captain Schneider had arrived, she was ready to begin. "Miss Soo Min, apprise the group of what you've uncovered."

"Right," said Doris. She knocked her shoes off the chair and slid into it, then tapped the keyboard.

"Getting the data off the chip was actually, like, a whole lot easier than I thought it would be. Whoever programmed this used the same algorithm the South Koreans use in their toy computers—the stuff they make for their kids. I worked on this kind of program in my uncle's toy factory in Oakland, so I recognized the pattern immediately. The encryption overlay that the North Koreans tried to hide the data behind was very basic, too. It was almost too easy to break, even without an encryption protocol, which I brought with me and downloaded from my own PC . . ."

While Doris babbled on, the large HDTV monitor sprang to life and a half dozen data windows appeared. In each display box, the digital representation of a different type of aircraft appeared. The image shifted so that each individual aircraft was displayed from various angles, followed by an image composed of its heat signature.

Dozens of aircraft were on display—all civil aircraft used in the West—passenger airliners, cargo craft, even research, firefighting, and weather monitoring aircraft were included in the chip's extensive database.

"What is all this?" asked Jamey Farrell.

"This is all the data I downloaded from the memory stick," said Doris. "There's nothing left beyond some random data strains here and there I have yet to decrypt. I'll continue working on them though; maybe I'll find something important."

"What exactly are we looking at?" Milo asked.

"It looks like a pretty thorough civil aircraft registry," said Tony.

"*Real* thorough," said Doris. "This software can recognize dozens of specific types of European, American, and Japanese aircraft by profile and heat signature, IFF frequencies, radio frequencies, you name it. And there's even a program to compress and download the necessary data into some other system which interfaces with the memory stick through the USB port—"

"That would be the computer guidance system inside the anti-aircraft missile itself," said Captain Schneider. "Once programmed and fired, the missile can guide itself to the target with the data downloaded from the memory stick."

Nina's face was tight with tension. "With this device at their disposal, terrorists could pinpoint and down any aircraft they wanted to. They—"

Captain Schneider raised her hand. "Not quite," she interrupted. "The effective range of a shoulder-fired anti-aircraft missile is very limited. A civil aircraft at its normal cruising altitude would probably not be at risk. A target aircraft would have to be flying at a fairly low altitude—as it is when it takes off or lands—for a Long Tooth missile to be truly effective."

"That explains why the terrorists were at the airport," said Tony. "They wanted to maximize their chance for success."

"But it doesn't explain their choice of target," Nina replied. "There was absolutely nothing aboard the cargo aircraft Dante Arete's gang was aiming at to warrant a shoot-down. It was a standard, cargo-configured 727 packed with overnight mail and packages. The cargo was checked after landing and cleared by National Transportation Safety Board screeners under our supervision."

"Maybe the shoot-down was supposed to be symbolic. Maybe the terrorists wanted to send a message," said Jamey.

"Or maybe it was a test," said Tony. "Maybe they wanted to see if the target recognition system really worked as advertised before they went after their real target."

Nina tucked strands of her short black hair behind an ear. "Whatever Dante Arete's goal, we know that with this technology, he and his accomplices have the ability to target *specific aircraft*, even in the crowded skies over a busy airport."

Nina faced Captain Schneider. "I'm turning the actual memory stick over to you next. Take it apart and put it back together, reverse-engineer the thing, trace each individual component to the original manufacturer or melt them down to their base minerals. I want you to do whatever it takes to find out where this device was made and where the maker got the parts."

Captain Schneider detached the memory stick from the data port it had been plugged into. She placed the device inside a static-free Mylar envelope and headed back to the Cyber Unit.

When she was gone, Tony confronted Nina.

"What are you doing giving Captain Schneider a spot on the Crisis Team? She's not an agent; she's a computer engineer. Captain Schneider doesn't have any field experience and she isn't even a member of CTU."

"We needed her expertise," Nina replied, still staring over Doris's shoulder at the images crawling across the HDTV screen.

Tony shook his head. "I don't accept your explanation. What does Chappelle have to say about all this?"

Nina rose to her full height, faced Tony Almeida. "Ryan Chappelle is on a conference call to Washington. He's working to control the damage, which is pretty important right now. That means he has no time to monitor the Crisis Team, so he left that task to me. In case you've forgotten, Jack left me in charge, too, so I'm handling the situation. My way."

12:11:18 A.M. EDT
Tatiana's Tavern

Georgi Timko cradled his friend's head in his blood-stained hands. Jack ripped away the ragged flannel shirt to check the downed man's wounds. Jack could see the man had taken three shots—to the chest, the shoulder, the abdomen. The shoulder wound was not life-threatening. It was impossible to tell how bad the abdominal wound was, but the largest injury was a sucking chest wound. When Jack tried to plug the hole and allow him to breathe, the man gasped, choked on the blood that shot up from his flooded lung and flowed from his mouth.

The man was doomed and Jack knew it. But at the

behest of the heavy-set man, whose piercing gray eyes both commanded and pleaded, Jack went to work, applying every first aid skill he'd acquired in fifteen-plus years of service in the Army, and later in the elite, anti-terrorist organization Delta Force. Jack managed to staunch the flow of blood, but the wounded man's eyes glazed over.

"Alexi, stay with me," Timko urged, shaking him.

"We have to move him," said Jack.

Together they lifted the man and placed him on a table.

"I need more light."

Timko ducked behind the bar and returned with a battery-operated lantern. Jack carefully rolled the man on his side to check for exit wounds. There were two. One, as large as a tennis ball, had taken out part of the man's spine.

The man on the table gasped in distress, opened his eyes, and thrashed about on the table. Despite his wounds, he fought with great strength.

"Alexi, Alexi! Keep looking at me. Stay with us," Timko urged.

He calmed when he saw Timko bending over him. Alexi coughed, then slumped back onto the blood-soaked table.

"I'm here, Alexi," Timko assured him, his eyes damp as he took the man's hand and squeezed it.

Alexi looked up at Timko and managed a smile. He closed his eyes and muttered in Russian. "I can hear the helicopter. They will be here soon to take me away . . ."

A minute later, Alexi was gone.

"I'm sorry," Jack said quietly.

Timko nodded as a tear escaped his eye, lost its

way in the stubble of his unshaven cheek. "Alexi was a decent man . . . for a Russian pig."

Jack studied the dead man's naked hide, criss-crossed with old scars. Someone had used a knife to inflict deep wounds that had shredded the flesh on his abdomen and chest. Jack knew that type of cut was meant to cause the most agony a human could endure. He looked up, met the heavy-set man's stare with his own.

"This man. He fought in Afghanistan," said Jack.

Georgi looked away. "Don't be absurd."

"Scars don't lie," Jack replied. "This man was tortured by the mujahideen."

"Who are you? What do you want from me?"

"My name is Jack Bauer. I'm not from around here. I'm in town for a job. I came right here from the airport because I was supposed to meet an associate—"

Timko snorted. "Now who is lying, Mr. Jack Bauer? Before I came to America, I was trained in the most difficult school in the world—the criminal underground in the former Soviet Union. I learned one thing while outsmarting the Communist enforcers. I learned to recognize the stench of police, no matter his country of origin."

Timko sniffed the air theatrically. "You, Mr. Jack Bauer, have a very strong odor."

A gun barrel dug into Jack's ribs. He turned to find a toothless old man pointing an Uzi at him.

"Meet my friend, Yuri. Do not let his looks deceive you. Yuri understands no English but he knows trouble when he sees it and can kill a dozen different ways."

Then Georgi Timko slapped Jack on the back.

"Once you have handed over your weapon, we will

sit down together, share strong tea, and talk like civilized men."

The black Mercedes moved along a dark stretch of Roosevelt Avenue under the elevated subway tracks. Steel support beams encased in crumbling concrete moved monotonously past the tinted windows. Though traffic was minimal at this time of night, cars were parked and double-parked along both sides of the busy commercial thoroughfare, making navigation tricky. Shamus Lynch skirted every obstacle.

He pressed the gas to beat a yellow light. The car hit a pothole and Shamus heard—or imagined he heard—the heavy missile launcher bounce in the trunk. Reflexively he glanced in the rearview, caught a glimpse of his ruddy, clean-shaven jaw, his fiery red hair, neatly cut—a professional look to go with the professional suit, the professional act.

For as long as he could remember, Shamus had despised looking younger than his years. Now, at thirty-five, crow's feet clawed his eyes. Creases gouged his brow. Shamus hadn't noticed the exact year, month, and hour his boyish face had fled—when the lines around his thin lips had deepened, his cheeks had become lean and angular like his brother's, his brown eyes as hard—but he was lately beginning to wonder if he'd been daft to ever long for it.

He couldn't remember a time when he hadn't admired Griff, ten years older, ten years wiser, the one to follow without hesitation. A stop sign compelled

Shamus to tap the brake and consider with a glance the man sitting beside him, staring intensely into the shadows between the streetlights.

In his beige, summer-weight suit, gold Windsor-knotted tie, and polished loafers, Griff could easily pass for your typical harried New York businessman. The handsome young freedom fighter was long gone. Not a strand of black Irish hair was left on his silver head and his normally pale features were looking downright ghostly. There was nothing faint, however, about Griff's resolve. For as long as Shamus could remember, he'd displayed more than enough raging certainty for the two of them, along with a vague paternal contempt toward any questioning of his decisions or plans. Not that Shamus had ever really challenged his brother.

Their father's death in '72, at the hands of the British Army had ignited Griff's sense of injustice. He'd spoken in church basements, organized civil rights protests, lobbied local politicians. Then their mother was murdered in a pub bombing. Gasoline on Griff's fire, that was. The IRA was Griff's family after that, vengeance his propeller. Shamus had been too young to sustain true hatred. He'd functioned mainly on need—need for his brother's affection and, eventually, his respect.

Even as a ruddy-cheeked child, he'd found a way to make Griff see his value. The cherubic freckles, which Shamus had always detested, allowed him to plant plastique unnoticed—at a bus stop near a Royal Ulster Constabulary post, a pub frequented by loyalist paramilitary groups, a British Army checkpoint. It had become a thing of pride for him, a measure of accomplishment to hide the thing and get away, to watch the explosion, to gain the approval of his brothers in arms.

They were fighting to free their countrymen, weren't they? From repressive, imperial, colonial rule. Human rights commissions were on their side. Hadn't the British allowed their army to detain and "question" his countrymen for as long as seven days without charges? Allowed their courts to convict based on confessions obtained through abusive treatment during that questioning? Taken away their right to a fair jury trial? Griff had made things clear for him back then, made things right . . .

"Ours is a justified war, and we're soldiers in it. The Brits . . . they try to label us 'terrorists,' but if that's so, then what are they, eh? Weren't the RAF 'terrorists' when they dropped two thousand tons of bombs on Dresden civilians? Weren't they guilty of 'terrorism' when they forced civilians into concentration camps in South Africa where thousands of 'em died?"

Whether their war was justified or not, in the end, Griff and Shamus both realized they'd been the losers. What was supposed to have been the highest achievement of their lives, the most important accomplishment for the Cause, had left them barely escaping the British Army, hiding on a tanker bound for North Africa. Everything had changed after that spring of '81. They could never again return to their homeland, never go back to using their real names. Yet Shamus had trusted Griff and he'd come through—found a way for them to continue the fight . . .

"Don't our brothers need arms?" Griff had told him. *"Don't they need explosives and weapons? That's what we'll provide. The Cause is still ours. Now we'll just be fightin' it another way . . ."*

Of course, Griff had said all that a long time go, almost seventeen years. Since then, their homeland—what they could remember of it—had changed its outlook. Peace agreements renouncing violence were now being struck by the IRA's political arm. While their comrades were rotting in hellishly long sentences in British prisons, the thrust of their people's will was being spent on disarmament.

Griff's cell phone rang. He pulled it out, flipped it open. Shamus's eyes were drawn to the twisted blast scars on his brother's hands, wrists, the callused knob that was once a finger. The wounds went deeper, spidering up his arms. The extent of their reach was hidden beneath the neatly tailored suit. For years, Shamus had seen them as badges of honor. Only in the past few weeks had he begun to ask . . .

"What are we doing, Griff? This job has nothing to do with the Cause."

"We didn't leave the Cause, Shea. It left us."

Griff had said the writing was on the wall. Adjustments were necessary. Shamus had disagreed. Weren't there still splinter factions like the real IRA who were still fighting the good fight? The Omagh bombing alone had proved the fight was still on. Wasn't a five-hundred-pound bomb tearing through a small town, killing twenty-eight and injuring hundreds, enough proof that peace under British rule was not a certainty? But Griff was unyielding. He claimed the real money for arms had dried up. And Shamus realized the real money was all he seemed to be after now.

"Chin up, lad," he'd told Shamus. *"With our new employer, we can ply our trade and get rich doin' it. We both know this is better than babysitting a stinking warlord in that stinking weapons market in Somalia."*

The red light blinked to green and Shamus gave the Mercedes gas. Listening in on his brother's cell phone conversation, he maneuvered the sedan along the narrow, congested streets. From what Shamus could deduce, there was some kind of snag—bad news, coming less than twenty-four hours before the whole operation was supposed to go down. By the deferential tone in Griff's voice, Shamus concluded their associate was not happy, and his brother was trying to fix the problem.

"Don't worry, I'll take care of it. Just like I took care of Dante and his Posse. Tell Taj the delivery will be there by morning. I guarantee it."

Griff ended the conversation, closed the cell, and stared straight ahead. "There's been a complication."

"Is that so?"

"Did you hear our boy Dante mention a lost memory stick?"

"Not a word," Shamus replied. "I figured it was blown up with the missile launcher."

Griff sighed in disgust. "That's the story he told our associate, but I think he has doubts and so do I. I'll be thinking the Feds got hold of that stick. Not the Federal Bureau of Investigation, but CTU."

"CTU! Can they crack it?"

"Of course they can . . . But it might take time."

"Enough time?"

Griff forced a laugh. "Ah, well . . . What's another three-letter word, eh? The SAS, the FBI, the CIA—now CTU—we took on all the others and we always walked away with our hides intact."

Shamus said nothing. Didn't smile or laugh. His hands tightened on the steering wheel.

"Pull over, right here," Griff commanded.

"But the pub's still a few blocks away—"

"Pull over." Griff's voice was tight, the forced levity gone.

On the mostly empty sidewalks, small knots of men and a few women gathered around Irish pubs to smoke, talk, and drink. This area, called Woodside, had for years been a haven for Irish immigrants. It still was, although these days it shared its sidewalks with the vast influx of newer immigrants. The century-old pubs and taverns were now interspersed between Korean greengrocers, Chinese and Filipino restaurants, and Arab-run newsstands and wireless stores.

Shamus guided the Mercedes into a spot in front of a darkened plumbing supply store. In the shadow of the overhead train, he cut the engine, killed the lights. The Number 7 Flushing-to-Manhattan train rumbled overhead.

"Wait here."

Griff opened the door and went to the back of the car. Shamus watched his brother through the rearview mirror. After the trunk opened, he could feel the weight shifting inside, though he couldn't tell what Griff was up to. A moment later, the trunk closed and Griff returned. When he sat down, he placed a silver metal attaché case on the seat between them—an identical twin of the one he'd handed off to Dante Arete.

Shamus eyed the case suspiciously.

"I took the memory stick out of our missile launcher and put it in here," Griff explained. "Have Liam deliver this case to the drop on Atlantic Avenue. He's to give the case to no one but Taj. And no taxis or car services. They keep logs that can be traced."

Shamus shook his head. "I can do it, Griff. Liam's just a kid, and it's one o'clock in the morning. Caitlin will have a frothing fit."

"I don't give a damn what your whore thinks. And you can't go. Neither of us can risk being seen anywhere near that dead drop. Liam's to do it and that's that. You were doing much more at his age, as I recall . . . Besides, he and his sister cost you enough of your money—those charity cases might as well be useful."

"Liam can take it in the morning—"

"Tonight. Get on it." Griffin seemed to regret his shortness. His voice became conciliatory as he added, "I know you'll be wanting to stay the night with Caitlin. Send Liam off and have your fun. Just be at the shop first thing in the morning. We need to close things down, tie up loose ends before our chartered flight takes off." He slapped Shamus on the shoulder. "Cheer up, brother. I know you don't much like pullin' up stakes again. But where we're goin', I hear the women are as beautiful as the beaches."

Attaché case in hand, Shamus nodded and climbed out of the car. Griffin slipped behind the wheel, made a fast U-turn, and sped away in the opposite direction. As another elevated train rumbled overhead, Shamus strolled the last few blocks to the corner pub called The Last Celt.

12:57:24 A.M. EDT
CTU Headquarters, Los Angeles

Captain Schneider climbed the metal staircase to the command center's mezzanine, a classified folder under her arm. She had been directed there by Jamey Farrell, who told her that Nina Myers had set up shop in Jack Bauer's office until his return.

She knocked twice, then opened the door. "Agent Myers? Can I have a moment of your time?"

Nina looked up, startled. She closed the file she was reading, sat back in the chair. "Come in, Captain Schneider."

The Marine slid into a chair. Her blond ponytail was unraveling, and there were bags under the woman's eyes, but Schneider's expression was alert, her voice strong when she spoke. "I have some progress to report."

Nina blinked. "On the memory stick. That was fast."

"When I opened the device up, it was clear the interior circuitry was manufactured in North Korea. The chips were made at their number two microchip plant in Pyongyang, and it was probably assembled there, too. But what is interesting is the fact that this stick was further engineered at a later date. It was retrofitted with the USB port, and inside I found some routers manufactured in Mexico."

"Any clue who did the retrofitting?"

Captain Schneider shook her head. "Not yet. But I did find this."

She reached into her folder and took out a digital photograph. "This is the surface of the main bus port, magnified fifty times. Note the serial number . . ."

Nina took the printout. A sequence of thirteen numbers and letters was stamped in the polymer surface.

"You can trace this?"

Captain Schneider nodded. "Given enough time. There are about five thousand firms in the United States, Mexico, and Canada licensed to manufacture this bus port. Each of these firms have thousands of clients who purchase these ports—"

"So you're saying it's impossible?"

"Not at all," Captain Schneider replied. "The Defense Department, the NSC, the Commerce Department, even the State Department keep tabs on the sale of such technologically sensitive devices. One of them is bound to have this serial number on file, but that's a lot of information to process, and from a lot of different locations."

"How can I help?" asked Nina.

"I need access to a computer with a large memory and a random sequencer. That's the only way I'm going to be able to collate so much data in a short time frame."

Nina didn't hesitate. She touched the intercom button.

"Jamey here."

"I want you to set up Captain Schneider at a station that interfaces with the mainframe. She needs a random sequencer and DSL access," Nina said.

"Roger. I'll put Milo on it. The sequencer should be up and running in five minutes."

"Okay?" Nina said to Captain Schneider.

"That's great. Thank you," Captain Schneider said, rising. "I should be able to determine precisely which computer firm did the retrofitting within the next few hours."

1 2 3 4 **5** 6 7 8 9
10 11 12 13 14 15 16 17
18 19 20 21 22 23 24

••

**THE FOLLOWING TAKES PLACE
BETWEEN THE HOURS OF
1 A.M. AND 2 A.M.
EASTERN DAYLIGHT TIME**

••

1:04:12 A.M. EDT
Tatiana's Tavern

Jack was treated like a guest. Yuri directed him to a private restroom in the back of the tavern. The old man even provided bandages and disinfectant for Jack's cuts and scrapes. As he was cleaning up, Jack heard engines outside in the parking lot. There were no windows in the bathroom, so he toweled off his face and slipped his shirt over his head.

In a typical New York neighborhood, shots fired in a bar would have brought down police, ambulances, press, and maybe even a fire engine. Since the gunfight here, however, the only sirens Jack had heard were in the far distance—the likely response to the JFK plane crash.

Tatiana's itself was isolated, the lone occupied building along a stretch of auto graveyards and vacant lots. The only way police would have known about the gunfire was if one of the patrons had called 911, and Tatiana's patrons clearly wanted as little to do with the police as its owner. So Jack wasn't all that surprised when he discovered the vehicles that had pulled up outside were not part of any government arm—local, state, or federal.

Yuri met Jack at the door and escorted him into the tavern area. The space was now filled with a dozen men, young and old, lean and fat. All of them appeared to be Eastern European, with blond hair, fair skin, and light eyes. They spoke to one another in Ukrainian. The bodies of Arete's men were gone. Alexi's corpse had vanished as well. The men swept the floor, moved broken tables and chairs outside. A carpenter hammered at the shattered, bloodstained floorboards. Others were slapping plaster and fresh paint on the bullet-riddled walls, while two bearded men, armed with AK–47s, guarded the entrance.

Georgi Timko waved Jack forward. "Too much noise in here. Come with me."

Timko's office seemed small for such a large man. Behind an old steel desk with an ancient Macintosh computer, a window looked out on a dark, deserted plot of weedy land. The chairs were comfortable, and the tea—hot and so sugary it was nearly the consistency of syrup—was surprisingly stimulating.

Also on the desk was Jack's watch, PDA, and CDD satellite communicator, which looked just like a normal cell phone. Timko slid the objects to Jack.

"You can have these back, my friend. No guns, though. Not yet. We've had enough shooting for tonight."

After some verbal sparring, Jack told Timko enough of the truth to make the man trust him. Timko freely admitted he operated a number of criminal enterprises, but denied any involvement in terrorist activities.

"That kind of thing is political, Mr. Jack Bauer. Since I came to America, I promised myself never to get involved in politics. It's a dirty business."

"Then why did Dante Arete's Posse try to kill you?"

Timko shrugged. "I think it may have something to do with the other men you spoke of. The Lynch brothers."

"The men in the Mercedes?"

The big man nodded. "I know them very well. They are not above assassination."

"Tell me more."

"The Lynch boys showed up . . . maybe a year ago. They went into business with the Columbia Street Posse around the same time. Griff Lynch came to me a few weeks ago, offered a business opportunity. I turned him down. But from his reaction, I'd say not many people have said no to Mr. Griffin Lynch."

"What kind of business opportunity did he offer you?"

"Something about airports and smuggling. He was looking for men with experience in certain types of weapons."

"Like shoulder-fired anti-aircraft missiles?"

Timko shrugged. "He didn't elaborate."

Jack raised an eyebrow. "But Georgi, you seem to be an intelligent businessman looking for an opportunity to make a buck. Why did you refuse this one?"

"The deal sounded political," Timko replied. "As I said before. I never get involved in politics."

The office door opened. Yuri entered. The assault rifle was slung over the old man's shoulder. In his arms he carried a tray.

"Ah, hot food at last," sighed Georgi. "Please join me, Mr. Jack Bauer. I don't know about you, but nothing makes me hungrier than getting shot at—especially when they miss, eh?"

1:16:38 A.M. EDT
The Last Celt

The place was nearly empty, the last customer trading jibes with Donnie Murphy at the bar. The pub was dim now that the bright sign in the window had been extinguished; the mahogany bar and booths, the oak paneling on the walls, the framed black-and-white photographs of forgotten boxers, baseball players, and local entertainers all seemed to absorb the light that remained.

"I got to tell you, Donnie. I took a bath on those damned Mets tonight," said Pat, a balding man with a well-known penchant for gambling.

"What can you do?" said Donnie in his rich baritone voice. "It's the fortunes of war. You place your bet and you take what comes."

With stooped shoulders, short-cropped gray hair, watery blue eyes and a loping limp, Donnie looked more like a senior citizen coaching a Little League team than the ex-con, ex-Westie turned pub owner. Only a few knew that Donnie's limp was the result of a vicious kneecapping masterminded by a prison rival decades before.

Alone at a table counting the evening's paltry tips, Caitlin sipped a cup of tepid tea. She'd only heard rumors about Donnie's past as an Irish gangster and enforcer on the West Side of Manhattan, though it was no secret he'd spent a decade or more in New York's notorious Sing Sing prison. Caitlin generally disregarded the rumors. She knew Donnie only as a generous and irascible old man who gave her the first real job she had in America, and a place where she and her brother could live when they were down and out and desperate.

" 'Night, Pat, see you tomorrow," Donnie called. "And next time, bet on the home team."

The New York Mets game—broadcast live from the West Coast—had ended half an hour before, and the pub had pretty much emptied out after a few celebratory rounds. On the television behind the bar, the post-game highlights had been replaced by silent images of an airplane crash at John F. Kennedy Airport.

Caitlin pushed an unruly strand of red-gold hair away from her face, messaged a neck that ached from carrying trays all night. With a sigh she rolled the bills up in a napkin and thrust the wad into her blouse. Once milky and smooth, Caitlin's pale skin was now sallow and uneven. Her formerly lustrous hair was frizzy and tangled. Her generous mouth frowned more than it smiled, and her lipstick—too red— exaggerated the emotion on her tired face.

The baby fat of her adolescence had melted away unnoticed in the past few months. Her long legs, once shapely, seemed thin and white under the short black skirt. But some of the changes were really improvements—age lent character and beauty to her face, her finely chiseled cheekbones more pronounced, green eyes large and lively despite the lines of exhaustion that edged them. Still, at twenty-two, Caitlin thought she was beginning to look—and feel—middle-aged.

"Better lock up, Caitlin," said Donnie. "Then get to bed."

Before she could rise, the bell over the stout oak door dinged once as it swung open. Caitlin's heart sunk when she saw Shamus Lynch on the threshold. Shamus had said he might stop by, but it was so late Caitlin, dared hope for a respite. But he was here now, a silver metal attaché case clutched in his hand.

Shamus pretended not to notice Caitlin, greeting Donnie and accepting a Sam Adams. Caitlin rose, carried the cold cup behind the bar, and dumped the tea into the sink. As he took his first gulp, Shamus caught her eye, winked. The smile Caitlin returned was forced. When Shamus waved her over a moment later, Donnie diplomatically moved to the opposite end of the bar and raised the volume on the television.

Shamus slipped his arm around Caitlin's hips. "Miss me?"

"Depends," said Caitlin. "Were you gone?"

Shamus planted a wet kiss on her lips, smearing her lipstick. Caitlin did not resist. Shamus rested his hand on the silver case. "Where's Liam? I got a job for him."

"Where do you think he is? He's sleeping. You can tell him all about it in the morning."

Shamus shook his head. "Sorry, darlin'. Can't wait. It's an important computer component. Has to be delivered tonight, so everythin's runnin' smoothly for business first thing in the mornin'."

"My little brother ain't going out in the middle of the night, Shamus, no matter what you or your brother say."

"It's a big job, Cait. I had to talk Griffin into giving Liam a crack at it. And the pay's real good. The kid does well and . . . uh, maybe he can apprentice in the electronics shop this summer."

Caitlin gave Shamus a sidelong glance. "You'd do that?"

"It ain't really up to me. Griff's the boss. But he likes Liam and if the kid shows himself to be responsible . . ." Shamus's eyes held steady, locked with Cait's green gaze.

Satisfied he meant what he said, she handed Shamus the key to her apartment. He squeezed the key, still warm from her touch, and winked again.

"See you upstairs," he said softly. "After you close up."

Then Shamus swallowed the rest of his beer, snatched the case off the bar, and sauntered to the back of the pub. He unlocked a small door and proceeded up the narrow stairs behind it to the cramped apartment Caitlin and her brother shared on the second floor.

Shamus found fifteen-year-old Liam tucked in a sleeping bag, eyes closed. There was only one bed in the two-room furnished apartment, and Caitlin used it.

Shamus gently kicked Liam's leg. "Wake up," he said, pulling off his suit jacket and loosening his tie. "I got a job for you, lad. Right now."

The youth sat up and rubbed his shaggy hair, red-gold like his sister's. "Hey, Shea. What time is it?"

Shamus laughed and tossed a pair of sneakers at the

boy. "Time for you to earn two hundred dollars up front, another hundred when you've done the job."

Liam was instantly awake. He rolled up the sleeping bag and tossed it behind the small couch in front of the tiny television set. Then he began to dress— jeans, white T-shirt under a navy blue sweatshirt, the dirty, scuffed sneakers Shamus had tossed him.

The man sat down on the couch, slid the case across the floor to Liam. "You're to deliver this to Taj and no one else. By subway. No taxi or car service. Remember how to get there?"

Liam nodded. Shamus reached into his wallet and took out two hundred in cash, thrust it into the boy's hand. "If there's any trouble, do what I told you to do. You remember?"

The youth nodded. Shamus eyed the attaché case warily. "And whatever you do, don't open the case. Got it?"

"I got it, Shamus."

"Then take off. And on your way out, tell your sister to get up here. I'm waiting for her . . ."

1:24:18 A.M. EDT
CTU Headquarters, Los Angeles

"Look, Tina. All I said was I wanted to go out with my friends on Friday night—"

Even from her chair in front of the monitor, Captain Schneider could hear the tearful sobs on the other end of Milo's cell connection.

"I never said I was bored with you, honey. I don't care what that magazine article said, I'm not like that," Milo insisted.

"Don't cry, I—"

Captain Schneider faced Milo. "I hate to interrupt, Mr. Pressman, but I'm having some trouble connecting to the DOD database."

Milo covered the phone. "That's because you're using the wrong routing protocol. Use our own network connection. CTU maintains a constant link with the Department of Defense, and the Central Intelligence Agency, too. The security code is thirty-three dash zeta zed backslash."

Captain Schneider tapped her keyboard. A moment later CTU's random sequencing program was searching through all of the DOD's stored digital files for a long string of numerals that matched the serial number printed on the memory stick.

"Look, Tina," said Milo, the cell phone close to his ear. "There's a situation here, I really have to go—"

"I think I just lost the feed from the Commerce Department," Captain Schneider said. She directed Milo's attention to a black data window on the massive HDTV monitor.

"No," said Milo, covering the phone. "See the blinking red cursor. Your search is completed. Engage the sequencer for a printout of your results."

"How do I do that?"

Milo lifted his finger, pressed three numbers, then enter.

"Yes," Milo said into the phone. "You did hear a woman's voice. It's my supervisor . . . Yes, Tina, you're right. That doesn't sound like Jamey because it isn't Jamey . . . Yes, Jamey Farrell is still my supervisor. But I'm talking to another supervisor right now."

"Mr. Pressman? What does this mean?"

Milo looked up, at the data window for the Department of Defense database. It was blinking yellow. His girlfriend chattered on, but Milo wasn't listening anymore. He rose to get a better look at the data window, absentmindedly closing his cell and dropping it back in his pocket.

"I can't believe it," gasped Milo

"Believe what?"

Milo blinked. "I thought this whole thing was a waste of time. Like finding a tiny needle in an immense digital haystack. But you did it, Captain Schneider. You located a match."

1:38:09 A.M. EDT
The Last Celt

Liam's scuffed, thrift shop sneakers bounded down the stairs. The pub was empty. Donnie Murphy had just left for Forest Hills where he still lived in the tiny brick house he and his late wife had shared for the past twenty years. Donnie trusted Caitlin to take care of the place when he wasn't there; it was part of the deal he made with her in exchange for access to the dingy apartment upstairs.

Caitlin handed Liam a cup of hot tea. "I'll need it to go, sis."

"You'll sit down and drink that before you go traipsing all over town in the middle of the night."

"But Shamus is waiting for you. He told me to send you up."

Caitlin bristled. "I'm not a servant that he can be summoning at will. Who's Shamus Lynch think he is, the Prince of bloody Wales?"

Liam laughed, slid into a booth. Caitlin brought him a sugar bowl and a dish of shortbread cookies. She glanced at the case on the floor. "What's in the case. Where are you going tonight?"

"Some computer thing, I think," shrugged Liam. "I'm taking it to a guy named Taj in Brooklyn—"

"Brooklyn!"

"Brooklyn Heights. It's no big deal. I'll take the 7 train to Times Square, then switch to the Number 2. That'll take me to close to Atlantic Avenue. I'll have to hoof it from there. It's a gatch walk but I've done it before—"

"But not in the middle of the night."

Liam swallowed the dregs of his tea, ignoring the cookies, and lifted the case.

"Are you sure you don't want something to eat?"

"Nah, ain't hungry."

Caitlin rubbed her hand through his mop of hair, the red-gold bangs hanging in his face like a sheepdog. How did it get so long, so quick? she wondered. First thing tomorrow, she was giving it a trim. "Tell me, Liam, and don't lie. Is this delivery on the up-and-up?"

"Sure, what do you think? Shamus owns an electronics store, he's not some criminal."

Caitlin sighed. She knew Liam looked up to Shamus like an older brother. They owed him for his help, that was certain. Finding her a job. Paying for Liam's Catholic school. But Shamus and his brother weren't exactly freshly washed sheets. She'd seen them talking quietly in this pub with enough shady types to guess they didn't get all their computer parts by way of legitimate wholesale. Whether they were moving stolen merchandise for small-time thugs or buying crates that "fell off" trucks driven by patsies for organized crime, she didn't know for sure. She just didn't want Liam involved in that part of their business. She wouldn't abide having her brother turned into a common thief.

"Liam, tell me what Shamus said. I want to know exactly what he's putting you up to."

He shrugged. "Taj has some store in Brooklyn—a deli. He has one of those computerized registers that takes credit cards and bank cards and stuff. It's probably broken. I'm taking him some kind of component, that's all."

"Anything else?"

"Chill out, Cait. I've done this before, you know."

"But not at such an ungodly hour."

Liam laughed. "And I'm bein' paid well for it, which is fine by me. Take it easy, will you? Shamus said he never even met Taj. He's just a customer. They do all their work over the phone!"

Caitlin sighed. "All right, all right . . . it sounds like it's on the up-and-up . . . and you might as well know that Shamus talked to me about giving you a job—"

"He did!"

"Hush. Yes, he did. But you're not to mention that I told you. I just want to make sure what Shamus is doing is honest work, that he won't involve you in anything shady."

"Who cares, so long as it's profitable?"

Caitlin shook her brother's shoulders. "Don't talk like that. There's more important things than money."

Liam threw his head back and laughed. "Not here in America, sis. In America money is everything."

"Hush your mouth."

"No way," Liam replied. "I'm sick of wearin' charity shop Nikes and listenin' to the radio instead of playin' CDs. I want a Nintendo. I want my own PC. And I'm tired of livin' in some dump of an apartment above an old pub. Aren't you?"

1:55:33 A.M. EDT
The lower level of the Fifty-ninth Street Bridge

"I'm tellin' you, man. You ain't seen anything this fine. These bitches ain't whores and they ain't hookers. They're high-class, know what I'm sayin'? *Carne dulce.*"

The white SUV bumped onto the ramp, climbing the bridge that spanned the East River from Queens to Manhattan. Dante Arete rolled down the window to disperse the fog in his head from too many beers, too much cocaine. For the last three hours, he'd been partying with his lieutenant at strip clubs on the Queens side of the Fifty-ninth Street Bridge. Now the stout drug dealer with the shaved head and tattoo of bloody thorns around his neck was driving him to a whorehouse that one of his Manhattan clients frequented.

"Word," the lieutenant told Dante, "these sluts . . . they'll make you feel like a fuckin' king."

The noise level increased as the van entered the mile-long lower level, which was enclosed in a steel support structure. Dark water flowed far below the span. Ahead, the lights of Manhattan twinkled in the warm spring night. Dante closed the window, sank deeper into his seat.

"A king, huh. Bring it on, 'cause that's what I am tonight."

More than a king, Dante felt downright immortal after surviving the last twenty-four hours. A CTU bust and a plane crash—neither had ended him. Now that it was over, Dante was gonna party till dawn.

"Royalty ain't cheap. These girls, they live on Sutton Place."

"Don't worry about money, *cholo*. Tonight, you talkin' to the ruler."

Dante reached over the back of his chair, pulled the silver attaché case from a bin under the backseat. He laid the case across his lap, patted it.

"In here, I'm tellin' you, I've got me a king's ransom."

The gang-banger nodded and licked his lips as Dante unsnapped the locks. Then he lifted the lid. Beneath the stacks of money that Griff had flashed him in Tatiana's parking lot, the one-pound block of C4 detonated.

There were two triggers on the attaché case. In the event one failed, the other would still set off the plastic explosives. Griff had activated both before handing over the closed case. The blast sent the SUV's sunroof upward, to dash itself against the roof overhead. The windows and doors flew off the white SUV, sending debris and glass blowing outward in a wide and deadly arc.

Sitting directly beneath the superheated blast, Dante Arete was instantly vaporized. The twitching body of his bald lieutenant—burned beyond recognition and still ablaze—was tossed out of the van and over the concrete wall that separated the traffic lanes.

A truck heading to Queens in the opposite direction pulverized what was left of the burning man.

The SUV, billowing orange fire and black smoke, rolled a few feet forward before it was ripped apart by a secondary explosion that spread wreckage and burning gasoline flowing across two lanes of the enclosed roadway.

1 2 3 4 5 **6** 7 8 9
10 11 12 13 14 15 16 17
18 19 20 21 22 23 24

• •

THE FOLLOWING TAKES PLACE
BETWEEN THE HOURS OF
2 A.M. AND 3 A.M.
EASTERN DAYLIGHT TIME

• •

2:02:03 A.M. EDT
CTU Headquarters, Los Angeles

Jamey Farrell divided her attention between the latest
Domestic Security Alert on her main screen—now
more than two hours old—and a data window on the
upper right-hand side of the HDTV monitor, where
Dante Arete's movements on the East Coast were
tracked by a GPS program that detected the signal
from the microchip embedded under the gang-
banger's skin.

Evaluating the daily Security Alert was an important part of Jamey's job. The highly classified watch
list was compiled by Richard Walsh's staff in Washington, D.C., and issued electronically every evening

at midnight, Eastern Daylight Time. The DSA cited every event occurring inside the continental United States, Alaska, and Hawaii within the next twenty-four-hour cycle that might pose a security threat, or attract the attention of terrorists. Every division of the CIA—including CTU—and all field agents posted in foreign capitals or the embassies of the world also received the DSA "hot list."

There were numerous events cited in the current Domestic Security Alert. In the next twenty-four hours a United States Navy Carrier Group would be docking in San Diego; the President of the United States would fly Air Force One on a courtesy call to a Colorado Springs congressman's district for a fund-raiser; and the Pennsylvania National Guard would conduct maneuvers in the hills of Central Pennsylvania.

Also listed on the DSA was a scheduled movement of spent nuclear fuel rods from the reactor at Three Mile Island, Pennsylvania; a charter flight from the Centers for Disease Control transporting dangerous biological specimens to New York City; and the First Lady's motorcade visit to a kindergarten in Falls Church, Virginia, to push the President's education agenda.

Jamey was about to catalog each item as "requiring no further action/CTULA" when she saw the red warning blip blinking inside the GPS data window. Dante Arete's signal had vanished.

"Oh, damn."

Jamey thought the problem might be a malfunction, or perhaps the battery in Arete's subdermal tracker failed much sooner than expected. But when she tried to send a signal to the device, she received no reply—though she should have gotten a single blip in response from the chip's fail-safe system, even if the device lost all power. The only way the tracker would completely fail to respond was if it was destroyed—which was only possible if Dante Arete's body had been utterly annihilated.

Heart racing, Jamey reversed the tracking mode camera and retraced the path of the GPS blip back to the second it vanished. The signal ceased transmitting thirty-five seconds before she'd looked up—more than a minute ago when accounting for the East Coast/West Coast signal delay. It took another minute for Jamey to switch from terrain mode, and to overlay the map grid of New York City on the GPS path. As the images were forming on her main screen, it first appeared to Jamey that Dante Arete's signal vanished over the East River. Finally, the three-dimensional image of the Fifty-ninth Street Bridge appeared. The blip had vanished in the middle of the span.

Jamey activated a subsystem that could immediately interface with emergency services departments in dozens of major American metropolitan areas. She keyed in the EMS code for New York City, and ten seconds later a massive log of 911 calls appeared on her monitor.

Before Jamey could even begin to scan the contents a new call appeared on top of the 911 roster—one that alerted the New York Police Department and Fire Department about an accident in the middle of the Fifty-ninth Street Bridge. According to the frantic 911 call, a white, late-model SUV was engulfed in flames—or possibly an explosion. A subsequent caller reported multiple fatalities.

Jamey stared at the screen in disbelief. The phone beeped and she hit the intercom. "Yes?"

"It's Nina."

"God, Nina I just lost—"

Nina interrupted her. "Listen, Jamey, we don't have much time. I have Jack on the line. He's just dumped new intelligence in our lap, including the possible identity of the men with the missile launcher. Now Jack needs an update on Dante Arete's position."

2:14:10 A.M. EDT
Tatiana's Tavern

Jack took the news about Arete's death hard. Their best lead—gone. He ended the call with Jamey Farrell and contacted Ryan Chappelle.

Diplomatically, Georgi Timko chose that moment to "get more tea." Cups in hand, the Ukrainian mobster left Jack alone in his office to speak to his superior in private, though Jack already assumed Timko had bugged the place.

"You heard about Arete?" Jack began.

"Nina just told me," Chappelle replied, "but I didn't have time for a thorough briefing—"

"Listen, I don't know if I mentioned the fact that the Lynch brothers slipped Dante an attaché case when they met up with him—"

"The Lynch brothers?"

"The men in the Mercedes. The ones who drove away with the missile launcher in their trunk," Jack explained, impatient that Chappelle had not bothered to keep up with the events he'd already relayed to the command center.

"What about these Lynch brothers, Jack?"

"I think they placed a bomb in that case to take Arete out."

"That doesn't make any sense. Weren't they the guys who shot the FBI airplane down to help Arete escape?"

"Maybe Arete's outlived his usefulness now that CTU's exposed his activities," said Jack. "Or maybe it had something to do with the deal Dante Arete made with Special Agent Hensley."

Jack heard a deep sigh on the other end. "What's wrong?"

"Special Agent Hensley is talking to his bosses, Jack. He fingered you for the murder of the two Federal marshals, for shooting the pilot, and for helping Dante Arete escape."

"That's crazy. I told you Frank Hensley's the traitor."

"Naturally the FBI is having a little trouble buying that. Hensley is a highly decorated field agent. He's been on the job for close to five years. That's longer than CTU's been around."

"So what are you telling me?"

"We're doing everything on our end to get to the bottom of things, but I've got to tell you some of the other agencies are shutting CTU out, and the FBI is not cooperating. The bad news is the FBI has issued a warrant for your arrest."

A long moment of silence followed. Then Chappelle spoke. "As it stands right now, you're on your own, Jack."

The line went dead and Jack lowered the cell phone. As if on cue, Georgi Timko returned with two mugs of sweet, steaming tea. He set one in front of Jack. Then he sat behind his desk and took a sip from his own cup.

"Bad news?"

Jack did not answer the question. Instead he leaned across Timko's battered metal desk. "The Lynch boys and Arete's punks tried to kill you, Georgi. Don't you want revenge?"

The Ukrainian chuckled. "Of course. And I will get my pound of flesh from those Irish punks and the Mexicans, too—but in *my* time, Mr. Jack Bauer. Not on *your* timetable, or your government's."

Jack frowned, rubbed his chin. The first signs of stubble were sprouting.

"But . . . since you saved my life, I feel I owe you something," Timko added. He pulled a Queens phone book out from under his desk, paged through it. He circled something on the Yellow Pages section, then tore a page out.

"Griffin and Shamus Lynch run a Green Dragon store in Forest Hills. It's part of a franchise. Computer sales and repair." He handed the page to Jack. "Here's the address and phone number. But they do most of their real work out of an Irish pub under an elevated subway train on Roosevelt Avenue. The pub is called The Last Celt. It's owned by a retired Westie gangster named Donnie Murphy, who is connected to the right people, even though he took himself out of the game a long time ago. Murphy has protected the Lynch boys ever since they arrived on the scene."

"Protected?"

"In this town, everyone needs protection, Mr. Jack Bauer. Even a remarkably resourceful man such as yourself."

"No. Right now, all I need is my weapon."

Timko folded his hands, held Jack's eyes.

Jack shrugged. "Okay, I guess I could also use directions to this pub, a car, and extra ammunition. Maybe a backup weapon, too, but nothing as flashy as an AK–47—if that's all right with you and Yuri."

Timko smiled, nodded, picked up the phone, and began to punch in numbers. "It's very late, Mr. Jack Bauer, but let us see what I can do."

2:27:56 A.M. EDT
CTU Headquarters, Los Angeles

Doris hit the delete key, then waited for the results. After five or six seconds, the cache registered zero percent memory and she moved on to the next bundle. After noting this data bundle's size, she pressed delete once again. This time the system seemed to stall, and Doris tapped her heel impatiently waiting for the program to obey her command.

After Captain Schneider had collected the memory stick for a physical analysis, Doris made a copy of the data downloaded from the device, then stored the original in CTU's main database. With a specimen safely preserved for the archives, Doris set to work "dissecting" the copy. First she isolated the different data streams, using a variety of self-invented techniques she created to hack programs for her uncle to replicate—and produce cheap knockoffs—in his Oakland, California, toy factory. With the data streams isolated, Doris began to delete them, one at a time. Her goal was to annihilate the program—eradicate it completely—in an effort to discover its architecture, to pick at its bones.

There were amazing things buried in the simplest programs, information of all kinds. Sometimes the creators of a subprogram inadvertently buried information, or hid it on purpose. Watermarks, access, security protocols, and slicing codes—sometimes complete software engineering documentation or embedded schematics were waiting to be discovered and decoded by just the right application of an outside program.

In the past Doris had tested the various reverse-engineering programs floating around in cyberspace or available commercially, but she never much cared for any of them. Instead she dismantled each program she'd come across and used the best pieces to create her personal reverse-engineering monster. She called it Frankie, short for Frankenstein, because her creation was a monstrosity cobbled together from bits and pieces just like the monster. And like the monster, Frankie was also a being that was much more than the sum of its parts. Using Frankie's phenomenal capabilities, Doris had dismantled the memory stick's software piece by piece, while mapping its secrets.

Frankie was nearly a decade old now, the first bones put in place back when Doris started working for her uncle. In those days, she never thought much of her hacking skills—not until she went to a conference sponsored by the Working Forum on Reverse Engineering to "pick up a few tips." The WFORE board members were so impressed by the young woman's innovative methodology for recovering buried information and systems artifacts from software, they invited her to join their organization. Doris had just turned sixteen.

An urgent beep shocked Doris awake. She blinked and rubbed her eyes, not sure she'd read the screen correctly.

"System failed to execute command!?"

That had never happened before. *Never.*

She sighed. "If at first you don't succeed . . ."

Doris called up the bundle again, checked the cache size—the same as before. But before she pressed delete she kick-started the dumping process by opening another bundle for the data to flow into. Sometimes that trick worked for stubborn programs that refused to go away.

Again there was a long lag time before she got a response.

"Failed again!"

Doris called up the cache—but found that all but approximately five percent of the program had indeed been eradicated. A stubborn subset of data remained in the cache, however. Doris suspected it was some remnant of an interfacing program, something that allowed the data she'd erased to be used in another program. Setting the problem aside for the moment, Doris moved on to the next bundle of data.

But five cache deletes later it happened again—a stubborn five percent of the memory cache refused to be deleted no matter what she tried.

Doris issued a tiny squeal of frustration.

2:36:19 A.M. EDT
Tatiana's Tavern

Yuri appeared at the office door, jerked his head. Georgi rose and roused Jack Bauer, who had fallen asleep in his chair after a long phone conversation with someone named Almeida.

"Your car has arrived, Mr. Bauer."

Jack rubbed sleep out of his eyes. "What time is it?" He blinked when he saw the weapons and ammunition on Georgi Timko's desk.

Jack ignored the shotgun, but lifted the Heckler & Koch Mark 23 USP, the .45-caliber self-loading version of the smaller, lighter USP Tactical, which Jack had used during his stint at Delta Force. The standard Mark 23 lacked the bells and whistles of the Tactical model—including the O-ring barrel that allowed the use of a KAC suppressor, and the rear target sight adjustment. But more important to Jack, the Mark 23 had the same ambidextrous magazine release just behind the trigger guard as the high-end Tactical. This allowed ejection of the spent magazine using the thumb or index finger without having to readjust one's grip on the weapon—an essential feature for quick reloading and accurate fire.

"The best I could do in such short notice," Georgi said apologetically.

Jack checked the pistol's extractor, which doubled as a loaded chamber indicator. The magazine was full, but to satisfy himself the readout was accurate, Jack pulled the slide back slightly and looked inside. There were additional magazines on the desk— twelve of them—each loaded with a dozen .45-caliber slugs.

Jack was accustomed to using 9mm rounds, not the bigger .45-caliber slugs. But with the Mark 23's recoil-reduction system, which featured a spring within a spring, Jack knew the felt recoil would be dampened enough for him to switch to the harder-hitting ammunition without difficulty.

Offering sincere thanks to Timko, Jack engaged the safety and slipped the weapon into his shoulder holster. Then he pocketed the extra ammunition in his pants, shirt, and jacket pockets.

"Take the shotgun as well, Mr. Jack Bauer," Georgi insisted. "You never know when you might have to shoot something bigger than a man."

Jack snapped up the double-barreled, sawed-off weapon and rested it on his shoulders. Then he followed Georgi outside. They avoided the bar area, where the sounds of construction continued, to exit through a back door hidden between the tavern's outdoor Dumpsters.

"My escape hatch," Georgi explained.

Emerging from behind the smelly garbage bins, Jack found himself in Tatiana's parking lot. Outside the night had cooled somewhat, but the humidity level remained high, much higher than LA. The sky was clear and cloudless, the parking lot nearly empty. Yuri was waiting for them, leaning against a 1998 cherry-red Ford Mustang Cobra convertible. He tossed the keys to Jack.

"I've given you directions to The Last Celt. Sadly I could not provide the proper paperwork for the automobile, so I advise you not to get stopped by the New York Police. They may ask some embarrassing questions . . ."

Jack slid behind the wheel. "I'll try to get the car back to you as soon as I can," he said.

"Do not worry about it," Timko replied with a dismissive wave. "The car is not mine."

Jack inserted the key into the ignition and the 305-horsepower V8 engine roared to life. A moment later Georgi Timko and Yuri watched as Jack sped into the night. When Jack was gone, Georgi shook his head. "I certainly hope the real owner of that superb automobile has taken out plenty of insurance. With Mr. Jack Bauer behind the wheel, he'll need it."

2:45:13 A.M. EDT
CTU Headquarters, Los Angeles

"The serial number on the bus port of the memory stick matches one manufactured in Shanghai and imported by a Swiss firm called Abraxsus-Gelder LLC," Captain Jessica Schneider began. "The shipment it came in passed through United States customs in May of last year and this particular component was purchased by a Green Dragon Computers store in Little Tokyo, right here in Los Angeles."

While she spoke, Captain Schneider tapped the blue folder that lay closed on the conference room table. She'd compiled the data herself, so she didn't have to refer to her notes to know what they said. Her update to the Crisis Management Team was concise and informative.

"Who owns this Green Dragon outfit?" asked Tony.

The woman turned to face Special Agent Tony Almeida. "A conglomerate out of Taiwan, with Abraxsus-Gelder as a partner. But a man named Wen Chou Lee holds controlling interest in the computer store franchise. They've been giving chains like Computer Hut and Cyber-Store a run for their money."

"Does this Wen Chou Lee have any ties to international terrorism? The Chinese Nationalist Movement, perhaps?" Nina asked.

"No," said Captain Schneider, still facing Tony. "But a 1995 report compiled by Interpol claims Wen Chou Lee was formerly the leader of a triad in Hong

Kong. He was forced to move his business interests to Taiwan just before the Communist Chinese government regained control of the island."

"I doubt a triad would have much interest in shooting down U.S. cargo planes," said Tony. He swiveled his chair to face Jamey Farrell. "Any luck tracing those license plates?"

"The Mercedes is registered to Griffin Lynch, which we knew already. The SUV was licensed to a company in Manhattan . . ." Her voice trailed off as Jamey searched the file in her hand for the printout. Jamey nearly groaned out loud when she realized she didn't have the information and must have left it at her workstation. She continued to fumble through the file even after she felt Tony's eyes on her, heard Nina's impatient sigh.

A knock interrupted them. The door opened before Nina could warn the visitor away. The conference room was off limits to everyone except members of the Crisis Team and unless the caller was Ryan Chappelle—who wouldn't bother to knock—he shouldn't have been there.

Doris stuck her head through the door. "Oh, there you are," she said, pushing up her oversized glasses. "I've been looking all over for you guys."

If Nina was impatient, she didn't let on. "Come in," she said. "And close the door behind you."

Suddenly shy, Doris stepped through the door. Milo wondered if he was the only one to notice the young woman wasn't wearing any shoes.

"Excuse me. I found something I think is important." Doris stepped forward and handed a printout to Nina, who glanced at it, then passed it to Milo and Jamey.

"There's a second layer of inscription that was buried inside the memory stick software."

Milo tapped a pen to his nose. "A watermark? Maybe a manufacturer's protocol?"

Doris shook her head. "This is a real program, and a big one. It's buried deeper and guarded better than the primary program data, which makes me think the whole first layer was a ruse, that the real important information is encrypted somewhere inside this buried code."

"Encrypted?" said Nina. "You mean you haven't cracked it yet?"

Doris brimmed with confidence. "Not yet, but Frankie's working on it, so it's only a matter of time."

Milo blinked. "Who's Frankie?"

2:55:30 A.M. EDT
Woodside, Queens

Liam stood on the raised platform, four stories over Roosevelt Avenue. A cool, humid breeze wafted in from the ocean, cutting the heat of the day. With a groan of impatience, he glanced at the cheap plastic watch on his arm.

It was nearly 3 A.M. He'd been waiting close to an hour for a subway. He knew service was bad late at night, especially on a weekday. But this was ridiculous. Only three trains had come in the time he'd been waiting. Two local trains going in the opposite direction, and a maintenance train that rolled right through the station without stopping.

He decided to wait another ten minutes. If it didn't come, he'd call it quits and hike the ten blocks over to

Northern Boulevard, where he could pick up an R train.

Liam peered down the tracks to the next station in the distance. Lights had appeared—another train at last. He set the attaché case down and rubbed the sweat off his hands. Lifting the silver case again, he wondered only briefly what was inside. Whatever it was, it didn't weigh very much. The most important thing, to Liam's way of thinking, was that taking this case to Brooklyn meant three hundred in cash.

Liam leaned over the edge of the open platform and peered down the track. The lights were approaching. Liam could clearly make out the purple circle with a seven emblazoned in the middle. In less than a minute he could sit down and rest as the train carried him to Times Square station.

When Liam finally boarded the Number 7 train, a cherry-red Mustang rolled directly beneath him. Behind the wheel, Jack Bauer cased the stretch of Roosevelt Avenue that ran under the elevated platform, then pulled into a parking spot directly in front of The Last Celt.

....

**THE FOLLOWING TAKES PLACE
BETWEEN THE HOURS OF
3 A.M. AND 4 A.M.
EASTERN DAYLIGHT TIME**

....

3:02:49 A.M. EDT
CTU Headquarters, Los Angeles

The meeting broke up soon after Doris interrupted it.
Jamey hurried back to her workstation. The printout
on Dante Arete's SUV was lying on her desk, right out
in the open—a clear violation of protocol. She
snatched it up and stuffed it into the blue "classified"
folder.

"Jamey?"

She jumped at the call, whirled to find Nina Myers
standing over her. "Yes?" Jamey replied, in a tone that
revealed her alarm.

"Are you all right?"

Jamey nodded quickly. "Just a little tired."

"We all are," said Nina, stepping forward. "But that doesn't excuse sloppy performance of a critical task."

"I don't—"

"The license trace on Arete's SUV," said Nina in a clipped tone. "I need the information now. I'm going to debrief Ryan."

Jamey yanked the document out of the blue folder, thrust it at Nina. She took the printout and scanned it. "The white SUV is registered to a Wexler Business Storage Company on Houston Street in Manhattan . . ."

Jamey nodded. "It has not been reported stolen. But that may change once the place opens up and someone notices the SUV is missing."

Nina looked up. "What do we know about Wexler Business Storage?"

"Nothing yet," Jamey replied. "I was about to run a check on the company, access their tax records, when the Crisis Team meeting was called."

Nina dropped the printout on Jamey's desk. "Get on it now. Top priority. I want a report within the hour."

Just then, Ryan Chappelle appeared at Nina's shoulder. "I need to see Tony Almeida. Do you know where he is?"

"He's over at financial. I've got him checking bank files and transaction histories on a Taiwanese computer firm and its owner."

"You mean Wen Chou Lee and Green Dragon Computers? Put Jamey on it. We're going to need Tony in the field."

Nina nodded, surprised. "Okay. But how did *you*

know about Lee and Green Dragon? I just found out about it myself and was on my way to brief you."

"Captain Schneider brought me up to speed a few moments ago."

Nina frowned. "Captain Schneider?"

"The captain is part of our Crisis Team, right? Good call on your part, Nina. It doesn't hurt to make political friends on Capitol Hill. Treat Congressman Schneider's daughter right, and he might return the favor someday. CTU can always use a political ally."

"I was only thinking of what was best for the current mission."

"And speaking of the mission, I'm putting Captain Schneider in the field with Tony. They're both ex-Marines, they speak the same institutional jargon, as it were. I think they'll work well together."

Nina hesitated but didn't protest. "I'll . . . I'll go find Tony."

"No. Keep doing whatever it is you were doing," said Chapelle. "I'll brief Agent Almeida myself."

3:11:19 A.M. EDT
The Last Celt

Caitlin had swept and mopped the floor, stacked the dried mugs on the rack, and polished the bar. More than an hour had passed since Liam had left for the subway, and Caitlin estimated he was halfway to Brooklyn by now. She looked around the bar, but there was nothing left to do. Tossing the last of her cold tea down the drain, she prepared to climb the stairs to her tiny apartment.

Caitlin had been stalling because Shamus was up there, waiting. He hadn't made a sound in more than half an hour and she was hoping he'd fallen asleep. Shamus did that, more often than not, on the nights he stayed with her—especially after he'd had two or three beers. Caitlin knew his routine and kept the tiny refrigerator upstairs well stocked with Sam Adams. Caitlin knew Shamus was expecting more from her than sharing a beer and some television. She never, ever offered, but he'd forced himself on her twice.

Over the past few weeks Shamus had felt increasingly pressured—something to do with his business—and the tension had revealed a cruel side to his personality. It was during this time that he began to pressure her for physical satisfaction, then forced himself on her.

The first time was two weeks ago. She'd tried to fend him off, but then she'd surrendered quietly rather than awaken her brother. The second time was only a few days ago. Liam had spent the night with a friend in the neighborhood. Shamus got a little drunk and a little rough, and so she'd surrendered again.

Upon reflection, Caitlin decided she had once liked Shamus, but she'd never loved him. Now she didn't even like him.

Even now Caitlin was torn about the situation. She and her brother owed their survival to Shamus's generosity. He'd helped them when they were both desperate, jobless, and nearly homeless. For a while Caitlin had even convinced herself that Shamus was genuinely fond of her. Only lately, when the relationship turned possessive, had she come to realize that Shamus was only exploiting the gratitude she felt toward him for his own ends, and that his generosity was a sham.

If a man demands something in return for his help, that's not generosity, is it? That's a transaction.

Caitlin started when someone pounded on the stout front door. She glanced at the clock, then tentatively approached the entrance, if only to assure herself the doors were locked, the bolt secure. The pounding came again, louder than before.

Caitlin put her face against the wood, peered between the cracks. In the dim glow of a nearby streetlight, she saw a man with an intense gaze and sandy-blond hair standing on the sidewalk. He was athletically built, dressed in dark clothes. He must have seen her shadow because he suddenly spoke.

"Please, you have to let me in," he said.

The accent sounded American to Caitlin. He didn't sound like he was from New York.

"I need to see the Lynch brothers. It's a matter of life and death."

3:14:49 A.M. EDT
CTU Headquarters, Los Angeles

Ryan Chappelle found Tony Almeida downloading Wen Chou Lee's financial records from the Taiwan Bank and Trust Company database.

"Want to engage in a little field work?" asked Chappelle. "With supervision, of course."

Tony nodded eagerly. "You bet."

"Send this data off to Jamey's workstation where she can evaluate it. Then I want you to reconnoiter the

Green Dragon Computers store in Little Tokyo. I've got a report which indicates there's a small electronics repair facility inside that store. Zoning and salary records indicate three shifts a day, which means that facility is up and running twenty-four/seven."

"How aggressive do you want me to be?"

Chappelle contemplated the question. "Don't run in with guns drawn, but get results. We know it was this facility that retrofitted the memory stick, so at least one person inside that firm knows about the device and how it was meant to be used. Find out what you can in a hurry. I don't want you to have to make a second trip."

"Should I talk to Blackburn, the team?"

Chappelle winced. "Definitely not. I'm keeping the Special Assault Team out of this, especially after that mess at LAX. You'll have a partner, but not someone from Tactical, or Division . . ."

Tony's eyes narrowed suspiciously. "Who exactly are you referring to?"

"Captain Jessica Schneider. She's the one who dug up the information on Green Dragon. She wants to go into the field to further investigate but she needs backup. That's you."

"No way," said Tony. "I'm not taking orders from a novice."

"I already told her she's going. And that she's in charge," Chappelle replied.

"She's active military. What about *posse comitatus*?"

"She's temporarily attached to CTU, which means Captain Schneider has an executive mandate to deal with domestic terrorists that overrules *posse comitatus*."

Tony frowned. "But she has absolutely no field experience."

"Captain Schneider found the link to Green Dragon everyone else missed. For that she's earned the right to follow up the investigation to the end. As far as field experience goes, everyone has to start somewhere. You had no field experience a year ago."

"It's political, isn't it, Ryan?"

Ryan Chappelle nodded. "Yes, Tony. It is."

"Get someone else, then. Special Agent Martinez, or that new guy, Curtis what's his name."

Ryan shook his head. "Believe it or not, Captain Schneider requested your presence, and you're going, Tony."

3:17:00 A.M. EDT
The Last Celt

"There's no one here. We're closed."

Caitlin was firm, but the blond American refused to go away. He seemed to search for another way in, then he spoke again. "I need to see Shamus or Griffin. It's urgent."

The man sounded sincere. "Who are you, then? The police?" Caitlin asked. "If you're a cop then show me yer badge."

The man shook his head. "I'm just a business associate. Listen, Shamus and Griffin are in danger. The people around them may be in danger, too."

Caitlin thought of Liam and the case he carried.

"At least give me some information," the man pleaded.

Caitlin took a deep breath. She unlocked the bolt

but left the chain in place as she cracked the heavy oak door. "You say you know Shamus?" she asked, nervously peeking through.

Jack nodded. "Yes. I've got to speak to him. I'm trying to keep him alive. His brother, too."

Caitlin gasped when a voice spoke behind her. "He's a damned liar, Cait."

She turned to find Shamus standing there, shirtless. He was flushed, angry. A gun with an absurdly long barrel was clutched in his right hand.

Through the partly opened door, Jack saw Shamus, too. He lunged, butting his shoulder against the thick wood between them. With the noise of splintering wood the bolt tore free. The door slammed against Caitlin, sending the young woman flying backward. She struck her head against the wall and slumped to the floor.

As Jack pushed through the open door, Shamus raised his arm and the weapon in his hand discharged. The blast was muffled by the noise suppressor on the barrel, but Jack felt the bullet whiz past his head, heard it slap against the elevated train's steel support beam in the street behind him. Jack leaped forward. Before Shamus could fire again, he slapped the weapon out of his hand.

Shamus stumbled backward but didn't fall. He bolted across the tavern, tossing tables and chairs in Jack's path. Jack caught up with him just as he burst through a door and started to climb narrow stairs to the second floor. Jack seized Shamus by the ankle and yanked. Legs jerked out from under him, the man hit the steps with his jaw, but still fought back. Jack grabbed the man's red hair as Shamus clawed at his face. Holding the man steady, Jack laid a hard right on the man's already bruised face—then another. He raised his fist for a third blow but Shamus went limp.

Jack hauled the man up the rest of the stairs and into the cramped apartment. He tossed him onto the floor. Using cords ripped from a phone, radio, and lamp, Jack hog-tied Shamus Lynch and muffled his mouth with some electrical tape he found in a drawer. When he was satisfied the man wasn't going anywhere, Jack ran back downstairs to check on the woman.

She had yet to stir when Jack got to her. He stepped over her limp body and closed the door, then he searched her clothing for a weapon. All he found was a wad of money in her blouse, some change in an apron pocket. The woman moaned softly. Jack hurried back to the bar and filled a glass with water, wrapped a cloth around a chunk of ice, and brought them back to her.

"Here, drink this," he said softly, cradling the woman's head and tipping the glass to her lips. "Can you talk?"

She nodded. "Yes."

"What's the name of this pub?"

"The Last Celt."

"Do you know what time of day it is? Before midnight or after?"

"After."

Jack checked her eyes. Her vision didn't appear glassy or vacant and her voice sounded strong, her answers comprehensible. So it didn't appear she'd suffered a concussion, but there was a nasty bump growing on her head. He placed the icy cloth against it and she winced.

"Do you feel nauseated? Dizzy?" Jack asked.

The woman waved him off. "You almost killed me, you did. All to get to Shamus. I hope you found him. Now what? You'll murder us both?"

"My name is Bauer. I'm a Federal agent. You are . . . ?"

"Caitlin." She clutched her head. "Help me up."

Jack lifted the woman off the floor, guided her across the tavern. Chairs and tables were overturned, strewn about. "Ohh," Caitlin sighed when she saw the mess. "I just cleaned this place."

Jack helped her into a booth. "Do you live in the apartment upstairs?"

"What business is that of yours?"

"Do you live upstairs?"

"Yes. With my brother, Liam."

"You're Shamus Lynch's girlfriend."

Caitlin pressed the icy cloth against the bump on the back of her head, winced again. "*He* thinks so."

"What does Shamus do for a living?"

"Owns a computer store. Surely you know that, if you've come lookin' for him."

"And you know nothing about his other activities? His ties to international terrorism?"

Caitlin stared at Jack as if he'd grown a second nose. Then she laughed out loud. "Terrorist! Are you daft? You can't be thinking about Shamus. The man might buy stolen goods here and there, but international terrorism? Mother in heaven, no."

They both heard a crash from above. Jack grabbed Caitlin's arm and dragged her across the tavern and up the stairs. In the small living room, Shamus was awake and struggling. He'd knocked over a chair trying to free himself. When Caitlin saw Shamus tied up on the floor, she froze; her green eyes went wide. Jack pushed her into the couch.

"Sit down and keep quiet," he told her. Then he reached down and tore the tape away from Shamus's mouth. The man spit out a bundle of cloth and launched into a stream of obscenities.

Jack grabbed what he could of the man's short red hair. "Why did you shoot down that airplane tonight?"

Shamus howled like an animal and spit at Jack. Bauer cuffed him, drawing blood. "Where is the missile launcher now?"

"You're from CTU," Shamus said. "The Counter Terrorist Unit."

"Where is the missile launcher?" Jack yelled.

Shamus clamed up. He glared darkly at Jack, spat a mouthful of blood.

"That attaché case you handed over to Dante Arete in Tatiana's Tavern. You remember, Shamus. The silver metal case full of money?"

Jack heard Caitlin's sharply drawn breath when he mentioned the case, pretended not to.

"It exploded a few hours ago. Right in the middle of the Fifty-ninth Street Bridge. Killed Arete and everyone else with him. Any more attaché cases like that one floating around, Shamus? Any more fatal surprises for the poor bastard who opens it?"

Shamus glared at Jack, but refused to speak.

"For God's sake, tell him," Caitlin cried.

"Shut up, Cait!" Shamus yelled. "Talk and I'll kill you. Don't say anythin' to this lyin' pig—"

Jack struck Shamus with the butt of his gun. The man's head snapped to the side, then dropped to the floor. Caitlin stared at Shamus in horror. He was either unconscious or dead. Caitlin couldn't be sure.

When she looked at Jack, he had fixed his gaze on her. "You know something." His voice was ice. "Talk to me now or I'll do to you what I did to him."

1 2 3 4 5 6 7 **8** 9
10 11 12 13 14 15 16 17
18 19 20 21 22 23 24

∙∙∙

**THE FOLLOWING TAKES PLACE
BETWEEN THE HOURS OF
4 A.M. AND 5 A.M.
EASTERN DAYLIGHT TIME**

∙∙∙

4:02:56 A.M. EDT
The Last Celt

"Don't hurt me, please. I'll tell you what I know, but not here." Caitlin gestured toward Shamus Lynch. Jack could see she was afraid of Shamus being conscious enough to hear.

"Let's go," Jack said, yanking the woman off the couch and pushing her ahead of him down the stairs. In the middle of the tavern, Jack set up a table and two chairs. Pushed her into one chair and sat down opposite her. "Tell me what you know."

"My . . . my fifteen-year-old brother has one of those cases you were talking about. Shamus is paying him to deliver it to someone."

"Your brother is part of this conspiracy?"

Caitlin shook her tangled mane of red-gold hair. "No, no . . . He just took the job tonight. It's a delivery. That's all."

"A name," Jack demanded.

But Caitlin lifted her chin. "No. Not unless you let me go with you."

"Why?"

"For one thing, you don't know what my brother looks like, and I don't have a picture, so you'll never find Liam without me." Then Caitlin glanced at the ceiling over her head. "And unless you plan on locking Shamus up, you know what he'll do to me."

"I can't lock him up . . . Not yet."

"Then he'll hurt me."

Jack couldn't explain to this woman what was really going on—that he was on the run, that the FBI and the NYPD were probably looking for him right now.

"Okay," Jack said softly. "I'll take you with me."

Caitlin nodded. "One more thing. Show me an ID. An official badge or something like that. Just so I believe you."

Jack reached into his jacket and produced his CTU identification card. Caitlin's brow furrowed as she studied the card, Jack's image. Then she nodded again.

"Brooklyn," she said. "Liam is on his way to Brooklyn."

"Who is he going to deliver the case to?"

"The man's name is Taj. He has some sort of business in Brooklyn. That's all I know."

"You don't know what's in the case?"

Caitlin shook her head. "Liam never opened it. Not in front of me, anyway."

"Any idea what part of Brooklyn?"

"Liam said he was taking the Number 7 to Times Square, then he's changing trains to get to Brooklyn. He'd be going to Atlantic Avenue, but I don't know which subway stop he'll use."

Jack stood, pocketed the key to the front door. "Wait here." As he walked back upstairs, he passed the tavern's phone. He ripped it loose from the wall and threw it into a corner.

Upstairs, Jack used his PDA to snap a digital image of Shamus Lynch and sent the data to Jamey Farrell's computer. Then Jack checked the bonds on Shamus Lynch and replaced the gag. Without resources on this coast, he was forced to abandon his prisoner here in the probably vain hope that Lynch could be recovered by the proper authorities before he managed to free himself. At least he would be out of action for the next several hours—long enough for Jack to locate Caitlin's brother and the other attaché case.

Satisfied he had done all he could do, Jack went downstairs, to find Caitlin waiting for him by the locked front door.

4:33:46 A.M. EDT
Green Dragon Computers, Los Angeles

"There seems to be a whole lot of activity on that loading dock, considering it's one o'clock in the morning."

They sat at a red light on East Third Street, Tony behind the wheel. At his side, Jessica Schneider slipped her mini-binoculars into a pocket. Out of uniform, she opted for tight black denims and stacked boots, lightweight summer blouse under a short leather jacket to hide her sidearm. Tony thought she looked fit.

And she probably skis Vail and rides thorough-breds, too, Tony mused. *The benefits of growing up the privileged daughter of a Texas congressman. A lot different pastimes than life for a Latino kid on the south side of Chicago, playing pick-up hoops on broken concrete and hustling your way into Cubs games.*

"I'm going to open your window a bit," Tony said, hitting the switch. Tinted, bulletproof glass descended a few inches, then stopped. Fresh night air filled the compartment—surprisingly cool for Los Angeles. A freak rainstorm had washed the late-night streets. Now the night was luminous with reflected light.

Tony twisted a knob on the dashboard, unspooled a long, thin, flexible wire. He passed it to Jessica.

"Use this."

There was an array of miniature lenses on the tip, and a mount that fit into a hook on the ceiling above the open window. Jessica slipped the tiny video camera into place. From his controls on the steering column, Tony popped the glove compartment and activated the video screen hidden inside.

"Camera's on. I'll roll by slowly. Watch the screen, not them. Let the camera be your eyes. Use the center control to zoom in or out. The onboard computer will record the images and send them back to CTU for further analysis."

The stoplight went from red to green. There was no one behind him, so Tony edged forward. Ahead, the reptilian neon glow of the Green Dragon Computers sign, a serpentine Chinese dragon forming the letters, was mirrored on the wet pavement.

The concrete block building that housed Green Dragon was located southeast of the Civic Center, in the heart of the redeveloped ethnic neighborhood called Little Tokyo. A maze of malls, restaurants, bookstores, and specialty and import shops, the area was the focal point of Japanese-American activity in LA.

According to their intelligence, the space now occupied by Green Dragon was formerly a Japanese supermarket, which explained the cavernous loading dock. Right now, the steel doors had been rolled up, the bright fluorescent lights filling the street.

Captain Schneider stared at the screen in front of her. "I've got a good picture. I'm zooming in."

The tires hissed on the pavement. Tony kept his face pointed straight ahead. "What do you see?" he whispered.

Jessica Schneider crouched low in the seat, straw-colored hair around her face, booted foot resting on the dash. Her pose was casual, almost sleepy, but her eyes focused intently on the screen as her fingers manipulated the controls.

"There are four men, one supervising. He's armed. An AK–47 is slung over his shoulder. A Dodge cargo truck—unmarked—is parked in the dock, the driver inside. The men are packing something up in a wooden crate, right there on the loading ramp. Can't tell what it is. I'll have to zoom in closer."

The SUV was almost past the open bay when Jessica Schneider spoke again. "It's a Long Tooth missile launcher. They're preparing it for shipment."

The building now behind them, the video screen went blank. Tony hung a left on Omar Street, pulled up to the curb. "I've got to call this in," he said, reaching for the radio. "We need backup to take this place down, seize that truck."

"No time to wait!" Jessica Schneider insisted. Before Tony could stop her, she was out the door and around the corner.

"Son of a—" Tony switched off the engine, secured the vehicle. Then he drew his P228 and took off after his partner. He rounded the corner in time to see Jessica race up East Third, boots clicking on the sidewalk. Near the Green Dragon loading dock, she drew a Marine Corps–issue Beretta 92F from her jacket.

Someone cried out a warning in Chinese. A shot struck the concrete near Captain Schneider's boot. She aimed her weapon in the direction of the roof, squeezed off two shots. There was a howl of surprise and pain; a body plunged down the side of the building, hit the sidewalk with a wet smack. Feet pumping, Tony was about ten yards from Jessica when the Dodge truck roared out of the loading dock so fast the woman barely had time to roll out of its way. The vehicle bounced into the street in a shower of sparks, crossed two lanes of traffic, and sped away.

Tony turned to check on Captain Schneider. She was running up the loading ramp, firing. One man pitched off the raised platform, the AK–47 still in his grip.

"Wait! It might be a trap!" Tony called.

Ignoring him, Jessica burst through the double doors and stormed into the building, gun blazing.

4:42:24 A.M. EDT
Tatiana's Tavern

"Don't lie to me, Mr. Timko. We know you helped a man named Jack Bauer last night."

Frank Hensley, flanked by a pair of FBI agents, leaned against the bar. Waiting for Georgi Timko to reply, he scanned the tavern's cheap yet suspiciously tidy interior: tables, chairs, booths, a wall-sized mirror behind the bar. Hensley could smell fresh paint.

Georgi gazed impassively at the FBI agent. Hensley and his men had swept in for a predawn raid, searching for Jack Bauer. By the time the Federal agents arrived, however, all evidence of the violence the night before had been eradicated, the bodies disposed of. Georgi was confident. He knew an FBI search would turn up nothing he did not want to be found.

"I don't know this Bauer fellow," said Georgi. "Perhaps if you describe him."

"We know he was here. We found Bauer's Glock outside, in the parking lot," said Hensley, displaying the weapon stashed in a clear evidence bag. "This weapon was used to kill two Federal marshals."

Timko shrugged. "Never saw it before. Perhaps it belongs to one of my customers. Many of them come from . . . how do you say it? Broken homes and troubled backgrounds." He smiled.

Another agent arrived, conferred quietly with Hensley. Timko knew the man was telling his superior that a search had turned up nothing but the Glock. Timko suppressed a chuckle, knowing he'd been successful. All they found was what he wanted them to find . . .

4:55:04 A.M. EDT
Brooklyn/Queens Expressway

The dark horizon bled color, dull purple edging out the black. Though the steel span of the Brooklyn Bridge was still swathed in shadows, the first hint of dawn was touching the sky. Jack drove past the ramp that would take them across the bridge to lower Manhattan. The city's skyline, dominated by the twin World Trade Towers looming over Battery Park, was a mass of mammoth black boxes dotted with bars of lights and topped with peaks, spires, spidery antenna arrays.

Caitlin, her fragile features pensive in the dim dashboard light, had said little beyond offering directions since they'd left Queens. Though Jack was itching to interrogate her further, he held back. He knew the worry she felt for her brother was clouding her thoughts, and Jack doubted he would get much useful information out of her in any case.

The cell chirped. It was Nina, with intelligence information on the leads he'd provided CTU.

"Interpol identified the man from the image you transmitted to us," she began. "Shamus Lynch is an alias for Patrick Duggan. For decades, he and his brother, Finbar Duggan, were international arms smugglers for the Irish Republican Army and the PLO. Both men are suspected of involvement in several bombings and attempted bombings in Northern Ireland. The brothers were born in Hillsborough, a small town south of Belfast. Their father was beaten by British soldiers during a protest march in 1972—just a week before the Bloody Sunday massacre. The man initially survived the beating but died weeks later. Their mother died a few years after their father. She was killed by a pub bomb believed to have been planted by a loyalist paramilitary group, possibly the Ulster Freedom Fighters, a cover name used by the Ulster Defense Association. Reading between the lines, it appears Patrick's older brother, Finbar, joined the Irish Republican Army after their mother's death. He would have been around twenty at the time, making Patrick no more than ten, but apparently he went along for the ride."

"What led to their flight from Ireland then?"

"Seems there was some kind of botched attempt on Queen Elizabeth II's life during her trip to the Shetland Islands in 1981 to mark the official opening of an oil terminal. The Duggan brothers were involved in handling and planting the explosives, but their information on the royal route was a setup. The explosion only destroyed property some miles away from the Queen's location, and the British swept up almost all of their associates in a dragnet.

"The Duggans very narrowly escaped, fled by ship with the help of IRA arms suppliers and PLO sympathizers. They surfaced in Somalia, where they began their gunrunning business by working for a local warlord. During that time Patrick's older brother was critically injured—there were even unconfirmed reports he'd been killed. Interpol was so sure Finbar Duggan was incapacitated, they moved his dossier to the inactive list."

"Apparently he's recovered," said Jack.

"Watch out, Jack. The Duggan brothers are tech savvy and well-versed in explosives and terror tactics. Finbar was trained by Dmitri Rabinoff—"

Former KGB, one of the best, Jack recalled. "Rabinoff trained Victor Drazen's Black Dogs . . ."

"Listen, Jack. Jamey also ran the name Taj through CTU's database of known terrorists and their associates. We tagged the search geographically, targeting the region around New York City and came up with a possible link. Are you familiar with the name Taj Ali Kahlil?"

"No."

"During the Soviet occupation, Taj Ali Kahlil became a national hero for downing Soviet HIND helicopters with Stinger ground-to-air missiles smuggled into Afghanistan by the CIA.

"After the fall of the Soviet Union and the rise of the Taliban in Afghanistan, Taj and an associate named Omar Bayat became Afghanistan's leading proponents of terrorism. Taj and Omar are suspected in the downing of a Belgian airliner over North Africa two years ago."

"I recall the incident but I don't see a connection yet," said Jack.

"Taj and Omar used a North Korean missile launcher in that attack—the forerunner of the Long Tooth missile system, to be precise. More importantly, Taj has a brother who fled the Soviet occupation in the 1980s. His name is Khan Ali Kahlil. He's now a United States citizen and currently runs a delicatessen on the corner of Atlantic Avenue and Clinton Street, Brooklyn."

"That's where the attaché case is headed," Jack replied. "I'm sure of it."

"I agree," said Nina. "I'm sending Khan Ali Kahlil's New York driver's license photo to your PDA, along with the most recent photos of Omar Bayat and Taj Ali Kahlil that we have in our database. Also some intelligence on the neighborhood."

Jack ended the conversation, checked his PDA. The photo of Taj Ali Kahlil was not much more than a blur. The driver's license photo of his brother Ali was almost a decade old and out of focus. The image of Omar Bayat, however, was crystal clear. It was taken by German intelligence agents in Libya in 1996. Bayat had blond hair, probably dyed, and could pass as an American.

Road construction slowed his progress so Jack reviewed the data Nina had sent him. After a few minutes waiting for traffic to proceed, Caitlin broke the silence. "What was that conversation about?" she asked.

"We may have found where your brother is taking the attaché case," Jack informed her. "A delicatessen on the corner of Atlantic Avenue and Clinton Street."

He could tell from Caitlin's blank stare that the address did not trigger any memories. Traffic began to move, and they passed a massive ditch in the roadway, heavy equipment moving tons of broken pavement.

"Caitlin, try to remember if Shamus mentioned anyone else in connection with his business. Anyone at all."

The young woman massaged her forehead. "He once mentioned a man named Tanner. A big client, he said. Had a funny first name, like Oscar or maybe— no! I remember now. It was *Felix*. Felix Tanner."

Jack nodded. "How well did Shamus know Taj?"

"I'm pretty sure they never met. Shamus told my brother he did all his business with Taj over the phone."

Ahead, Jack saw the sign for the Atlantic Avenue exit and pulled off the highway. Five minutes later, they were on the avenue itself. From the intelligence

Nina sent him, Jack knew this area—called Cobble Hill—featured the largest concentration of Middle Eastern shops and businesses in the city. The area was occupied by Yemenis, Lebanese, Palestinians, and other immigrants from Muslim countries.

"That's the place," said Jack. Caitlin saw the sign: KAHLIL'S MIDDLE EASTERN FOODS.

Face grim, Jack studied the shop, which sold groceries and prepared foods, exotic spices, Arabic newspapers and magazines.

"I'm going to circle around and park."

Jack located a spot almost in front of the delicatessen. The store took up the ground floor of a century-old, three-story brownstone. The security gate was up, and a *New York Post* truck rolled up while Jack parked, delivered a stack of the morning edition hot off the presses.

"I want you to hold this stuff," said Jack.

He handed Caitlin his cell phone, the PDA, and the revolver Georgi had given him. Jack reached into his jacket and gave Caitlin his CTU ID, too. After a moment's hesitation, Jack slipped off his wedding ring and added it to the pile. He kept the wallet he'd taken from Shamus Lynch, slipped it into his hip pocket. Then Jack popped the door.

"Where are you going?" Caitlin asked.

"Inside," he told her. "I'm going to try to pass myself off as Shamus Lynch. If Liam shows up, stop him from delivering the case—and don't open it, no matter what."

Caitlin touched Jack's hand. "What about you."

"If I don't come out of there in two hours, I want you to call 911."

....

**THE FOLLOWING TAKES PLACE
BETWEEN THE HOURS OF
5 A.M. AND 6 A.M.
EASTERN DAYLIGHT TIME**

....

5:00:01 A.M. EDT
Green Dragon Computers, Los Angeles

Tony Almeida ran through the empty loading dock and up the concrete incline. Exhaust fumes from the Dodge cargo van still lingered, though the vehicle and the missile launcher it carried were long gone. Half expecting a sniper's bullet to cut him down, Tony felt his skin prickle as he moved without benefit of cover. He found the supervisor lying at the top of the ramp, dead eyes staring at ducts that crisscrossed the ceiling.

He found the AK–47 on the ground, popped out the banana-shaped magazine, and thrust it into his pocket. Then he checked the assault rifle's chamber for an extra round. Finally he tossed the empty weapon into a Dumpster, satisfied no one could use it against him now.

Tony moved to the door, but before he entered the factory he used his cell phone to call for backup. Ryan Chappelle was unavailable to authorize direct action, so Nina Myers dispatched the Special Assault Team on her own authority as Chief of Staff. Estimated time of arrival: eight minutes.

Tony wasn't happy about calling out Blackburn's men—Ryan Chappelle had been against using the assault team—but neither he nor Nina could see any other way to go. The LAPD weren't equipped to handle potential terrorism, and would ask for things CTU could not provide—like a warrant to enter the premises.

Tony ended the call, pocketed the cell phone. From somewhere inside the factory a shot boomed. Two followed in reply. Tony gripped his P228 with both hands and burst through the factory doors, startling the only occupant—an elderly Chinese woman with skin like old parchment, trembling beside an overturned bucket and fallen mop. She threw her hands in the air when she saw Tony.

"Relax! I'm not going to hurt you," Tony said in what he thought was a reassuring tone. The woman calmed for a moment, then spied the 9mm in Tony's hand and began to scream.

"Look, I'm leaving, I'm leaving," Tony said, lowering the weapon.

He quickly moved into a maze of cubicles and workstations. The area was lit by overhead fluorescent lights, crammed with gutted computers, loose motherboards, wire bundles in rainbow colors, dangling circuits, soldering irons, and tools.

Progress through the factory was slow because Tony feared ambush. After a thorough search of each cubicle he finally found someone else. An Asian man with a long ponytail, perhaps twenty-five years old, was lying facedown on the concrete floor, blood pooling around two holes punched into his abdomen. A .45 was still clutched in the man's right hand. Tony kicked the weapon into a corner, cautiously checked for a pulse, found none.

Then Tony discovered a staircase partially hidden behind a large bulletin board. He took the steps two at a time. At the top he pushed through a steel fire door, into a suite of offices. The area was large and dimly lit by recessed fixtures in the ceiling, the space broken up by cramped cubicles, sparsely furnished. A bank of chipped and dented metal filing cabinets ran along one wall. The carpet was stained and shabby.

Down a short hallway Tony found glass double doors; beyond that, a brilliantly lit, spotless, air-conditioned, air-scrubbed space dominated by a massive mainframe computer and two large workstations. Captain Schneider was in one of the stations, looming over a young Asian man slumped in an office chair. She gripped him by the scruff of his chic sports jacket, the barrel of her service revolver pressed against the back of his skull.

When Tony pushed through the doors, captor and captive looked up. Captain Schneider's relief was evident, though she quickly tried to hide it.

"About time," she said.

"I had to call for backup."

Tony drew a pair of plastic cuffs from his jacket, slapped them on the prisoner's wrists. The man was missing the little finger of his left hand; on his fore-arm the edges of a purple tattoo were visible below the cuffs.

"Watch the material, daddy-O," the man complained. "This is an Italian suit. The jacket alone costs more than an American flatfoot earns in three whole months of taking bribes."

Tony leaned close to the man's face. "Tough guy, eh?"

"His name is Saito," Captain Schneider said. "A visitor to our shores, from Japan—"

She was interrupted by a crashing sound, loud voices. Seconds later, Agent Chet Blackburn and another member of the assault team—clad in head-to-toe helmets and body armor, assault rifles raised and ready—hustled into the computer room, their chukkas scuffing the polished floor.

Blackburn put up his weapon, flipped the visor open. "Nice assault, Almeida. You, too, ma'am. Doesn't look like you guys needed our help."

"Wasn't me, Chet. Captain Schneider's the gung-ho jarhead."

Chet chuckled. "Maybe CTU should sign the lady up."

Tony couldn't hide his irritation. Captain Schneider holstered her weapon, helped the prisoner out of the chair. Blackburn noticed a long decorative chain dangling from the man's belt. He reached out and tore it off, rolled the silver links around his leathery black hand.

Saito studied the faces around him, then displayed an arrogant smirk. "This has been a lot of fun and all—" He winked at Jessica. "Especially meeting you, missy. But right now I need to confer with legal counsel."

5:11:54 A.M. EDT
Kahlil's Middle Eastern Foods

Hands in his pocket, eyes downcast, Jack entered the grocery store. Brass bells chimed as he pushed through the door. The interior of the store was surprisingly small and cramped. Narrow aisles and far too many goods piled one atop the other made the place feel claustrophobic. There was a vast array of products jammed into a limited space, but unlike most New York delicatessens, which copiously stocked beer, wine, and malt liquor in their refrigerator cases, no spirits of any kind were here—only soft drinks and dairy products. Jack wasn't surprised since alcohol was forbidden to Muslims.

Behind refrigerated glass at the deli counter, Jack saw tubs of water-soaked feta; trays of black, brown, and green olives; stuffed grape leaves; hummus; mast—a kind of Afghan yogurt—flat *nan* breads; and other foods Jack didn't recognize.

Somewhere a radio was playing, the volume low. The announcer spoke Dari, a common language in Afghan cities. From his quick reading of the CTU dossier in his PDA, Jack knew the Khalil brothers were nomadic Pashtuns by birth, so their first language was Pashto. Nomadic Pashtuns were raised according to an ancient tribal code called Pashtunwali, which stressed honor, courage, bold action, and self-reliance. They were also warriors by tradition, and undoubtedly by bitter experience, given the recent Soviet actions in Afghanistan.

Behind the register, a tall, thin man with a gray-streaked beard and an Afghan turban sat on a high stool. Jack waited patiently until a Hispanic man in a security guard's uniform paid for a copy of the *Post* and a cup of coffee. Jack noticed a well-thumbed copy of the Koran at the man's arm. Finally the security guard was out the door, and Jack approached the proprietor.

"Excuse me. I'm looking for Taj. Is he here now?"

The man barely glanced at Jack. His eyes were deep brown, reflective. They were the eyes of an aesthetic, not a terrorist.

"Who is asking?"

"My name is Shamus Lynch. I need to see Taj. I have something for him . . ."

The man's gaze grew suspicious and he did not reply. The moment stretched, until Jack began to think his masquerade had failed.

"Go to the door at the back of the store," the man said at last. "Follow the stairs to the basement."

Jack nodded, walked through the aisles to the rear of the market. When he was out of sight, the turbaned man reached under the register and pressed a button.

A few moments later Jack reached the bottom of the rickety and uneven wooden stairs. The three-story building that housed the market was more than a century old, so the basement walls were made of crumbling sandstone, the floor bare earth, covered here and there with rotting planks. The ceiling was so low, Jack had to crouch a bit to move around. For illumination two glowing bulbs dangled from wires wrapped around the plumbing. The place was dark, damp, and stank of mildew. Instead of a large, expansive area, the basement had been partitioned into sections by walls fabricated from unfinished wood already beginning to rot.

"Hello," Jack called softly.

From the partition behind him, a fist lashed out, cuffing Jack on the side of the head. The blow was not meant to kill, or even stun him, just put him down. It worked.

The man who'd struck emerged from the shadows, pinned Jack to the floor. He wore an Afghan skullcap, his scraggly beard dangled in Jack's face. One of his front teeth was missing and his hot breath reeked.

Jack did not struggle, even when a second and third man emerged from the shadows. One was a youth, his face twitching nervously. The other was past middle age, stocky and powerfully built. He also wore a turban, along with a clean if slightly shabby suit and a too-wide-to-be-fashionable tie. This man knelt next to Jack and fumbled through his pockets until he located a wallet. Inside the worn black leather he found cash, several credit cards, and a New York driver's license, all belonging to Shamus Lynch.

The older man lowered a lightbulb from the ceiling and shined it into Jack's face. Blinking against the glare, Jack wondered if his passing resemblance to Shamus Lynch—along with the fact that he held the man's ID—would be enough to convince these men he was the real deal. Though Jack could not see beyond the light in his eyes, he heard footsteps and knew more men had arrived.

"It must be him," someone grunted.

"As I said. Who else could it be?" the older man replied.

The man pinning Jack to the floor rolled off, then stood. He extended his hand, helped Jack to his feet. Jack rubbed the glare out of his eyes, focused hard to pierce the darkness. Soon he discerned five men surrounding him. Two were armed with U.S. Army–issue .45s, a third man had an AK–47 slung over his shoulder. Jack scanned the crude wooden walls around him, but could not figure out where the others had come from.

The older man closed the wallet, returned it to Jack.

"I am sorry for the rough treatment, Mr. Lynch. We had to be sure you are who you say you are."

5:35:23 A.M. EDT
Brooklyn Underground

Liam jerked awake, glanced at his watch. He'd been dozing for nearly thirty minutes. At Times Square there'd been a long delay because of bollixed-up track work. He'd waited forever to transfer from the Number 7 to the 2. Now the subway ride to Brooklyn was moving slower than bottled shite. He sat on a dead-still train in a dark tunnel between two stations. Which stations? He couldn't be sure since he couldn't remember when he'd fallen asleep.

Hugging the metal case in his lap, he sat up in the orange plastic seat and stretched his jeans-covered legs. The train started up again, rumbling toward the next station. He rubbed his tired eyes, fighting fatigue. For a long time during the seemingly endless underground journey, Liam had kept himself awake by visualizing all the stuff he was going to buy with the money Shamus was paying him.

New tackies first, he'd decided—not the gacky no-name brand from the discount store. Maybe a pair of Air Jordans, black with blue stripes. And a pair of new shoes for Caitlin, too. She was always complaining about how much her feet ached after working twelve hours in the boozer.

Liam's biggest dream was to own one of those new MP3 players. Two of his friends from St. Sebastian's had them, and they were downloading free music from their computers all the time. Liam thought that was bleedin' deadly. Of course, he didn't even own a computer so for now, having an MP3 would only work if he used his friends' machines. But if Shamus let him work the summer in his store, who knows? He might be able to afford a used PC and an MP3 before school started in the fall. That would be bloody brilliant.

Soon the train began to slow; the metal-on-metal screech of the brakes drowned out the garbled station announcement that simultaneously crackled over the intercom. Liam sat up, gazing through the window to see which station they were pulling into. Finally he saw the platform, the dirty beige ceramic tiles lining the walls. Then a strip of black tiles spelling out the name of the stop: Hoyt Street.

The train slowed as the conductor's voice crackled over the intercom.

"Attention passengers, attention passengers. This train is going out of service. Hoyt Street is the last stop on this train. Anyone wishing to continue on to Atlantic Avenue, exit here and wait for the next available train. We are sorry for the inconvenience."

Bloody hell, thought Liam. *One stop away and I gotta change trains.*

Liam stood, still groggy. Clutching the overhead rail, he moved to the door as the train squealed to a stop. The doors slid aside and Liam stepped onto the concrete platform. No one else exited the train, and he saw no one else on the platform. He discovered he was far from the nearest exit—two or three subway car lengths, at least.

The doors closed again. With a hiss the brakes were released and the train lumbered forward, gaining speed as it moved into the tunnel. Finally it disappeared, a steady blast of air in its wake. When the noise of the subway receded, Liam heard footsteps behind him.

As he began to turn, a hand snatched the case swinging at Liam's side. A powerful tug nearly yanked him off his feet. Liam quickly shifted his weight and pivoted to face the mugger. There were three. Black kids. Maybe two years older than he, one chubby, two lean. They wore oversized, dark blue jogging clothes, sneakers, baseball hats. Their eyes were focused on the metal case. But Liam refused to let it go. Gripping it with both hands, he began a tugging match with the fat git who'd grabbed it. For the moment, the two skinny ones held back, letting the big homey do all the work.

The chubby mugger was pulling hard, but Liam surprised him. Instead of tugging back harder, he pushed the case forward, thrusting it into the git's round face. With a crack the case smashed the kid's nose and cheek. He stumbled backward and released the attaché, then doubled over howling and groping his battered face with both hands.

Liam turned to flee, but a movement caught the corner of his eye. Something flashed close to his head, then connected with his upper arm. He stumbled under the impact. His arm went limp and the case clattered to the concrete.

One of the skinny kids stood over him with a nightstick while the other rushed forward to pick up the case. But the stupid plonker approached it too fast, kicking it forward.

"Shit—"

Time stopped as they all watched the case slide over the edge of the platform. The git with the nightstick swung it again. This time Liam saw it coming and dodged the blow. Sensation was coming back to his left arm along with throbbing pain. But Liam swung out with his good arm, determined to drive off his attacker.

The plump kid with the battered face was kneeling on the platform now, coughing. A stream of blood flowed from his nose and he cried out in alarm at the sight of it. The wanker who'd kicked the case glanced back to check on his friend, then freaked when he saw the blood.

"Shit—" he yelled again.

The git with the nightstick stared at the place where the attaché case plunged over the side. He took a half step in that direction when they all felt a breeze, heard a distant roar. A Brooklyn-bound train was coming, rolling along on the very same tracks where the case had fallen . . .

5:45:13 A.M. EDT
CTU Headquarters, Los Angeles

"Hey, that code sequence doesn't make any sense." Milo gestured toward the sequential stream of letters and numbers on the screen.

Doris stopped typing. "You're reading it from left to right. It's Korean. Read it backward."

Milo sat back. "Yeah, that's right. You said that before."

"Uh-huh," Doris replied, her fingers again tapping the keyboard.

"Why does Frankenstein—"

"Frankie."

"Why does your program depend on such old protocols?" Milo asked.

"Lots of reasons. North Korean programmers aren't always up to speed and they build their programs on top of preexisting computer models. Most of them are pretty old."

"Oh."

"And Frankie is pretty old, too. I started building him when I was in junior high school."

"What? Last week."

Doris paused, pushed up her oversized glasses. "Ha-ha. You're a real laugh riot."

She shook her head and went back to work. Milo Pressman was supposed to be helping her, but all he was doing was asking questions—when he wasn't arguing with his girlfriend. Frankly Doris didn't know what was worse, Milo's stupid questions or the stupid one-sided conversations with his stupid girlfriend he'd been having all night.

Suddenly the workspace reverberated with the

theme from the movie *Titanic*. Ugh, thought Doris. Tina's land line again. At least Milo had programmed Green Day to ring when his girlfriend called on her cell. But for the last few hours Doris had been subjected to that nauseatingly insipid "Sad Boat" song. She rolled her eyes as Milo flipped open his phone.

"Tina? I can't believe you're still awake? . . . What do you mean you're crying . . . Of course I didn't hang up on you. I told you what happened . . ."

Doris tried to block out the conversation, focus on the stream of data she had just managed to separate from the rest of the memory bits. This one looked promising.

"Don't cry, Tina . . . I can't stand it when you cry."

Doris pretended to gag, then silently mimicked Milo's and Tina's insufferable conversation. Something happened on her monitor, and Doris stared at the screen.

"A time code? What's a time code doing in here?"

"What?" said Milo, suddenly interested.

"I found a time code—date specific, too. It's in the heart of the program. The start time is twelve hours ago. The time code runs out—well, let me see . . ."

Milo leaned forward, to gaze at Doris's monitor. "Word. You're right. It is a time code . . ."

Tina, meanwhile, continued to speak over the phone, her voice a tiny squeak. Deciphering the data, Milo, not for the first time, forgot about the conversation with his hysterical girlfriend, closed the phone.

"What do you make of it?" he asked.

"The entire sequence is a long series of instructions. For what I don't know—yet. But from this time code one thing is certain. Today, this afternoon at five

P.M. Eastern Daylight Time to be precise, something really big is going to happen."

5:50:59 A.M. EDT
Hoyt Street Subway Station

Liam was still shaking when the Brooklyn-bound train pulled into the station, bringing with it the possibility of help from a motorman or conductor. The three punk muggers ran for the stairs, giving up on the case. Liam slumped down on a wooden bench, panting, in a cold sweat. His left arm throbbed. In a few hours, he'd probably have a bruise the size of Staten Island, but he could move it, so he knew bones hadn't been broken.

After the train closed its door and pulled out again, Liam began to search for the lost attaché case. It had fallen onto the tracks, he knew, and he was worried the train had run over it. Then he'd really be in the shitter. He walked to the very edge of the platform, scanned the tracks below. There was no debris, no sign of the case, though its silver finish should have made it visible even in the shadows of the subway tunnel.

Liam figured the drop from the platform to the tracks was about six feet—about six inches taller than he was. He could get down easily enough, but would have to pull himself back up again using upper body strength alone. For a moment, he hesitated, his mind jumbled. He thought about the money he'd lose if he didn't retrieve the case. But what panicked him more was the money he might owe.

Shamus had done a lot for him, for his sister, but the man could be a real tool. He'd either take the cost of the lost case out of Liam's hide or make him work off the debt for months—or both. Earning three hundred was one thing, but owing thousands or more for a lost computer part, or *whatever* was in that bloody attaché, scared Liam shitless.

No matter what, he had to find that case and deliver it to Taj.

He leaned over the edge, gazing into the tunnel, listening for the sound of an approaching train. Liam heard nothing, so he sat down, his legs dangling over the edge of the platform. Then he lowered himself to the tracks, careful to avoid the electrified third rail.

Oil and layers of filth covered everything at track level. Rats scurried around him, one ran over his foot. Liam yelped and shuddered. Then he exhaled and began to search the area, keeping one ear cocked for an approaching train.

His sneaker caught on a switching circuit and he stumbled and fell. His hand came within an inch of touching the electrified third rail. Liam carefully pulled his hand back. As he began to rise, he spied a bit of shiny silver metal—the attaché case. It had ended up under a cluster of signal lights, hidden from view above.

Liam moved quickly to the case, picked it up, and examined it in the station's dim light. Except for a few scratches and dents, it appeared to be fine. He was tempted to open the case, check the contents for damage—but Shamus had commanded him not to open it under any circumstances. Figuring there might be some sort of alarm or something, he decided to leave the case shut.

With a rush of relief, Liam stepped to the edge of the still-deserted platform. Boosting himself up wouldn't be easy. And there was no way he could do it while holding the case. Reluctantly, he swung the case over his head, heard the attaché land with a hollow clatter. Then Liam jumped and grabbed for the platform's edge. His fingers slipped almost immediately and he dropped back to the tracks.

Liam spit into his palms and rubbed his hands together. Under his scuffed tackies, the ground began to rumble. This time he put all his strength into the leap. He caught the platform's cold concrete edge with a firm grip and hung on tight. Legs kicking, he pulled himself up until one elbow rested on the platform. A few feet in front of his face, the attaché case lay on its side. Under him, Liam could feel the platform vibrate, hear the roar of the approaching train.

He kicked his legs again, rose a few inches—and then stopped. Something sharp had caught the pocket of his Levi's. No matter how he squirmed, he could not free himself. Lights appeared at the end of the tunnel, reflected off the dirty beige tiles.

At the opposite end of the tunnel, a Number 2 train roared into view.

1 2 3 4 5 6 7 8 9
10 11 12 13 14 15 16 17
18 19 20 21 22 23 24

. . . .

THE FOLLOWING TAKES PLACE
BETWEEN THE HOURS OF
6 A.M. AND 7 A.M.
EASTERN DAYLIGHT TIME

. . . .

6:05:08 A.M. EDT
Hoyt Street Subway Station

The motorman sounded the train's horn, activated the
emergency brake. A shrieking squeal filled the subway
station, but the train was too fast and too heavy to
stop on a dime. Its continuous forward motion bore
down on the terrified boy dangling off the platform.

Liam kicked wildly but couldn't free himself from
whatever had snagged his clothing. "Hail Mary, full
of grace, the Lord is with thee . . ." In seconds the
train would cut him in half. Liam closed his eyes. "Jesus, God, help me."

Strong brown hands gripped his forearms.

"Come on!" a deep voice boomed over the roar of the approaching train.

Liam felt someone pulling him upward. There was a tearing sound and he was suddenly freed. The man who'd tugged on his arms stumbled backward, dragging Liam onto the platform and out of the path of the steel monster a split second before it crushed him.

Trembling, Liam lay on the platform, hugging the concrete. From what seemed like very far away, he heard the train stop, then a voice over the chugging noise of the idling motor.

"You okay, son?"

In mild shock, Liam lifted his head, stared blankly at the black man speaking. The Transit Authority policeman took Liam by the shoulders and lifted him to his feet. The officer's brown eyes were wide with concern. Sweat stained his bronze-colored, pockmarked cheeks.

"I'm okay." Liam's voice was strained, even to his own ears.

"He okay?!" called the train's conductor from the open window in the middle of the Number 2.

"Yeah," called the cop. "Kid's okay." The officer turned his attention back to Liam. "Man! For a second there I thought we'd have to scrape you off the wall." The policeman smiled, his relief evident.

"Thanks . . . thanks for helping me," Liam muttered, knowing full well how inadequate his words sounded.

"What the hell were you doing down there? Did you slip? Or did somebody push you?" The transit cop glanced around the deserted platform.

"I lost my case and I had to get it back." Liam pointed.

The officer saw the scuffed and dented case lying on its side. He brought the case to Liam. The boy snatched it back, hugged it to his chest.

"Thank you, sir," he said quickly.

He felt the cop's searching gaze, refused to meet his eyes.

"What the hell's so important about that case that you'd risk your life for it?" the officer demanded.

Liam could hear the peeler's tone was a little less friendly now. Still dazed, Liam searched for an answer, but his mind drew a blank. Finally, he stammered, "It . . . it's my laptop computer."

The policeman studied the boy's expression, then the attaché case. "Is that right? Okay, then maybe we should open that case up and see if your 'laptop' is damaged."

6:08:36 A.M. EDT
CTU Headquarters, Los Angeles

Tony Almeida handed his prisoner over to an armed detention team.

"Take him to room eleven. Prepare him for interrogation."

"What's with the third degree, man? So my visa expired. So what?" Saito cried, squirming against his cuffs. "This is America. Even illegal aliens have got rights."

Captain Schneider fell into step with the guards. "I'm going with them. I don't want to let Saito-san here out of my sight."

The Japanese man smirked. "I'll bet you've got great gams under those Hepburns, missy. Put on stiletto heels and you can punish me any time."

The guards dragged the young man away. Tony signed his name on the entry log, then spied Ryan Chappelle approaching. He braced himself for a dressing-down.

"Good work, Agent Almeida. Great work, in fact," said Ryan, slapping his back. "You and Captain Schneider are to be commended. I just got off the phone with Chet Blackburn. He told me you two captured a mainframe computer with its database intact."

"That's right, Ryan. Unfortunately we got there too late to stop the transfer of another Long Tooth missile launcher to another location. We don't know where it's headed, yet, and that should be our priority. Has Jamey dug up any information on that truck?"

"She examined the footage you sent her, but even with enhanced imaging filters she couldn't get a license number off the plate. Nina issued an all-points bulletin, but there are a lot of white Dodge cargo vans in Los Angeles . . ."

"We should start with the vehicles registered to Green Dragon and all the factory's current employees. Then we should check the airports. Cargo shippers especially—"

"Jamey and Nina are on top of it, Tony. It's more important that CTU gets access to the data on that computer, so I've dispatched Milo Pressman with a Cyber Unit."

Tony nodded. "Captain Schneider also captured a prisoner. I'm on my way to interrogate him. His name is Hideki Saito, a Japanese national from Tokyo. He came here about eighteen months ago. His visa expired a month ago."

Tony displayed his PDA. "I'm going to run his name and picture through the Japanese National Police database. I'm certain Saito is Yakuza, so the Tokyo Prefecture will probably have a file on him."

Ryan was surprised "Yakuza? You're sure?"

"Definitely," Tony replied. "A member of an old clan, too. Very traditional. Somehow he messed up in the past so maybe I can use that against him during the interrogation. It might be the psychological hook I need to get inside of him."

"How do you know all this, if I may ask?"

"The little finger on Saito's left hand is missing. As atonement for his mistake—whatever it was—he was compelled to sit in the presence of those he offended, cut his own finger off, and wrap it in silk. Then he presented it to the head of his clan and asked for forgiveness."

6:12:52 A.M. EDT
Hoyt Street Subway Station

Liam stared at the policeman. "I can't go with you, Officer. I have to go to school . . ."

"That answer doesn't cut it, son," the man replied tersely. "You've already broken the law by going down onto those tracks, and I think you're lying about what's in that case, too—"

He was interrupted by the radio on his shoulder. "All available units. Emergency alert. Immediate backup requested. Tactical law enforcement action imminent. All entrances to Atlantic Avenue are to be secured immediately, the avenue to be closed off to all vehicular traffic. All available units respond . . ."

The officer keyed his microphone. "This is MTA, Hoyt Street. Moving to respond, over."

He faced Liam, and the man's expression hardened. "I have no choice but to let you go this time. But if I ever see you again I *will* find out what the hell you're up to."

6:39:09 A.M. EDT
Kahlil's Middle Eastern Foods

Four Afghanis in traditional garb led Jack through a maze of partitions under the century-old Brooklyn brownstone. Soon they came to a flat wooden wall with a single door hanging on two shiny steel hinges and ushered him inside.

Jack scanned his surroundings warily. The basement room was triangular-shaped with crumbling sandstone walls on two sides. Wooden crates were stacked against the stone wall; above them a small, barred window peered onto the street from sidewalk level. A massive water heater ticked in the corner, and the space was hot, dry, and stuffy. The only illumination was provided by a naked sixty-watt bulb mounted in the ceiling, and the tiny glimmer of sunlight that managed to penetrate the decades of grime layering the window.

Someone slammed the door, shaking the cheap partitioned wall. The burly Afghani in a skullcap pushed Jack onto the pile of crates. The older man in the ratty suit nodded to his comrades, spoke a command in Pashto, and the others left without a word. Before the door closed behind them, another man entered the dingy chamber.

This one was tall and wiry, perhaps fifty years old, with long stringy arms and legs under a loose-fitting shirt and cotton trousers. A .45 was slung in the man's belt; on his knobby feet he wore leather sandals. Though not particularly muscular, the Afghani man seemed to exude strength, and he was tall enough that he had to stoop slightly as he faced Jack. His face was narrow, flesh sallow and leathery. His intelligent eyes burned with fierce intensity. His hair was covered by an Afghan turban; the beard that dangled to his chest was streaked with gray. Under his prominent nose, the man's yellow teeth protruded slightly.

"Are you Taj?" Jack asked. "My brother Griff sent me here with a package."

The Afghani stared silently at Jack. It was the man in the ratty suit who spoke.

"Why did you break with protocol?" he demanded. "Why did you come here yourself, instead of sending that boy?"

"You need the case—"

"The boy was supposed to bring us the case," the man interrupted. "Where is he? Where is the case?"

Jack knew from the man's response that Caitlin's brother had not yet made his delivery, which was good news. If the boy *had* made the drop, these Afghanis would probably have killed Jack on the spot. Instead they hesitated, despite their obvious suspicions. Jack knew it was because they were so desperate to take possession of the contents of that case they were willing to take the risk that Jack was an impostor.

"I was being followed," Jack lied. "I had to ditch the case in case I was captured."

Jack sensed the man in the suit was wavering, not yet ready to believe Jack's story, but willing to be convinced. The silent man's expression was unreadable, so Jack decided to push the envelope, go for broke.

"Listen," he said in an urgent tone. "The whole plan may be unraveling. I think the Feds are on to us—that's who was following me, I'm sure of it."

The older man raised an eyebrow. "What do you propose to do about it?"

"I have to see Felix Tanner. Tanner has to be warned that the whole plan might be compromised."

The man in the suit became instantly alarmed. The silent man seemed implacable.

"Didn't you hear me?" Jack cried. "The whole plan is in jeopardy. I have to warn Tanner now, before it's too late."

The silent man spoke at last. His voice was soft, but firm. "We must retrieve the attaché case first. Lead me to it, then I will take you to see Tanner."

"Listen, Taj, we're all in danger. Just let me speak with Tanner—"

The older man stepped backward, perhaps alarmed by Jack's urgency. Before he could speak the high window burst inward, showering them all with shards of dirty glass. A dark object landed on the dirt floor. Instinctively, Jack threw himself backward, to land behind the crate he'd been sitting on. But the older man stooped over the object, reaching to pick it up. Jack opened his mouth to cry a warning—then the grenade exploded.

The powerful concussion tossed the man backward, against the wall. Though the older man absorbed the brunt of it, the blast was powerful enough to bowl everyone else over as well. Partially deafened by the noise, Jack could not hear the hissing noise as the gas canister released its noxious contents. But he immediately felt the stinging pain in his eyes, his nose, and he choked against the rising tear gas mist. Through the roaring that still filled his ears, Jack heard a loudspeaker blaring outside.

"This is the FBI. We've surrounded the building. There is no way you can escape. Come out with your hands up and you won't be harmed . . ."

••

**THE FOLLOWING TAKES PLACE
BETWEEN THE HOURS OF
7 A.M. AND 8 A.M.
EASTERN DAYLIGHT TIME**

••

7:00:06 A.M. EDT
Atlantic Avenue at Clinton Street, Brooklyn

After Jack Bauer had entered Kahlil's Middle Eastern
Foods, the night's events finally caught up with
Caitlin. Alone for the first time, she tried to make sense
of what was happening, think through any options.

Caitlin wondered why her brother had not yet arrived at this destination. Had she and Jack missed
Liam somehow? Had he delivered the attaché to Taj
before they arrived, and was on his way back home to
Queens? If so, her unsuspecting brother was heading
into the waiting arms of a spitting mad Shamus
Lynch, still bound and gagged in the dingy room
above the pub.

What if Jack Bauer doesn't come back? she wondered. *What am I supposed to do then?*

Jack had ordered her to surrender to the police if he did not return within two hours, but that was something she would never do. She and her brother had overstayed their visas and were illegal aliens. Caitlin didn't even have a bloody green card—Donnie Murphy was paying her off the books—and there would be hell to pay if the Immigration and Naturalization Service ever caught up with them. If Caitlin were to turn herself in to the authorities, and Jack Bauer was telling her the truth about Shamus's ties to terrorism, then she and her brother would be tainted by association. And if Liam had done something illegal by delivering that case to Taj, then her brother might be facing criminal charges, trial, and imprisonment.

At best they would be branded undesirable aliens and deported back to Northern Ireland. Though Liam would probably end up in the Londonderry Home for Boys. Caitlin was too old to be housed by the state and would end up on the streets. With no job, no home, no skills to speak of, Caitlin was about as useful as a leaky teapot. What future could she have in Ireland?

No, I'll never go to the police, no matter what happens.

Caitlin chewed her thumbnail, sweating under the increasing intensity of the early morning glare. Despite her proximity to New York harbor and the Atlantic Ocean beyond, there was no cool morning breeze off the water to stir the still air. The temperature was rising along with the humidity. In the front seat of the car, the sun beat down on Caitlin until heat became intolerable.

She opened the windows, but was unwilling to leave the car or even step outside. Instead, Caitlin searched the backseat for something to fan herself. That's when she noticed the black, late-model sedan parked across busy Atlantic Avenue, in front of a four-story brick building that housed an Arab meat market. Though the driver's eyes were shielded behind dark sunglasses, observing the man through the back window soon convinced Caitlin he was watching her.

Caitlin wondered how long he'd been there, if he'd seen Jack enter the Middle Eastern deli. Less than two minutes later that question seemed to be answered when an identical vehicle rolled slowly past her car with another man in a dark suit and sunglasses behind the wheel, trying hard not to stare at her. Shifting nervously in her seat, Caitlin looked around and immediately spied a third vehicle parked across Atlantic, this one along Clinton Street. Then a fourth vehicle pulled up behind the first one. Two men sat inside, behind tinted glass. One of them was speaking into a microphone strapped to his shoulder.

Caitlin began to panic.

Whoever these people were—friend or foe—they were arriving in greater numbers. More alarming, they seemed to be surrounding Kahlil's store and her car. Now Jack Bauer's story about Shamus's involvement with international terrorists did not sound so ridiculously far-fetched. Suddenly, Caitlin felt like an animal sitting in a trap about to be sprung.

Though Jack had ordered her to stay put and wait at least two hours before leaving the car and turning herself in to the police, Caitlin's instincts warned her of immediate danger. With shaking hands she stuffed Jack Bauer's belongings into her bulging shoulder bag, rolled up the windows, and stepped out of the car. Stamping a foot that had fallen asleep, Caitlin draped the heavy bag over her shoulder and used the keys Jack left her to lock the car door.

Adopting what she hoped was a casual manner, Caitlin used the reflection in the car's windows to adjust her hair, her clothing. Then she turned on her heels and strolled away from Atlantic Avenue. With each step she felt—or imagined she felt—suspicious eyes on her back.

In her initial panic, Caitlin sought only escape. She walked quickly down Clinton Street, passing century-old brownstones fronted by iron gates and high sandstone stairs. But after several blocks, her steps slowed. Caitlin thought of her brother. It wasn't a given that he'd come and gone already. He might still be making his way to Kahlil's, or he might already be inside. Either way, Liam would likely face the imminent danger she was fleeing unless she did something to find and stop him.

Ashamed of her sudden cowardice, Caitlin stopped and checked her watch. By now two hours had passed since Jack went inside the market. He was sure to come out any minute, she decided, as she turned around and headed back toward the car. She was still two blocks away from Atlantic Avenue when Caitlin found the way suddenly barred. She watched while half a dozen vehicles blocked off the corner of Atlantic Avenue and Clinton Street. Meanwhile an army of NYPD officers moved down every street in an effort to cordon off the surrounding blocks of all traffic.

Stumbling forward, Caitlin could just make out the front of Kahlil's market between two black vans. She stared while two men swathed in black body armor and helmets dragged a struggling Afghani out of the store and pinned him to the sidewalk, where they cuffed his hands behind his back.

"Miss?"

Caitlin jumped, startled. A tall, broad-shouldered New York City cop stared down at her. He offered Caitlin a reassuring smile, even as he blocked her path. "Sorry, miss. You'll have to go another way," the young policeman said. "There's a law enforcement action in progress and traffic is blocked from here."

"But my car—"

The policeman nodded sympathetically. "This whole thing might be over in a few minutes. Then we can get you to your car."

Caitlin nodded, but did not move. Instead, she stared at the drama unfolding less than two blocks away. The cop's eyes followed her gaze and they both watched as an Afghani man in traditional dress was dragged away by the two men in assault gear. Meanwhile other armored men moved forward, to aim what appeared to be short-barreled shotguns at the basement window. Caitlin saw white letters emblazoned on their uniforms: FBI.

With a blast and a gust of smoke, one man fired into the building. Even from this distance Caitlin could hear the sound of breaking glass—then the muffled explosion. Before the noise of the first detonation faded, another man fired a grenade through the delicatessen's plate-glass window.

"Jesus, Mary, and Joseph," Caitlin whispered.

As shards from the shattered window rained down

on the sidewalk in a silver shower, the armored assault team charged into the market, weapons raised and ready.

7:11:58 A.M. EDT
Kahlil's Middle Eastern Foods

Jack threw his left arm across his face, buried his nose and mouth in his shirtsleeves to ward off the choking CS gas quickly filling the hot, grimy basement. Jack knew from experience that a cloud of chemical smoke tended to rise, so he remained on the ground, crawling across the floor to reach the dark form crumpled in the corner.

The older man was sprawled on his back, clothes smoldering from the heat of the explosion he'd absorbed. His frayed suit was in tatters, gore staining the shabby fabric from head to toe, and the man's head lolled to one side, jaw shattered. When Jack finally reached him, the man's blackened eyelids opened and their gazes met. He gripped Jack's hand, crushing it with the last of his strength as he tried to gasp out a final word. The sound rattled in his throat and he lay still, fingers limp. Jack fumbled at the man's throat for a pulse, found none.

"Dammit!" Jack knew from the flash and the force of the grenade's concussion that the FBI was using military-type CS gas grenades, in clear violation of federal law enforcement guidelines. They were the same devices the Bureau had used during their ill-fated siege at Waco. According to a still-classified government report Jack had read, those grenades had contributed to the fire that had swept the Branch Davidian compound almost as soon as the assault began.

Eighty people had perished at Waco, including a dozen children that the FBI was supposed to have been rescuing. The fires had been fed by that military-type tear gas—a gas with incendiary properties when used in a confined space like the Branch Davidian compound or the basement of a Brooklyn tenement.

So what was the FBI doing using the same type of incendiary tear gas canisters? Did they really want to botch another raid? Either the FBI was refusing to learn from its previous fatal blunder, or someone was out to *kill* Taj and his comrades, not capture them.

But even that scenario didn't make sense to Jack. Wasn't FBI agent Frank Hensley using Taj, along with the Lynch brothers, to carry out his scheme? So why wouldn't Hensley try to protect his accomplices? Why would Hensley let Taj die if the Afghani terrorist still had a role to play? The only thing that made sense to Jack was the notion that Taj and his men had outlived their usefulness and had to be disposed of before they talked to the wrong people. But if that was the case, then why the frantic delivery of the attaché case, unless it contained another bomb like the one that killed Dante Arete, but meant to kill the Afghanis?

Jack's head was spinning, as much from the mystery he was trying to solve as from the gas. The only two people who could answer Jack's questions were Taj Ali Kahlil and Special Agent Frank Hensley. The FBI agent was out of reach, so Jack's only choice now was to stick close to Taj.

Suddenly Jack felt a crushing grip on his forearm.

A wet cloth was slapped onto his shoulders. He looked up to find Taj standing over him. The man had a cloth wrapped around his own nose and mouth to block the gas. He gestured for Jack to do the same.

From the floor above, Jack heard a stampede of booted feet followed by several shots. A long burst from an assault rifle ended with a howl, then a body struck the floor with a solid thump. The smoke in the claustrophobic basement intensified. Now the smell of burning wood mingled with the CS gas fumes. Face wrapped, Jack stood with Taj and an Afghani youth—perhaps fifteen—gripping an Uzi in his trembling hands.

The rickety door opened and another Afghani emerged from the billowing smoke. This man was short but powerfully built, perhaps fifty years old or older. He wore a turban, loose trousers, and a robe. An AK–47 assault rifle was slung over his arm, its muzzle bumping the low ceiling. The newcomer locked eyes with Taj and the men embraced. With whispered words spoken in Pashto, Taj held the man close, and Jack realized he was witnessing a farewell. Finally the man turned, yanked the rifle off his shoulder, and vanished once more into the billowing clouds of tear gas.

Jack grabbed Taj by the arm. "They're using CS gas," he cried over the chaos. "This whole building could burn."

"We are leaving now," Taj replied. "We must retrieve the attaché case immediately or all our sacrifices will be for nothing."

"Forget the case. I need to see Tanner," croaked Jack, choking back a cough.

"The attaché first, Mr. Lynch. Then I shall take you to Felix Tanner."

**7:17:19 A.M. EDT
CTU Headquarters, Los Angeles**

Nina Myers emerged from Jack Bauer's office and walked to the head of the metal stairs. Below, the Mission Center was a hive of frantic activity. She watched the action in silence, contemplating her next move.

Nearly every member of the Crisis Management Team was preoccupied. Tony Almeida and Jessica Schneider were interrogating the prisoner Saito, and with Milo Pressman and half of CTU's Cyber Unit dispatched to the Green Dragon Computers store in Little Tokyo to crack their mainframe, pretty much every analyst was doing double duty. They were stretched too thin as it was, and things were about to get worse.

"Listen up," Nina called in a loud voice. "I'm starting a second Threat Clock—"

Shock and disbelief greeted the news. Nina continued to speak over the noise.

"This second Threat Clock is a countdown. Zero hour is five P.M. Eastern Daylight Time—nine hours and thirty-six minutes from right now."

"What about a briefing," someone called from station six.

"It's on a need-to-know basis right now, which means I'll need a second Crisis Management Team immediately. I expect all daily and hourly logs to be kept up-to-date, even if it means triple duty. All shifts are to remain in position until further notice—no one's going home."

Nina ignored the moans of protest, knowing full well some of her staff had been on duty for more than twelve hours already. She'd been working fourteen hours straight herself.

"Station managers will inform their staff and rearrange duties accordingly. The new team leaders are to assemble for a briefing in thirty minutes."

7:19:43 A.M. EDT
Kahlil's Middle Eastern Foods

The young Afghani led Jack and Taj to another basement room. As they stumbled through choking smoke, staccato bursts of gunfire continued in the store above them. At one point an armed Afghani pushed past Jack and pounded up the stairs. More gunfire erupted.

The youth kicked through a door, into a corner room where a wide hole had been dug into the dirt floor. Jack followed Taj to the edge, peered into the dark pit but could not see the bottom. A rope dangled over the center of the yawning chasm.

Without hesitation, the youth thrust the Uzi into his sash and jumped for the rope. He caught the thick hemp, hung for a moment, then climbed down.

"Go!" barked Taj.

Jack leaped, caught the rope. Fingers digging into the rough hemp, Jack wrapped his legs around the swinging cable and lowered himself into the dim abyss. Jack wondered how far he had to go, then perceived a bright glow under him. The young Afghani had switched on a bank of naked light bulbs that had been strung through a narrow earthen tunnel. The walls were supported by the same untreated wood used to make the partitions under the store, and Jack smelled freshly turned earth. This told him that Taj and his men had fashioned this escape tunnel themselves.

Jack's feet touched the dirt floor and he let go of the rope. Taj landed in a crouch at his side a moment later.

"Through here!" The youth hurried forward, toward the far end of the earthen pit where a narrow crawlspace had been cut into a solid stone wall. Following the man's lead, Jack squirmed through the hole, to emerge into a cool dark space, pitch black. His labored breathing echoed off distant walls, as if the chamber he had entered was large.

"Come!" called the youth.

"I can't see anything," hissed Jack in reply.

Jack heard a click as the youth tripped another bank of electric bulbs, blinked against the sudden glare. As his vision cleared Jack was amazed by his surroundings. "What is this place?"

"The Atlantic Avenue Tunnel," said Taj. "It was built in 1844 by the Long Island Railroad, but the tunnel was sealed up in 1861, during America's Civil War."

Jack marveled at his surroundings. The smooth walls were made of chiseled stone, the curved ceiling towering eighteen feet above his head. Though no tracks remained, Jack could believe that trains had once moved through this shaft because the tunnel was more than twenty feet wide.

"How far does this go?" Jack asked, staring down the dimly lit shaft.

Taj shrugged. "Only about two thousand feet—

roughly five blocks. The rest of the shaft is completely filled, but there are many side tunnels no one knows about."

"How did you find this place?"

"The tunnel was rediscovered in the 1980s, and the city government had electricity installed before sealing the tunnel off again. Now the shaft is inspected once or twice a year, but we have obscured our tracks and the authorities suspect nothing."

"So you've been using this tunnel for a long time?"

"Several years, Mr. Lynch. Like you, we have been planning this event for a long time." Then Taj smiled. "Our work ends soon, Mr. Lynch."

What event? What plan? Jack was straining to ask. "Your patience is commendable. You must bear a great hatred for America," he said instead.

Taj faced him. "When the Soviets invaded Afghanistan, the chieftain of my clan greeted the agents of the Central Intelligence Agency as the protectors of our tribe. The Americans provided us with the weapons we needed to fight the Russians—"

"Stinger missiles, you mean?"

Taj nodded. "At the start of the invasion, Russian HIND helicopters dominated our skies, slaughtered our people. Then the CIA brought us shoulder-fired missiles. They were the arrows we used to bring the Russian vultures down. After the Stingers came, the Russians feared us."

"What went wrong?"

"Someone from my clan—a renegade, an outcast I later murdered with my own hands—this man provided intelligence to the Soviets. The Russians used that knowledge to seize the CIA weapon shipments, capture American agents. After that, the CIA stopped trusting my chieftain, and they stopped supplying weapons to my clan."

Taj's expression darkened. In the dim lighting, his eyes seemed to burn with hatred. "Then the Spetsnaz came—"

"Soviet special forces?"

Taj nodded. "They hunted down our clan leaders, ran them to the ground like dogs and blew them up in their caves. They came to our settlements, raped our women and murdered our children, stuffing their mouths with forbidden pork so they could never, ever sit at the table with their God. And it was not enough for the Russian demons to destroy my people, they also ravaged the land, slaughtered our goats, and poisoned our wells."

Taj paused, working his jaws under his sallow skin. "In time, we dealt with the Soviets. We butchered them. Drove the infidel from our lands and brought jihad to their homeland. Now I have come to America, to New York, to deal death to America, to take my revenge on the great power who left us defenseless in the face of our enemy."

A sudden burst of gunfire echoed through the tunnels, reaching their ears.

"We have to move now," said Jack. "If you know about this tunnel, the FBI will know about it, too. They're going to follow us."

"No," Taj replied.

"But—"

"Keep silent and listen, Mr. Lynch."

A moment later, they all heard the roar of a muffled explosion, then the crash of tons of masonry. Jack knew the century-old building that housed the delicatessen had been blown up by the men inside.

The young man grimaced, blinked back tears. Taj clapped his hand on the young man's shoulder, squeezed it.

"*Inshallah*," Taj whispered. "You must be strong," he reminded him. "This is what God demands of us. Who are we to question Him?"

1 2 3 4 5 6 7 8 9
10 11 **12** 13 14 15 16 17
18 19 20 21 22 23 24

THE FOLLOWING TAKES PLACE
BETWEEN THE HOURS
OF 8 A.M. AND 9 A.M.
EASTERN DAYLIGHT TIME

8:00:01 A.M. EDT
Centers for Disease Control, Atlanta

Boxy and utilitarian in design, Building One on Clifton Road at the Centers for Disease Control and Prevention was the venue for many of the CDC's press conferences and media briefings. On this sunny, sweltering Georgia morning, the main conference room was not open to the press or the public, but the space was already crowded for the history-making teleconference.

As one of thirteen major operating components of the federal Department of Health and Human Services, the CDC served as a sentinel for the health of people in the United States and throughout the world.

One of the CDC's mandates was to protect the health and safety of the public through the prevention and monitoring of infectious diseases and the creation of new, more effective vaccines—the very subject of the briefing that was about to begin.

At precisely eight o'clock, Dr. Henry Johnston Garnett's digital wristwatch issued a series of quiet staccato beeps. The Director of the Centers for Disease Control quickly muted the alarm on his wrist and promptly called the briefing to order. The tall, white-haired African-American physician and researcher offered the audience his greetings, then turned the floor over to Dr. Colin Fife, Head of Immunology Research and Development for Paxton Pharmaceuticals in New York City.

Dr. Fife, stocky man with a thick red beard and a partially bald head, stepped up to the podium. Waving away the scattered applause, he began to speak.

"As the former Administrator for the Bacterial, Viral, and Infectious Diseases Registry, my colleague Dr. Garnett was instrumental in setting today's historic events into motion, and for that I thank him."

This time Dr. Fife waited patiently for the applause to fade.

"As many of us know, the worst outbreak of Type A influenza in history was the 1918 pandemic that killed more than twenty million people worldwide. Striking America just as the nation was gearing up for the First World War, the disease ultimately killed more soldiers than combat in that conflict. If that same influenza strain were to return today, up to a hundred million Americans would die for one reason—because there is still no effective vaccine in existence, or under development."

Dr. Fife glanced at his notes before continuing.

"In 1918, the Type A strain of influenza, which seemed no different from the Type B and C strains of previous years, suddenly and inexplicably turned lethal, killing its victims within hours of the first signs of infection. The virus induced in its victims an uncontrollable hemorrhaging that filled the lungs, and the victims drowned in their own body fluids.

"This strain was so virulent, the normal age distribution for flu mortality was reversed—instead of children, the old, and infirm, in the 1918 pandemic the vast majority of the infected were young healthy adults. Thus society's very infrastructure was ravaged as the bulk of those responsible for civilization's day-to-day maintenance perished of the disease. Those who survived believed the social order was breaking down—it very nearly did."

Dr. Fife paused. "So you see why Paxton Pharmaceuticals' breakthrough experiments are so important. With our new techniques in vaccine development and production, we at Paxton are optimistic that using the 1918 influenza cultures the CDC is providing, our researchers will be able to develop the first wide-spectrum Type A influenza vaccine ever developed."

Dr. Fife looked up from his notes. He did not need them for the next part of his talk.

"Think of it, ladies and gentlemen. Imagine a time when, like polio or typhus, influenza might be eradicated completely. Within a decade influenza will pass from one of humanity's greatest threats to a minor health problem solved by the proper vaccinations."

No longer able to hold back, a young woman in a business suit stood up in the second row. "But Dr.

Fife," she began, "is it not terribly dangerous to move these cultures?"

Dr. Fife seemed unfazed by the outburst. "Of course, if these cultures were to be released into the general population, the nightmare scenario I just described could be repeated. That is why every possible precaution has been taken."

"But are those precautions enough?" the woman demanded in an urgent tone.

Dr. Fife nodded, acknowledging her concerns. "You tell me if our precautions are adequate," he countered. "For instance, hazardous material and biological contamination specialists will be present to facilitate the movement of the cultures at every step of the transfer, from the time they leave the CDC labs until they reach Paxton's research facilities in Manhattan.

"There will be a team at the Atlanta airport, another at JFK to meet the aircraft when it arrives. And a third biohazard team will be aboard the aircraft, riding with the cultures in full hazard gear. The FBI will be notified of the flight, and will send out alerts to all pertinent local and federal law enforcement agencies."

Dr. Fife offered the woman his most benign smile. "When those influenza cultures are placed aboard a chartered 727 jet in just a few hours, you may rest assured that all steps have been taken to assure safety, and that absolutely nothing has been left to chance."

8:09:12 A.M. EDT
Court Street and Atlantic Avenue, Brooklyn

In a state of stunned bewilderment, Liam watched the three-story brownstone on the southeast corner of

Clinton and Atlantic—his destination—collapse in a rolling rumble of brick, plaster, wood, and glass.

"Jesus, Mary, and Joseph . . ."

Well over an hour before, Liam had emerged from the Hoyt Street subway station on the heels of the transit cop who'd been summoned to a police action. He watched as the officer hopped into a waiting Transit Police car driven by another cop. They sped down Fulton Street and turned toward Atlantic Avenue, out of sight.

Liam had followed Fulton until he'd reached Boerum Place, a quiet, shady boulevard only a few blocks from downtown Brooklyn. Even from a distance, Liam had been able to see the emergency vehicles rushing down Atlantic Avenue, hear the sirens wailing. He hadn't thought much about it then, and when he caught the smell of bacon frying, he could no longer ignore his exhausted condition.

He'd been through a lot—the long ride, the mugging, the subway train nearly killing him, then the cop getting suspicious. He felt cold, clammy, shaky all over. He hoped getting some food into him would help him make the final hike to Taj's store. So he'd sat at the counter of a small neighborhood diner and ordered up a good fry—bacon, sausage, eggs, toast—then washed it all down with a cup of hot tea.

The food had done the trick. He was still bloody fah'ed out, but the hot food and the caffeine in the *cha* had revived him enough to finish the job for Shamus. By the time he'd made his way over to Atlantic, however, he'd found his way blocked by a police barrier.

The officers had seemed preoccupied with watching the drama unfold, so Liam had followed the line of yellow tape and wooden barricades until he'd found an unguarded spot and slipped through. He'd walked another block, to the corner of Court Street. It had been impossible to go farther than that. Police were everywhere, and emergency vehicles had blocked every street. Fire trucks were scattered about, and fire hoses jutted from hydrants and snaked along the pavement. Finally Liam had joined a group of Middle Eastern men who'd emerged from a greengrocer to watch the action from a fairly close vantage point.

Liam had been stunned to discover that black FBI vans had circled Kahlil's delicatessen—his destination—and armored assault teams had just entered the store. Sirens had continued to blare, emergency lights flashed as more vehicles moved through the cordon. Police, fire department, and traffic helicopters were circling overhead, the sound of their beating rotors reverberating from the surrounding buildings. Among the air traffic a chopper belonging to Fox Five News dipped low, cameras rolling to provide live coverage to its millions of viewers.

Then the staccato sound of gunfire had shattered the bright blue morning. Shocked outcries had greeted the shots and many had fled the sidewalks, taking shelter in the surrounding stores and shops. A second assault team entered the building to join the first, and Liam had heard another burst of gunfire. Then he'd heard the muffled explosion, saw the flashes inside the brown-brick building, and the brownstone literally folded in on itself, to vanish in a massive cloud of billowing dust and debris that washed over emergency vehicles and law enforcement officials close to the collapse. Almost immediately, a dozen fires sprang up among the rubble.

"Back! Everyone back!"

A fireman was on the sidewalk now, in helmet and full gear. He was waving everyone into the surrounding buildings. As he forced the crowd back, away from the toppled structure, a dozen more firemen hurried forward, toward the conflagration.

Liam knew that the law enforcement officials who had charged into that building had been buried in tons of rubble. As fires began to spread, Liam was amazed by the courage of the firemen who rushed toward the site of the explosion instead of away from it.

"Clear the area!" a fireman's bullhorn blared.

Liam considered retreating, but didn't. Instead, he slipped through the crowd and moved forward. He was only half a block away now, and his flesh prickled with the heat of the fire. A thick column of black smoke rose from the rubble, pushed along Atlantic Avenue by a faint breeze off the water. The smoke hit Liam, choking him. He smelled burned wood, smoldering plaster, and something else—gas.

A fire chief in white helmet stood in the middle of the street, yelling into a bullhorn. "Get out! Get away! Clear the area now—"

Inside the rubble, among the trapped and moaning FBI agents, hot flames touched the ruptured gas main. Liam was blinded by an impossibly bright orange flash. Behind him, the plate-glass window of a furniture store shattered. A wave of superheated air washed over him, and Liam was bowled over by the force of the blast. Deafened, scorched, trembling, he curled into a ball around the attaché case while the sidewalk quaked beneath him.

8:12:57 A.M. EDT
Atlantic Avenue Tunnel

Jack, Taj, and the young Afghani felt the stones under their feet tremble before the thunder of the gas explosion reached their ears. Then they heard it. Dust fell from the ceiling and smoke billowed out of the narrow shaft they'd climbed out of. First a dusty powder, then oily curls of hot smoke. The young man's gaze found Taj. His lips trembled.

Another sound made itself known—alien, alive, angry. Tiny, tittering squeals merged into a sustained shriek, the chattering click of thousands of tiny claws brushing stone. In the weak light of the electric bulbs, a rippling brown carpet seemed to flow along the floor, the walls, at the far end of the tunnel. Stampeded by the explosion, they rushed toward the men in a snarling mass of teeth and claws.

"Rats!" Jack shouted.

"This way," Taj called, turning away from the maddened swarm. Jack followed the man for a few steps before he realized the young Afghani was not with them.

"Taj!" Jack cried.

The man turned, saw the young Afghani. "Borak!" he cried. "Follow us."

But the young man shook his head. "I will stop them."

"No!"

The Afghani turned his back on them, lowered the muzzle of the Uzi he drew from his sash, naïvely fired. The bullets chewed through the squirming, squealing tide without effect. The brown flow swarmed around the young man even as he emptied the magazine into the panicked horde. The rats nipped at his sandals, clawed at his legs. The young man howled and dropped the useless weapon. Reaching into his loose shirt, he pulled out an old, Soviet-made grenade.

"Not in here!" Taj screamed.

But the boy was too frightened to hear him. As the rats swarmed over him, forcing the boy to the ground, he popped the pin on the grenade.

Without a word, Taj and Jack ran away from the rats, the impending explosion. Jack figured on a ten-second fuse and counted down in his mind.

Eight . . . seven . . . six . . .

"Get ready to hit the ground!" Jack cried.

Five . . . four . . . three . . .

"Down!"

Jack leaped forward, skidded along the hard stone floor. He curled into a ball, covered his ears. As expected, the explosion seemed massive in the enclosed space. The sound reverberated off the walls, bringing down dust and jarring more masonry loose as it rocked the one-hundred-and-fifty-year-old structure.

As the smoke cleared, Jack jumped up. Taj was already on his feet, running forward. Over the startled squeals of the swarming rats, they heard another sound—crashing masonry, crumbling earth, and the roaring rush of water. The grenade or the gas explosion—or perhaps both—had ruptured a water main.

Running behind Taj, Jack glanced over his shoulder to see a tidal wave of foaming black water engulfing the horde of rats and following them down the length of the tunnel.

"Here!" Taj cried, "the ladder."

Jack saw the Afghani scramble up iron rungs embedded in the stone. His fingers closed on the cold metal a split second later, just as the foam washed over his feet, his ankles, his legs.

8:45:41 A.M. EDT
Federal Bureau of Investigation
Pennsylvania Avenue, Washington, D.C.

The FBI received an urgent electronic message from the Centers for Disease Control. The memo informed the Bureau that the long-planned transfer of disease cultures to Paxton Pharmaceuticals in New York City was taking place as scheduled. A flight plan was included in the memo, providing the FBI with the radio frequencies the pilots would use, the airplane's flight path, altitude, and cruising speed, departure and arrival times and destinations, files on all personnel involved in the transfer.

Signed by Dr. Henry Johnston Garnett, Director of the Centers for Disease Control, the directive urged the FBI to contact all pertinent agencies and alert them to the transfer of the potentially deadly cargo. Immediately, the FBI analyst in charge of intelligence redistribution alerted state and federal law enforcement officials in Atlanta and New York City about the potential biohazard threat coming their way.

Because of the Frank Hensley accusations about Jack Bauer, however, FBI Headquarters in New York City instituted a Bureau-wide intelligence blackout with CTU. Beyond the routine security alert issued eight hours before, no one at the Counter Terrorist

Unit was notified about the chartered CDC flight, or the deadly cargo it contains.

Dennis Spain, a bundle of nervous energy in a stocky, compact form, entered the Senate office precisely on time. As Chief of Staff to Senator William S. Cheever of New York, Spain felt his duty to be sleek, smart, and imperially efficient was surpassed only by his obligation to appear that way. Today's ensemble was one of Spain's favorites, a lightweight Italian suit and Bruno Magli loafers. The impression, he felt, was "chic competence," but the finely tailored clothes also left Spain feeling crisp and comfortable, no easy feat during the muggy summer months of the glorified swamp that was Washington, D.C.

After picking up his own mail, Spain's next stop was his boss's in-box, where his daily routine of browbeating the staff began. "These letters are all dated three days ago," he said, shaking a blue folder at a quaking intern sitting behind her desk. The young woman pulled a lock of long, dark, stringy hair away from her face.

"I . . . I know, Mr. Spain. But the Senator was away on a junket and he couldn't sign them until today."

Spain read the names and addresses on the letters. "None of these people matter one bit. Why didn't you use the signature machine?"

The young woman—an undergraduate at Columbia

University and daughter of a rather large donor to the Senator's last campaign—seemed to shrink in her chair as she avoided his angry stare.

"The . . . the Senator . . . Senator Cheever . . . He said he didn't want me to do that anymore. Said it was too impersonal."

"Well, Senator Cheever certainly can't sign *these*. They're as stale as old fish." He tossed the folder on her desk. "Do the letters over with *today's* date, then give them to the Senator to sign. Let's hope he can find a pen around here."

"Yes sir, Mr. Spain. Right away."

Her reply was barely heard and certainly not acknowledged. Dennis Spain had already entered his office. He closed the door behind him, dropped into his leather chair, and brushed back his blond-streaked brown hair, exposing a broad forehead over thin eyebrows and narrowly set eyes with a constantly critical gaze that made him appear shrewd. That's the word his friends used—shrewd. His opponents preferred shifty.

Like everyone in Washington, Dennis Spain had enemies, more than his share considering he'd never run for or been elected to a political office. He'd served only as the Senator's campaign manager and then his Chief of Staff. Not quite out of his thirties, he occupied a powerful position that had been well earned in Spain's own estimation.

Five years before, Senator William S. Cheever had been a political dinosaur, an endangered species—just another fading Northeast politician with a penchant for bloated government programs even his constituents no longer favored. His chances for reelection were so bleak that his own party endorsed his rival in the primary campaign. After that blow came, Senator Cheever did the first smart thing he'd done in a decade—he fired his old campaign manager and put Dennis Spain in charge of his reelection.

As a political strategist, Spain was magic. While still in college, he'd ingratiated himself with New Jersey state politicos and key members of the tristate media. From his decade aiding then running local election campaigns—in New Jersey, then New York—Spain had learned all the simple but effective tricks, and in Cheever's senatorial race he used every one of them with ruthless precision.

Most effective were the Sunday morning press conferences Spain had instituted. In the campaign manager's deft hands, they became a forum to announce programs and initiatives, to spotlight "problems and concerns," to highlight studies by think tanks that supported his political stands. Whether, in the end, anything truly useful came out of Cheever's announced agendas was beside the point. The press conferences became a way for Senator Cheever to showcase himself. On a slow news day like Sunday, Senator Cheever always got his mug on the evening news, complete with a pithy sound bite penned by his campaign consultants. Constituents would be left with the impression of the Senator's diligence and effectiveness, which would be the basis for his next reelection campaign—because, of course, when it came to politics, impressions were always, always more important than results.

It was Dennis Spain who taught Cheever how to cozy up to the policemen's union and the professional class of political malcontents and activists at the same time, using the very same tactics with both. "Just tell them all what they want to hear," Spain advised his boss—and it worked. Within six months of Spain's coming aboard, with a handpicked advance team, speech writer, and key media contacts, major magazines and newspapers were all publishing stories about "the new Senator Cheever."

Under Spain's tutelage, the former lame duck breezed through the primary and won reelection with a handy two-to-one margin over his rival. Since that time, Dennis Spain had guided Cheever's political activities as well. Spain drafted legislation for the Senator to propose, wrote policy speeches for the Senator to deliver. More importantly, Spain used the Senator's years of senatorial service as clout. Using Cheever's seniority, Spain muscled him onto several important committees and steering commissions. One of them was the newly minted Air Transportation and Travel Committee, established to recommend ways in which the deregulated airline industry could more efficiently operate in a climate of rising oil prices and falling revenues.

It was a powerful committee, and one that immediately attracted the attention of lobbyists for the airline industry, and through them, the top airline CEOs themselves.

Dennis Spain reached for his telephone. He would begin today's frantic schedule by phoning the CEOs of those very airlines, to remind them of a critical video conference on the future of the American airline industry, hosted by Senator William S. Cheever, Chairman of the Air Transportation and Travel Committee, scheduled for four-forty-five P.M. that very afternoon.

```
 1  2  3  4  5  6  7  8  9
10 11 12 13 14 15 16 17
18 19 20 21 22 23 24
```

9:01:00 A.M. EDT
CTU Headquarters, Los Angeles

Nina dropped her reading glasses onto the desk, rubbed her tired eyes. When she refocused on the monitor she had to fight to keep the lines from blurring. For the past hour she'd been examining the last five years' worth of state and federal tax records for the Green Dragon Computers store in Little Tokyo.

Hundreds of digital pages had to be scanned, but no computer could do the job right. Only a human analyst possessed the skill and intuition to find the tiny jewels buried in the reams of worthless data. The process was time consuming and labor intensive, but at the end of sixty minutes, Nina had managed to narrow her search to four promising references.

During a second pass, two of those items were eliminated immediately. But a third clue produced unexpected results. According to the records, one of the most lucrative customers in Green Dragon's Little Tokyo store was Prolix Security, a New York City firm with no offices in Los Angeles.

Nina knew immediately that the facts didn't compute—why would a Manhattan company do business with a store in LA when there were plenty of franchises in New York City?

A cross-check of Prolix Security records produced a revelation, and a clear connection to terrorist activities. In the last eighteen months, huge sums of money had been funneled from Prolix's Security to several Banque Swiss accounts in Zurich, Switzerland. Other transactions involved the Iraqi government—though U.S. businesses were restricted from trade with Saddam Hussein except through the United Nations Oil-for-Food Program.

But Nina knew those weren't the real leads.

The important discovery involved the ownership of the firm. Though the company had been established in 1986, Prolix had just recently been acquired by a former insurance executive named Felix Tanner—the same name Jack's female informant Caitlin had mentioned during an interrogation about the Lynch brothers.

Putting aside her other tasks, Nina Myers concentrated on finding out everything she could about Felix Tanner.

9:18:54 A.M. EDT
The Last Celt

Griffin Lynch tramped on the gas. Tires shrieking, the Mercedes swung around the lumbering delivery van, then swerved in front of it. The Boar's Head meats truck skidded to a halt, the driver bellowing a curse at what looked like the typical New York asshole businessman—silver hair, well-dressed, and in a hurry. In seconds the black Mercedes was gone, zooming down Roosevelt Avenue under the shade of the elevated train tracks.

The day was already hot. With the window down, the clattering subway rolling overhead drowned out almost everything else. Cars double-parked along the busy avenue made vehicular progress slow. Griff clutched the steering wheel impatiently, even though the pub was only a few blocks away.

He was more than a little bit cheesed at Shamus. Bloody brilliant of the boy not to show at the shop, this morning of all mornings, thought Griff. With so much to do, so many loose ends to tie up and final decisions to be made, Shamus was behaving like a tool. Bad enough he'd been more interested in fast-money deals with the local swains than taking care of their real business. Now the boyo'd vanished, along with the pub sketch he'd been shagging. Griff had been calling Shamus repeatedly since eight-thirty, but no one at The Last Celt would answer the bloody phone. With zero hour less than half a day away, Griff had no choice but to get in the car himself and drive to the pub.

It was bloody reckless of Shamus to act so irresponsibly, but Griff wasn't all that surprised. He'd noticed changes in his brother over the past few months. At first Griff assumed it was Caitlin. Since the explosion that maimed Griff so badly, the joys of women were denied him, but he hadn't forgotten the power of the mating urge. Griff indulged his younger brother's need to get his hole now and then—but when he compared his brother's professional attitude in Somalia to his fuck-ups lately, he realized Shamus hadn't been the same since they'd set up shop in New York City.

It was the seductive lure of the fast-money American way that warped him, Griff knew. Shamus would rather remain in New York and exploit the opportunities at hand than go for a really big score and retire in a banana republic with a fat bank account. Not that his little brother had directly challenged Griff's plans. But it was obvious enough to Griff that Shamus wanted to stay.

The boy just didn't understand. Living in America was an impossible dream. It hadn't taken Frank Hensley very long to track them down. The fact that the FBI agent was as crooked as a turf accountant was a bit of luck. Griff had been able to make a deal with Hensley, but sooner or later another FBI agent—an honest one—or someone from the police department, the DEA, or CTU would find them and the bomb would explode in their faces.

Griff understood that there was no future for them anywhere in America or Europe. He and Shamus had already done too many things for the Cause to turn back now. In that sense, the Duggan brothers had already made their choice, back when they became Provos.

Griff topped a small rise, and The Last Celt was in sight. Luck was with him—he spied an empty spot on

the corner, right in front of the pub. As he parked, he
calmed down a bit. Most likely Shamus got royally
flustered and had simply slept in. He'd be hungover
this morning, but after coffee, food, and a bitch slap
from his elder bro, Shamus would be up to the task at
hand—and not so crazy over Caitlin's melt that he'd
balk when the time came to say adieu. Griff would off
the ninny and her brother himself if it came to that.

Griff exited the car and crossed the sidewalk. He
halted mid-stride when he saw the splintered wood on
the pub's door. Reaching into his linen sport coat,
Griff eased the 9mm Beretta out of its shoulder holster before he touched the knob. No surprise the door
was unlocked. Griff pushed through it and slipped inside. In the tavern's dim interior he saw toppled tables,
overturned chairs, the phone ripped out of the wall.

Griff found Shamus upstairs a few minutes later, on
the floor of Caitlin's shabby digs. He ripped the tape
away from his brother's mouth, untied his hands and
legs, and dashed cold water in his face. Shamus
moaned, then reached for his head. Suddenly he
opened his eyes, focused on his brother, bolted up-
right. "Where's that bleedin' CTU agent?"

Griff scowled. "What CTU agent?"

"He took her away at gunpoint."

"Who, Caitlin?"

Shamus nodded. "He forced her. Made her go
with him."

Griff wasn't so sure. "What about the attaché
case?"

"Liam took off with it." Shamus glanced at his
watch. "Taj should be holding the damned thing by
now."

"We'll have to clean up this mess," said Griff.

"Caitlin and her brother are liabilities now. So is Donnie. Before this day is over, everyone we ever did business with in the States—*everyone* who knew us here—must be permanently silenced."

Shamus looked away, said nothing. Then they both heard a noise from downstairs in the pub. Tables and chairs being moved, then someone cursed. Shamus spoke. "It's Donnie. He'll be real cheesed about the mess."

"Shut up and wait here," snarled Griff. He led with his gun as he silently glided down the stairs.

9:31:21 A.M. EDT
CTU Headquarters, Los Angeles

Crisis Management Team Alpha, formerly *the* Crisis Management Team, met in the main conference room at the behest of Ryan Chappelle, who wanted to be brought up to speed on the latest developments.

Ryan was surprised when Nina Myers arrived— late—and informed him that a second Threat Clock and Crisis Management Team Beta had been established. When Nina closed the door to officially begin the conference, Ryan blinked in surprise. "This is everyone?"

The only other person at the conference table was Doris Soo Min, who rocked nervously in her chair and played with the cover of the laptop computer on the table in front of her.

Nina brushed her short dark hair away from her face, sank into a chair. "Milo Pressman is in the field, supervising the Cyber Unit at Green Dragon in Little Tokyo. Tony and Captain Schneider are interrogating a prisoner in holding room three. And I've excused Jamey from the meeting because I've asked her to follow up on a new lead."

Ryan sighed theatrically. "Then why am I here, Nina?"

Because you called the meeting instead of taking the trouble to read the hourly logs, Nina thought. She said something else. "Actually, Miss Soo Min has had something of a breakthrough."

"I thought the memory stick had been pretty much decrypted and mined."

Nina shook her head. "Did you know that Doris found a time code encrypted within the aircraft recognition program?"

"I'm aware of it *now*."

Chappelle swung his office chair to face the young woman. He fixed her with his best managerial gaze. "So, tell me what you found, Doris . . ."

Doris cleared her throat, tapped the computer keyboard. In the center of the conference table, the square block of HDTV monitors sprang to life.

"Along with the time code there was also a series of longitude and latitude points in the encrypted data," Doris explained. "Watch what happens when I cross-reference that geographical data against a map of the continental United States."

On the monitor, the map of America appeared in blue outline. Then a crimson grid appeared superimposed over the image. Six geographical markers blinked, all positioned in or near major metropolitan areas—two around New York City.

"The exact longitude and latitude pinpoint six locations," Doris continued. "JFK and LaGuardia airports in New York City, Logan Airport in Boston,

Ronald Reagan National Airport in Washington, D.C., O'Hare in Chicago, LAX here in Southern California."

Ryan Chappelle placed the palms of his hands on the table, leaned closer to the screen. For a long moment he studied the grid in silence.

"That's it," Ryan said at last. "As I see it, there's no other conclusion possible. The aircraft recognition software in the memory stick, the Long Tooth shoulder-fired anti-aircraft missiles, the time code, now this. They all add up to one thing—the terrorists are planning to shoot down commercial aircraft all over the United States at the same time, in a nation-wide act of coordinated terrorism."

9:41:21 A.M. EDT
CTU Headquarters, Los Angeles

Captain Jessica Schneider stared across the interrogation table at Saito. The Japanese man was slumped in his chair, his arrogant confidence gone, replaced by exhaustion and anxiety.

"Listen, miss. I'm telling you the truth."

Jessica sighed and shook her head. "I think I liked your Rat Pack persona better."

"It was just part of the act." Saito pushed his slick hair back with his left hand. The gesture displayed the stump of his missing finger.

The steel door opened. Tony Almeida walked in, slapped a file folder on the desk, slumped down in the chair next to Jessica Schneider. They both fixed their gazes on Saito. Tony spoke.

"I had a conversation with the Japanese Ambassador. He confirmed everything. He's telling the truth."

Saito grinned, slapped the table with the palm of his hand. "See, I told you."

Jessica's jaw dropped. "You're a cop?"

"Agent Ito Nakajima, Special Assault Team, Tokyo Prefecture." The Japanese man offered a respectful bow.

"What are you doing in Los Angeles, Special Agent Nakajima?"

"As Saito, I infiltrated the Machi-yokko crime clan two years ago, when they began to diversify."

"What do you mean by diversify?" Tony asked.

"For decades the Machi-yokko clan was strictly *bakuto*—illegal gambling, numbers, some loan sharking. But a couple of years ago the Kumicho of the Machi-yokko clan—"

Jessica blinked. "Wait a minute, who or what is a Kumicho?"

"A leader. A clan elder. Think *The Godfather*, missy," the Japanese man replied with something of his old bravado. "Anyway, last year this Kumicho made a deal with a Taiwanese businessman named Wen Chou Lee."

Tony nodded. "The triad leader who owns the Green Dragon Computers franchise."

"Yes." Agent Nakajima nodded. "Only this deal wasn't for bootleg computer parts or hot microchips stolen off a Malaysian cargo ship. This deal was the same one the Kumicho made with Shoko Asahara."

"The Aum Supreme Truth Cult leader? He's the man responsible for the sarin gas attack in the Tokyo subway system. Why isn't your Kumicho behind bars?"

"The Machi-yokko clan's contributions and behind-the-scenes activities are very important to a certain political party. That gives the Kumicho and his men a measure of protection."

"What did your Kumicho do for the Aum cult?"

"Helped them build their secret death lab, Satian Six, at the base of Mount Fuji. It was there that the cult's scientist, Hideo Murai, produced the poison gas. The Aum also fried their political enemies and dissident members of the cult in industrial-sized microwave ovens, dispatched terrorists to murder an innocent lawyer and his family, and ultimately masterminded the worst terrorist incident in my nation's history."

A moment of silence followed the man's outburst. Finally Tony Almeida asked, "So what's really going on at Green Dragon?"

"The Kumicho has taken a lot of money in exchange for smuggling North Korean–made missile launchers, that's a fact. But lately I've heard talk about other things—biological weapons, pandemics, that kind of thing."

"Here? In the United States?" The notion seemed to surprise Jessica. Tony was unruffled.

The man faced Jessica. "I couldn't tell you for sure if the attacks are going to be here or somewhere else. I'm just a *kobun*—a soldier. Nobody tells me anything. But I have eyes and ears, and I don't like what I'm seeing and hearing."

"You're free to go, Agent Nakajima." Tony Almeida reached into the file folder, handed Agent Nakajima a one-way ticket for a flight back to Japan. "The airplane leaves in an hour. If you're not on it, you will be arrested and deported by the Immigration and Naturalization Service."

Agent Nakajima glowered, snatched the ticket out of Tony's hand.

"Fine," he said. "My cover's blown anyway."

A CTU security man opened the steel door, ushered the Japanese agent out. When they were gone, Jessica faced Tony.

"Do you think he was right? Do you think some sort of bio-terrorism attack is possible?"

Tony nodded. "More than possible, but I'm not sure it has anything to do with the threat we're facing right now."

"But if it does?"

Tony rubbed his jaw, itchy from the crop of stubble that had sprouted overnight. "Right now Milo Pressman and a Cyber Unit are setting up shop at the Green Dragon facility. They should be able to crack the computer security codes. The data will be ours in a few hours. If a bio-attack is imminent, we'll find out all the details—hopefully before it happens."

9:52:50 A.M. EDT
Near the Brooklyn Promenade

Coughing, hungry for fresh air, Jack and Taj put their backs against the cold steel manhole cover and pushed upward until they slowly moved it aside. Jack climbed out first and sprawled on the sidewalk. Blinking against the sudden daylight, he turned and reached back to help Taj out of the darkness.

They emerged on a quiet, shady street with tall

granite apartment buildings on either side. Jack read the street sign: Grace Court. From a canopied apartment entrance a half block away, a uniformed doorman gaped at them.

Taj eyed the doorman as he rose. "Come, we must move before we attract more attention."

"Where are we going? What about the attaché? Don't you need it?"

The man's narrow face grimaced. "It's too risky to retrieve the case now. We must proceed to the safe house."

Jack nodded. "Will Tanner be there?"

"Perhaps," said Taj.

After escaping the rats and the flood, Jack and Taj had moved through the sewer system until they were blocks away from Atlantic Avenue. Even now they could still hear the sirens blaring, but the noise, the chaos, the death seemed far away from this peaceful, sun-washed block.

At the end of Montague Street, Taj guided Jack through a shady park entrance and around a flagpole. A sign told Jack they had arrived at the Brooklyn Promenade. They entered a concrete strip of public space built over the busy Brooklyn/Queens Expressway. The Promenade offered a panoramic view of the East River and Lower Manhattan beyond. Behind them were rows of pricey townhouses and apartments. Roaring up from directly beneath was the steady noise of rush hour traffic.

Beyond the raised Promenade, the Brooklyn piers jutted into the East River, its muddy water dotted with tugboats, barges, and pleasure craft. Then came the banks of Manhattan Island. Beside the green expanse of Battery Park rose the granite buildings of the

Financial District. At its heart stood the gleaming, massive twin towers of the World Trade Center. The towers dwarfed everything around them. Reflecting the bright June sky, the golden sun danced across their mammoth glass facades.

Taj touched his arm. "We cannot linger here, Mr. Lynch."

The Afghani gestured for Jack to follow him. They walked the length of the esplanade until they reached the last bench. Beneath a nearby guardrail, cars and trucks moved on the expressway below.

"There is a cell phone hidden under that park bench," said Taj. "With it we can speak with our associates, summon transportation. The phone is to be used only once."

Several dog walkers passed them, along with a woman pushing a stroller. The bench was empty, its wooden surfaces covered with scratchffiti. Jack sat down. Taj kept watch. "The phone is taped under the seat, Mr. Lynch."

Jack stooped over, reached under the seat and felt around. "I can't find—"

A garrote made of strong hemp dropped over Jack's head and closed around his throat. He grabbed for the thin cord, his fingers digging into the flesh of his own neck. The noose only tightened.

As Jack's breathing was cut off, Taj loomed over him. Jack felt hot breath on his cheek as a voice hissed in his ear.

"If you were *really* Shamus Lynch, you would know I am not Taj, but his brother, Khan Ali Kahlil. Remember the name for it is the last you will ever hear . . ."

1 2 3 4 5 6 7 8 9
10 11 12 13 **14** 15 16 17
18 19 20 21 22 23 24

....

THE FOLLOWING TAKES PLACE
BETWEEN THE HOURS OF
10 A.M. AND 11 A.M.
EASTERN DAYLIGHT TIME

....

10:00:00 A.M. EDT
Green Dragon Computers, Los Angeles

"All in all it's a pretty shoddy operation. The technicians didn't even bother to take out the old bathroom pipes in the ceiling before they set up shop. And yet they went through all the trouble of glassing in this computer room and installing air-conditioning and high-tech scrubbers. What were they thinking?"

Mickey Chen couldn't keep the disdain from his voice as he lumbered to a chair and settled in. At five-foot-nine and close to three hundred pounds, Mickey managed to fill the tiny workstation, forcing Milo into a corner.

"Just look at that mess up there."

Milo followed the man's gaze to the broken plaster over his head. Through that ragged hole and several others, he saw a web of crisscrossing rusty pipes.

"What about explosives? Booby traps?"

Mickey shook his head. "The CTU bomb squad's been here and gone." He laid a meaty arm over the monitor screen. "She's a sweet baby, this one. You gonna give her a go?"

"Oh, you first. Be my guest," Milo replied.

Mickey had a habit of referring to all computers in the feminine form. Jamey Farrell said it was because a computer with a girl's name was the closest the Hawaiian programmer was ever going to get to a romance.

The glass doors hissed. A short, curly-haired brunette entered the computer room, bringing in her own briefcase computer. It contained the decryption programs she would need to bypass or overcome the mainframe's security and download the data.

Mickey grinned at Danielle Henkel. "About time you showed. This little lady was getting impatient."

"Blow it out your ass, Mickey," said Nell.

"Speaking of an impatient lady, I have to make a phone call before we get started." Milo pulled out his cell, tried to get a signal.

"Not in here, dude," said Mickey. "This room is shielded."

"Okay, I'll be right back." Milo walked to the door.

"Don't expect us to wait for you," called Mickey. "Me and this little lady have been waiting too long for this night."

Mickey swung around in the chair and began tapping the keyboard to probe the computer's security system.

On the other side of the glass wall, the temperature

was much warmer, but at least Milo could acquire a signal. Turning his back on the others, he called up Tina's number from his directory and pressed send.

Milo placed the phone to his ear, but the sound of the first ring was drowned out by the hiss of a gushing spray, followed by shrieks of confusion, terror, and agony.

Milo turned, gagged, dropped his cell.

Inside the glass-enclosed computer room, Pyrex tubes inside the "rusty pipes" in the ceiling ruptured the moment Mickey Chen tried to gain access to the data without first entering the proper security code. But it was not water pouring down on Milo's colleagues. Mickey had inadvertently triggered the computer's real firewall—a downpour of scorching acid. While Milo watched helplessly, the caustic chemical shower rained down on Mickey Chen and Nell Henkel, burning great smoking pits in their living flesh.

Mercifully the screaming stopped almost as soon as it began. A white chemical mist instantly filled the computer room as the acid fumed. Inside the haze, flashes of sizzling electricity erupted as thousands of volts of electricity crackled through the computer room. The searing, melting bodies flopped in an obscene dance before they toppled to the gouged and pitted concrete.

Somewhere in his horrified mind, Milo deduced that the caustic chemical was probably hydrochloric acid, an excellent conductor of electricity. A shower of the stuff would effectively fry the circuits along with anyone tampering with the computer before any data could be recovered.

Choking back the hot bile that rose in his throat,

Milo watched as the chemical soup continued to cook away flesh, muscle, hair—until nothing remained but twitching, smoking mounds of flesh and bone.

10:00:01 A.M. EDT
Brooklyn Promenade

Jack's vision fogged as oxygen deprivation scrambled his brain. Though weakening, he continued to claw at the noose around his throat and struggle against the man who loomed over him. But the Afghani's full weight was on Jack, pinning him to the bench. Ali Kahlil grunted with the effort as he pulled the noose tighter.

Jack could not break the man's grip, so he tried a desperate bid to fool his assassin. Abruptly Jack ceased struggling, went limp. After a long moment the pressure of the noose and the man's weight eased slightly—enough for Jack to suddenly shift position and push upward with all his strength.

The top of Jack's head slammed into Khan's jaw with a satisfying crack. Jack saw stars, felt a sharp pain, but he knew the Afghani was hurting more. Khan Ali Kahlil attempted to choke him again, but Jack managed to get both hands around the cord. Though the rough hemp ripped the palms of his hands, the rope no longer strangled Jack. Now the dog was controlling the leash, and Jack used his weight to throw Khan Ali Kahlil backward, against the aluminum guardrail. He felt the man's ribs crack, heard the Afghani howl.

Khan Ali Kahlil still gripped the garrote, and that was his mistake. Younger, stronger, and better trained, Jack recovered immediately. Now he used his own weight to press Khan against the rail while he pummeled the man with his elbows, the backs of his arms. Finally Jack seized the Afghani man's wrist and twisted out of his grip. The bones in Khan's forearms twisted, then snapped. He howled and released the cord. An elbow to his face shattered Khan's nose, sending black blood cascading down the front of his loose cotton shirt.

Jack could easily finish the man, but he needed Khan alive and as cooperative as possible. He whirled, pinned Khan's good arm behind his back.

"Surrender," Jack cried, pressing the man against the Promenade's aluminum guardrail. "Tell me what your brother is doing with the Lynch brothers and Felix Tanner. Tell me where the missile launchers are hidden. Cooperate and I can guarantee the President of the United States will grant you immunity from all past crimes."

Eyes bright, Khan ceased struggling as he seemed to consider Jack's words. He grinned behind the ooze of blood that gushed from his flattened nose. "I will help you."

Jack stepped back, released the man. "Listen to me, Khan Ali Kahlil. I know that you've made a life for yourself here. Don't throw it all away for a struggle that is not yours, for a dying cause—"

Khan lashed out, slamming Jack's jaw with a balled fist. The blow was meant to crush his throat, but Jack saw it coming and dodged it. Khan turned and jumped over the guardrail. Jack made it to the fence in time to see the man land headfirst on the roadway forty feet below, in the path of rushing traffic. Horns blared, brakes squealed, a woman screamed.

Jack looked away, stumbled to the bench where he'd almost lost his life. The flesh around Jack's throat was raw, his palms gouged and sticky with blood. He stared at the wounds. As the adrenaline drained out of him, his hands began to tremble uncontrollably.

He felt weak and nauseated. He thought of his wife, Teri, his daughter, Kim—now almost a teenager. Who would take care of his family if he had died here, a wanted fugitive three thousand miles from home, hunted by the FBI?

Glancing up, Jack's gaze traveled across the river and up the gleaming glass walls of the World Trade Center. Those towers, the city around them—it all seemed so massive and permanent. Was this city, this country really in mortal danger? Could this enormous city, this entire nation, ever really be hurt by a haphazard cadre of individual terrorists? As he gazed at those twin towers, so solid, so substantial, the concept suddenly seemed absurd. Yet Jack knew from experience the kind of acts such men as Taj and Khan Ali Kahlil and the Lynch brothers were capable.

Jack reached for his cell phone to check back with CTU. With Khan Ali Kahlil dead and his brother Taj missing, Jack had run out of options. Then remembered he'd given the phone, ID, PDA, and even his .45 to Caitlin—and right now he didn't even know where she was.

10:19:45 A.M. EDT
Aboard the Manhattan-bound R Train

A battered Liam immediately left the scene of the lethal explosion. Delivery was impossible, and he still clutched the silver attaché case. The first time he'd made a delivery to Taj, several weeks ago or more, Shamus told him that if something happened and he couldn't make the delivery, he was to return the case to the Lynch brothers' Green Dragon store in Forest Hills. With no other plan, Liam now followed those same instructions.

Unfortunately, the blast and subsequent rupture of a water main had forced the closure of the 2 and 3 train routes, so it took him nearly forty-five minutes to walk across downtown Brooklyn to the nearest working subway, the Manhattan-bound R train.

Now, as he sat in a corner seat in the crowded subway, the attaché case on his lap, his sister Caitlin's words from the night before came to mind. *Was this delivery on the up-and-up?* If it was, then why did the police, the FBI, raid Kahlil's store? Was Taj some kind of crook?

And what if I'd been inside when the FBI charged the building? Liam thought. *Then I'd be dead, too. What is in this case that's so bleedin' important that it had to be delivered in the middle of the night? Am I carrying what the FBI and the police were looking for?*

Liam fingered the case, noting for the first time that one of the clasps had already been broken and hung loose—probably by the fall onto the subway tracks. He touched the other latch and it sprung open. Liam paused, looked around.

If the case was full of money or cocaine or something, he didn't want anyone else in the packed subway to notice. But everyone was minding his own business, reading the paper or dozing or listening to music on their Walkmans so he decided to risk it.

Taking a deep breath, Liam opened the case.

Inside he found sponge packing material and a black plastic device lying in a formed depression. Long and thin, the black plastic object seemed innocent enough. Liam touched it, picked it up. On the smooth unbroken surface he saw a serial number, a plug-in port of some kind, and nothing else. Obviously the object was just what Shamus said it was, some bloody part for a computer.

Liam placed the device back into the depression, lifted the sponge packing. Under it he saw two black squares, each the size of a pack of coffin nails. They were completely covered with electrical tape. More tape held the squares to the side of the case. Liam figured it was just more packing material. He closed the case and leaned back with relief.

In another hour or so he'd be in Forest Hills. He could return the case to Shamus, go back to The Last Celt and catch some zeds at last . . .

10:34:40 A.M. EDT
CTU Headquarters, Los Angeles

Jamey was following Nina Myers's sole lead—the identity of Felix Tanner. Using state, federal, and local databases, banking information, tax records, and corporate registers, she found some interesting connections.

For one thing, according to tax records from the Lynch brothers' Green Dragon franchise, most of the shop's income was generated by a vaguely worded contract Griffin Lynch had signed with Prolix Security, the firm taken over by Felix Tanner.

Even more interesting, with some electronic digging Jamey also discovered that Wexler Business Storage—

the company that owned the SUV that had served as Dante Arete's deathtrap—had only two clients renting space in their Houston Street storage facility. One was Green Dragon Computers of Forest Hills, the other firm was Prolix Security of Manhattan.

Jamey grinned as she added the intelligence to her electronic data log.

Let's see Nina Myers accuse me of "sloppy performance" now!

10:59:56 A.M. EDT
Montague Street, Brooklyn

Following the homing technology embedded inside his digital watch, Jack located the narrow-band beacon signal constantly broadcast by his CTU-issue Personal Digital Assistant. There was a lot of interference, and sometimes he stumbled into blind spots and lost the signal, but Jack knew that Caitlin must be close or he would not be receiving the signal at all.

Along a trendy, upscale commercial area on tree-lined Montague Street in Brooklyn Heights, the signal became very strong. As Jack wove his way through throngs of late morning shoppers, the watch began to emit tiny beeps—a warning that he was within fifty yards of his PDA.

Jack scanned the busy street, noticed a small café tucked between a bakery shop and an antiques store. A few tables, shaded by umbrellas, were on the sidewalk in front of the café. Jack spied Caitlin sitting at one of them, a cup of coffee untouched at her arm. Her head was down, her eyes red from crying, her skinny arms wrapped around her.

Jack crossed the street, moved among the tables. Caitlin looked up just then, blinked in disbelief, then launched herself out of the chair and clasped him tightly.

"Jack! Oh, Jack! Mother of God, you scared me. I thought you were dead, sure!"

Jack held her close, felt the young woman tremble in his arms.

"Did you see my brother? Did you see Liam?" she asked, frantic.

"Don't worry. I know Liam never made it to Kahlil's store, they told me so. I'm sure he's safe, Caitlin. We just have to find him before anyone else does . . ."

....

**THE FOLLOWING TAKES PLACE
BETWEEN THE HOURS OF
11 A.M. AND 12 P.M.
EASTERN DAYLIGHT TIME**

....

*11:09:56 A.M. EDT
CTU Headquarters, Los Angeles*

Nina Myers jerked, snapped back to reality by the insistent three-tone ring. She looked away from the computer monitor, punched the button for the speakerphone. "What is it Jamey?"

"I have Jack on the line."

Nina snatched the receiver. "Jack. My god. It's been close to six hours since . . ." She took a breath. "After the reports coming out of Brooklyn, Ryan was ready to write you off. Did you make contact with Taj Ali Kahlil?"

"Only his brother, Khan. He's dead now. So is everyone else, thanks to that FBI raid. I've hit a wall."

Jack was reaching for a lifeline and Nina tossed him one. There was a tiny pause in which he could almost feel Nina's smile over the phone. They had worked so closely and so intensely, Jack sometimes felt he knew what Nina was thinking.

"Listen, Jack. We're not out of leads yet. Jamey's dug up some new intelligence; so have Tony and Captain Schneider."

"Who?"

"Never mind, just listen." Nina told Jack everything they'd learned about Felix Tanner, his connection to Prolix Security, and that company's connection to the Lynch brothers through their Green Dragon store in Queens. Then she briefed him about Wexler Storage and the company's connection to both Prolix Security and the Lynch brothers' computer store.

"Have you found out anything more about Special Agent Frank Hensley?"

"Sorry, Jack. Only what's public knowledge—and by public I mean in the newspapers. The FBI has effectively cut us off from their database. Some of the other agencies are starting to get nervous, too. The walls are getting higher."

"Because of Hensley's accusations about me?"

Nina said nothing. They both knew the answer.

"Listen, Nina . . . I have a problem. It's Caitlin, she's done her part but she's a civilian. I can't drag her all over town, put her in jeopardy again. And I can't leave her on her own. If the Lynch brothers find her she's dead."

"I've already discussed this issue with Ryan. He's dispatched a CTU agent named Carlos Ferrer out of the D.C. office. Special Agent Ferrer is scheduled to arrive on the Amtrak Acela in less than an hour. He'll contact you then. Agent Ferrer will take custody of Caitlin, escort her to a safe house."

"Good work, Nina. I'm going to Wexler Storage next."

"Why there, Jack?"

"I'm figuring that the missile launchers for the New York attack have to be stored somewhere—a central location where the leader of the terrorist cell can keep tabs on them, and a place from which the weapons could easily be dispatched. Wexler Storage fits the bill. It's in the heart of Manhattan, within driving distance of three major airports."

"It's your call, Jack."

"It's going to take me some time to get to Houston Street. The car's been compromised so I'm taking the subway. I'll be out of touch for a while."

"What about the package?"

"Caitlin is coming with me. Keep gathering data on Felix Tanner, and find out what you can about Frank Hensley."

11:19:11 A.M. EDT
Office of New York Senator William Cheever
Hart Senate Office Building, Washington, D.C.

Dennis Spain had just ended a conversation with WestWing Airlines CEO Gilbert Hemmer when his intercom buzzed.

"I said I was not to be disturbed," Spain snapped at the woman. "You know the Senator's teleconference is this afternoon. I have more calls to make."

"It's Mr. Reichel, sir. You said I was supposed to notify you immediately whenever Mr. Reichel calls."

"Put him on."

A moment later, Spain addressed the Assistant Undersecretary of Budgetary Affairs for the United States Government Travel Office. "Hey, Ted. What's up?"

"Listen, Dennis. You asked me to tell you when travel vouchers are issued to anyone at CTU. We got one this morning. For an Agent Carlos Ferrer, D.C. to New York City."

"I'll need Agent Ferrer's itinerary," Spain said, examining his fingernails.

"The usual fee?"

"You bet."

"I'll fax that information right over to you."

"Wait. I have another number I want you to use." Spain read it off.

"212? That's a New York City area code."

"That's right. Fax the information ASAP."

"I'll do it now."

Dennis Spain ended the call, buzzed his secretary. "Get me Felix Tanner at Prolix Security's Manhattan office."

11:20:09 A.M. EDT
CTU Headquarters, Los Angeles

A shaky Milo Pressman finished recounting the disaster at Green Dragon Computers to the members of Crisis Management Team Alpha. Jamey Farrell was especially affected. She had known Nell Henkel quite well. Sometimes they went clubbing together.

Ryan Chappelle listened with the others, then spoke. "First let me say what happened was a tragedy, but no one in this room should blame themselves. My assistant will compose letters of condolences to the families of Michael Chen and Danielle Henkel. Needless to say, their loss has further strained our manpower resources. Mr. Pressman and Ms. Farrell will have to take on additional responsibilities—"

"What about the plan, Mr. Chappelle?"

All eyes turned to Captain Schneider, still clad in the civilian clothes she wore when she single-handedly assaulted Green Dragon, her blond hair loose and falling around her shoulders.

"I really don't think this is the time—"

"I think it is," Captain Schneider replied. "You want to find out more about FBI Agent Frank Hensley, right? This might be the only way to gain access to such information. The California Senator's running feud with the Bureau is something we can exploit."

"What you're suggesting is nothing less than a raid on another government agency."

Jessica Schneider shrugged. "A potentially corrupt agency, Mr. Chappelle. At the very least an agency that has been compromised by a traitor or double agent."

"You can't be serious," Nina Myers protested. "CTU has already been marginalized by the other agencies. If word of this ever gets out—"

Chappelle waved Nina's concerns aside. "What do you think, Tony?"

Agent Almeida's eyes shifted from Nina to Jessica. "In this case I'd have to go with Captain Schneider. We need to know if Frank Hensley is the mastermind behind this operation, or if he's another cog in a bigger wheel. We need to know why the FBI chose today to raid Kahlil's market. And we need to know what the FBI knows—about Felix Tanner, Green Dragon, Wexler Storage. If they're going to withhold that intelligence from us because of some bogus accusations against Jack Bauer, then we should go in and grab it ourselves."

"Is there any other way to gain access to this information?" Ryan asked. "Any suggestions, Jamey? Nina?"

"Withholding information is nothing new," Nina replied. "The wall this Administration and the Attorney General's office erected between the intelligence agencies is too high for CTU to climb. And with Jack Bauer under suspicion, nobody is willing to cut us any slack."

"I'll take that as a no," Ryan said. "Therefore I'm going to authorize this mission. When can you go?"

Tony rubbed the stubble on his chin. "Some software protocols will need to be established—"

"We can go right now," said Jessica. "Who's the FBI Bureau Chief in Los Angeles?"

"His name is Jeffrey Dodge. I met him at an interagency conference three months ago. Middle-aged, recently divorced."

Jessica nodded. "Good, I can exploit that."

The meeting broke up minutes later. Tony fell into step with the Captain. "You're right. We do need the information the FBI is keeping from us. But you poured it on a little thick back there. This isn't the Corps. We can't just charge into every situation and hope for the best. Stop thinking like a Marine all the time."

Jessica's eyes flashed cold. "Maybe you should *start*

thinking like a Marine again, Agent Almeida. You might get better results."

11:59:34 A.M. EDT
Boulevard Diner, Forest Hills, Queens

Liam hung up the receiver, heard the quarter rattle in the return slot. He pocketed the coin and headed back to the counter. Following Shamus's instructions, he'd gone directly to the Lynch brothers' store on Queens Boulevard, only to find the place mysteriously closed.

He hung around for a while, then decided to cross ten lanes of Queens Boulevard to a local diner. The place was jammed with a lunchtime crowd, so he grabbed a seat at the booth and ordered a burger and chips. He left his jacket on the seat and took the attaché case to the pay phone. The steel case was starting to feel like a ball and chain.

First he dialed the number for the Lynch brothers' store, got the electronic message giving business hours and directions. Next he dialed The Last Celt, looking for his sister. Strangely, no one answered the phone there, either. But Donnie Murphy should have been there; he was as punctual as the sun when it came to running the pub, and he was always there before nine o'clock to accept deliveries and such.

Liam hung up the phone and carried the case back to the counter. His food was waiting for him, but he'd lost his appetite. He just couldn't shake the feeling that trouble was heading his way.

....

**THE FOLLOWING TAKES PLACE
BETWEEN THE HOURS OF
12 P.M. AND 1 P.M.
EASTERN DAYLIGHT TIME**

....

12:00:00 P.M. EDT
Penn Station, New York City

The Acela had rolled into New York's Penn Station at
11:57 A.M., four minutes ahead of schedule. Exiting
onto the cavernous underground platform, Special
Agent Carlos Ferrer shifted his heavy suitcase, followed the tide of passengers to the escalator and up to
Penn Station's main concourse.

When Ferrer departed Washington that morning,
he had been told that CTU Los Angeles had not made
contact with Jack Bauer in more than four hours.
Reestablishing communication was Ferrer's first priority. He paused under the massive hanging sign that
displayed arrival and departure times and track num-

bers of trains with names like the Yankee Clipper, the Metroliner, the Pennsylvanian, and the Washingtonian. Agent Ferrer doubted that finding Bauer would be as easy as making a phone call, but he had to give it a shot.

Unfortunately he could not acquire a signal—probably because he was beneath massive Madison Square Garden. Agent Ferrer turned, searching for an exit when he saw a man approaching him. The stranger had a dark tan, deep brown eyes, and sunstreaked yellow-blond hair. He grinned as he stepped into range, extended his hand in greeting.

"Special Agent Ferrer? I'm Jack Bauer, CTU." The man flashed his ID. "I just got word you were on your way in from D.C., so I came to meet you."

12:21:06 P.M. EDT
FBI Headquarters, Los Angeles

The FBI's Los Angeles headquarters was one of a cluster of Federal buildings on the corner of Wilshire Drive and Veteran Boulevard, between the UCLA Medical Center and Westwood Park. Despite rush hour traffic, Tony Almeida and Captain Schneider drove there in thirty minutes. They displayed their false IDs to security and were immediately cleared.

Jeffrey Dodge, the Los Angeles District Administrator of the FBI office in Los Angeles, met them at the elevator. A balding, heavy-set man of middle age, Dodge displayed the instant affability of a trained bureaucrat. "Ms. Van Dyne, Mr. Newsom, welcome to the Bureau. I had no idea you were coming."

Tony smiled, shook the man's beefy hand. Then Jessica stepped forward, brushed aside her windblown, straw-blond hair. "Things have been just a whirlwind since Senator Baxter accepted a chair on the Senate Intelligence Committee," she said breathlessly. When they shook hands, Jessica's lingered in his.

"Please, follow me." Dodge ushered the pair into his spacious corner office, closed the door behind them. He had trouble keeping his eyes off Jessica Schneider, who wore a black pin-striped jacket over a matching mini-skirt and stiletto heels that emphasized her tanned, athletic legs. Under the jacket, her wispy blouse was open to display the Captain's other attributes.

While Dodge escorted Jessica to a chair, Tony studied his surroundings. The Bureau Chief's office was spacious, its faux wood-trimmed walls decorated with framed diplomas, portraits of his two adolescent children, along with vacation snapshots. Images of the former Mrs. Dodge were noticeably absent, suggesting a bitter split. There was a photo of Bureau Chief Dodge posing with the current President. On a large, polished oaken desk, Tony spied what he was looking for—Dodge's keyboard and monitor. The computer was idle; on-screen the FBI insignia floated on a red, white, and blue background.

Dodge took position behind his desk, waited politely for Jessica to sit down. She did—directly in front of him, crossing her long, naked legs.

"Well," Dodge said, visibly nervous, "how can I help California's esteemed Senator?"

Jessica leaned forward, smiled. "I'll just get right to the point, Mr. Dodge. During her long political career, Senator Bonny Baxter has been unfairly cast as a politician who is hostile to our nation's law enforcement and intelligence services—"

"Oh, now I wouldn't go that far," said Dodge.

"No, no, Mr. Dodge, it's true. My boss is fully aware of her reputation; that's why I came here today. You see, Senator Baxter would like to show America that she can forge strong relationships with America's premier law enforcement agencies, starting with the FBI."

"I think that's a fine idea."

"The Senator thought you'd feel that way."

"She did?"

"She even mentioned you by name. And I can see why she chose you, Mr. Dodge. You're quite . . . *photogenic.*"

Dodge grinned shyly, fumbled with his tie. Tony noted how pronounced Jessica's Texas drawl had become. He smiled to himself. Obviously that whole debutante thing was something she could turn off or on at will—and, he had to concede, a fairly handy little tool for undercover work.

"Well, Ms. Van Dyne—"

"Call me Tandi, Mr. Dodge."

"Well, Tandi. What can I do to help?"

"The Senator was thinking a photo opportunity, right here at FBI headquarters, with its director. A nice dramatic shot, with a really interesting background."

"How about our new training facilities? They're located right here in the basement. We just opened the newly renovated wing last week."

"Why that would be simply delightful, Mr. Dodge. Could you possibly show me around?"

"By all means." Jeffrey Dodge rose, placed a hand on Jessica's shoulder. On their way out Dodge completely ignored Tony—and that was the plan.

While Jessica kept the man distracted, Tony leaned

across the desk and flipped the keyboard upside down. He slapped the tiny self-adhesive device in the palm of his hand onto the bottom of the keyboard, then put the keyboard down. In less than three seconds the job was done.

Tony knew that a routine security sweep would immediately uncover the CTU spyware device, but such measures were taken only once or twice a week. In the meantime the tiny transmitter would broadcast every keystroke on the FBI director's keypad back to CTU headquarters. The next time Jeffrey Dodge logged onto his computer, Jamey Farrell would have his password. Using it, she could then download the classified FBI files on Frank Hensley from the Bureau's own database.

12:36:54 P.M. EDT
Wexler Business Storage
Houston Street, Lower Manhattan

Wexler Business Storage was housed in a dreary six-story brick building on Houston Street in the West Village. The chipped, over-painted cornerstone revealed the date of construction as 1908. A cast-iron fire escape climbed the front of the red-brick edifice. The arched windows had once admitted sunlight, but were now shuttered with dense black glass.

An SUV identical to the one Dante Arete had perished inside was parked at the curb. Behind it, a New York City police car with three officers gathered around it.

Jack dragged Caitlin back, peered around the corner.

"What's the matter, Jack? Don't you want to go in there?"

"I can't. Thanks to a corrupt FBI agent, the police are looking for me. I can't risk being spotted."

Caitlin peeked around the corner, studied the building for a moment. "Why don't I go?"

"That's crazy."

Caitlin faced him. "Look. There's a help wanted sign on the door. I'll pretend to apply for the job. Maybe I can check the place out. If you tell me what you're looking for I can—"

"No," said Jack. "I have a better idea . . ."

12:41:12 P.M. EDT
CTU Headquarters, Los Angeles

"I've got Jeffrey Dodge's password," Jamey said, her fingers poised over the keyboard. She typed the code into a secure data line. "Okay, I'm in."

Five minutes later, Nina was scanning Special Agent Frank Hensley's personnel file on screen. She learned that Hensley had many Bureau citations, most earned for undercover assignments. But as they thought, Hensley's most recent investigation centered on Dante Arete's Brooklyn gang, the Columbia Street Posse.

The case had not gone well; at least that's what Hensley reported to his superiors. The Posse outsmarted the FBI at every turn, rooted out informants, and when Hensley's partner tried to take extraordinary means to get a conviction, he was murdered by Dante or his lieutenants—at least that's what Hensley told his bosses. But Nina knew Hensley was a liar, so he might be lying about his partner's death, too.

Going back through his personnel file, Nina discovered Hensley was a 1991–92 Gulf War veteran of the U.S. Army. He had been a prisoner of war, too. A captive of the Iraqis in Baghdad for nearly three months.

The capture took place when Hensley had been on routine patrol along the border of Occupied Kuwait. His men had been killed by an elite Iraqi unit, but since Hensley was the highest-ranking officer, his life had been spared and he was spirited to Baghdad to act as a human shield. Hensley was released at the end of hostilities, along with all the other American and Coalition prisoners. He left the Army, finished earning his law degree, and took a job with the Bureau.

Nina cursed. The files revealed nothing. They were the history of an exemplary citizen—war hero, law enforcement officer, dedicated civil servant.

"He's divorced," said Ryan Chappelle, startling Nina. She turned to find him staring at the monitor. "It says so right there. He was married for three years. Her maiden name was Katherine Elizabeth Felloes and she was born in Los Angeles, attended Beverly Hills High School."

Jamey cross-referenced the name on a dozen databases. The New York files came up without hits, so she widened her search parameters.

"Got her," Jamey declared a moment later. "Mrs. Katherine Hensley returned to Los Angeles a year ago. She lives in Brentwood now. Runs an art studio out of her home."

12:50:14 P.M. EDT
FBI Headquarters, Federal Plaza, Manhattan

The silence was cut by a gentle chirp. Hensley swung his chair away from the window and its view of Foley Square, placed the cell phone to his ear.

"My brother is dead." The voice on the other end was flat, emotionless.

"I know. I just received word," Hensley replied. "You said your brother could handle Bauer. Apparently you were wrong. Do you want me to take care of him myself?"

"No," Taj replied. "Thanks to Felix Tanner and our mutual friend in Washington, Bauer will die very soon."

Taj Ali Khalil ended the conversation. Hensley cursed, tossed the cell on his desk.

Since Dante Arete's capture by CTU, things had become increasingly more complicated, until he was forced to sacrifice the entire Atlantic Avenue cell just to stop Jack Bauer. Taj went along with the plan, confident his brother could finish Jack Bauer. But somehow the CTU agent managed to escape the trap they had set for him.

Now it was up to Taj and his personal assassin, Omar Bayat.

12:51:42 P.M. EDT
CTU Headquarters, Los Angeles

Shoeless, Doris walked into Jamey's workstation and plunked down on a chair. Jamey and Milo had been surfing through the FBI database. They both looked up.

"I cracked the final code," Doris said. "This new-type North Korean security software is tough, but with Frankie's help I broke down the last firewall two minutes ago. I've got all the data on screen right now."

"What did you find?" Milo asked.

Doris waved the question aside. "It's, like, instructions, I'm sure. But I can't read them."

"Why can't you read them? Are they in some kind of code?"

"It's in Korean. I just need a translation program."

Jamey and Milo were both puzzled. "Aren't you Korean?" Jamey asked.

"Duh, I was born in *California*," Doris replied.

"But it says on your profile you're a linguist."

"I am a linguist. I speak fluent French and Russian. I wanted to be a ballerina when I was a little girl, so what's the point of learning Korean? Have you ever heard of any great Korean ballet companies?"

Jamey passed Doris a zip drive. "Here's a translation program. Let me know when you're finished . . ."

12:52:14 P.M. EDT
Wexler Business Storage
Houston Street, Lower Manhattan

Caitlin crossed the sidewalk, walked in front of the squad car parked at the curb. Only one officer was there now, sitting behind the wheel. He offered Caitlin a polite smile as she passed.

A bell rang when Caitlin entered the waiting room of Wexler Business Storage. Sunlight streamed through the streaked plate-glass window; rickety steel chairs lined the dirty beige walls. A large poster listed storage bin sizes and rental fees, on a monthly and yearly basis. The waiting room was deserted, so she approached the counter.

She leaned over the scratched and dented surface, to peer behind the counter. Caitlin noticed a door, completely papered over with a huge five-year calendar. Next to that Caitlin saw a small office through a window in the interior wall.

The door opened and an elderly, heavy-set black woman emerged. On the jacket of her pantsuit a plastic nametag identified the woman as Mamie Greene. A blue cap with the Yankees logo topped her short, tightly curled white hair. She smiled at Caitlin. "Bin number?"

Caitlin blinked. "I beg your pardon."

"What's your bin number, miss?"

"Oh, I'm not here about a storage bin. I saw the help wanted sign on the door and, well, I—"

The woman made a face. "You'll have to fill out an application. Follow me."

Mamie Greene lifted a section of the counter and Caitlin stepped through to the other side. They went through the door, into the office where the woman ushered Caitlin to a chair in front of a cluttered desk. Mamie crossed the room, rifled through a filing cabinet. When she returned she laid a sheaf of papers in front of Caitlin.

"Do you have a copy of your résumé?"

"My what?"

"Your résumé. You *have* worked before?"

"Yes, oh yes," Caitlin replied.

"Can you use a computer? Word processor?"

"No, not really. But I learn quick."

"Can you use a Xerox machine? We only use Xerox around here. Company policy."

"I used one once. In a Staples store."

"You better fill out the form, miss."

"But I don't have a pen."

Mamie Greene threw up her hands. "I'll give you a ballpoint, we have lots of those. But nobody's using my felt tip."

A suitable pen was found, and Caitlin began filling out the application. A moment later the doorbell rang again.

"I'll be right back," said Mamie.

Caitlin watched through the window as Mamie Greene spoke with the UPS man. Then she reached into her pocket and took out the lighter Jack had bought for her at a convenience store. She quickly stuffed a bunch of loose papers into the bottom of a nearly empty aluminum trash can, touched them with fire. Flames leaped up immediately, too many.

As per Jack's instructions, she tossed more paper onto the fire, not quite smothering it but almost. She wanted a lot of smoke and a little bit of fire, nothing more dangerous than that.

She looked for a place to hide the trash can, heard Mamie Greene say goodbye to the delivery man. Hurriedly Caitlin slid the smoldering can into a walk-in closet, too quickly to see what was inside. She only just made it back to her chair when Mamie returned.

"You aren't done yet?"

Caitlin smiled sheepishly. "There's a lot of writing."

"That's why we have computers."

"Are you the manager, then? Or is it Mr. Wexler?"

Mamie Greene chuckled. "Mr. Wexler died in 1957. I was working here then, too. I was the assistant office manager when Mr. Wexler was in charge. I was the office manager when his son took over the business. And I'm still the office manager now, after Junior sold the company to that Arab fellow last year."

"I see."

Mamie cocked her head, sniffed the air. "Do you smell smoke? I smell smoke . . ."

The woman spied brown smoke wafting out of the closet. "My stars!" she cried.

With a speed that was impressive considering her advanced age and considerable girth, Mamie hurried across the room and yanked an unwieldy fire extinguisher off the wall. Before Mamie could drag the heavy extinguisher to the fire, Caitlin hit the red emergency button on the wall next to the desk.

Shrill fire alarms echoed throughout the building. Stubbornly, Mamie crossed the room with the bulky extinguisher. But when she yanked the closet door open, roaring hot smoke rolled out, followed by licking orange flames. The woman squawked and dropped the canister. Caitlin peered inside the closet. In the rippling flames, she could see cardboard boxes and reams of papers lining the walls.

"My god!" Caitlin gasped. She wasn't supposed to set a real fire, only make some smoke. She jumped when she felt a heavy hand on her shoulder.

"Honey, let's get out of here," Mamie cried.

Caitlin raced into the waiting room, hands clutching her head. She didn't even have to fake panic as she began to scream.

"Fire! Fire! Mother of Mercy, the whole building is on fire!"

12:59:26 P.M. EDT
Boulevard Diner, Forest Hills, Queens

Three cups of joe and two Cokes. Liam had to piss but he was still knackered. He'd been up all night, mugged, almost run down by a subway, caught in a police raid, then an explosion—no wonder he couldn't keep his bleedin' peepers open!

He swung the stool around, ready to make a trip to the head, when he spied the Lynch brothers' Mercedes swing into a parking spot in front of the computer store across the road.

Finally.

Liam fumbled in his pockets, dumped money for the bill and a tip on the counter. Then he lifted the metal attaché case and left the diner. He would be glad to get this over with. Tell Shamus about the raid in Brooklyn, and get rid of the case—he'd been carrying the damned thing for nearly twelve hours!

·······································

**THE FOLLOWING TAKES PLACE
BETWEEN THE HOURS OF
1 P.M. AND 2 P.M.
EASTERN DAYLIGHT TIME**

·······································

*1:01:03 P.M. EDT
Houston Street, Lower Manhattan*

Jack Bauer watched the entrance to Wexler Storage from a recessed doorway across busy Houston Street, waiting for Caitlin to make her move. Around him the bohemians of the West Village—women in black dresses, stacked shoes, and wide-rimmed glasses; men with shaved heads, tattoos, and multiple body piercings—crowded the sidewalks, the shops, the side-walk cafés. Jack ignored the locals, focused attention on the police car parked at the curb, the lone officer inside.

When the fire alarm wailed, Jack was ready. He

burst out of hiding, into the street. Dodging cars, he watched the policeman hurriedly report the fire on his radio, then climb out to offer assistance.

A large black woman stumbled out of the store-front, collapsed with a coughing fit on the sidewalk. Caitlin appeared a moment later, screaming her head off. She spotted Jack and the cop at the same time.

Thinking fast, the woman literally jumped into the young policeman's arms.

"There's smoke and fire! The building is burning."

As she babbled, Caitlin swung the cop around so Jack could race past the man unseen.

The waiting room was already filled with black smoke. Jack blinked against the burning haze. Through the window behind the counter, he saw orange flames racing through the inner office. The plasterboard wall around that window began to smolder; beige paint bubbled and curled from the tremendous heat.

He'd wanted Caitlin to set a small fire with enough smoke to empty the building. Clearly, she had gone overboard. Jack thought about escaping the building, too, but a sudden noise changed his mind.

Jack heard a clang as a steel door burst open. A Hispanic man in a gray uniform stumbled out of a stairwell, choking against the billowing smoke. Jack pushed the man toward the exit, then ran into the stairwell and slammed the door behind him.

The stairwell was relatively free of smoke. There was no way down; the stairs ended on the ground floor. So Jack climbed the stairs to the second floor. He found another steel door, this one locked from the other side. Cautiously Jack peered through a small wire-lined window in the center of the door. He saw long rows of storage bins, each with its own door and padlock—none of them large enough to hold a North Korean missile launcher.

At the opposite side of the room Jack saw sliding metal-mesh doors blocking an empty elevator shaft. Smoke was beginning to penetrate the second floor through the floorboards and elevator shaft. It hung in the air.

Jack climbed to the third floor, the fourth, then the fifth. On each floor the steel doors were locked, the floors themselves seemingly deserted—just row upon row of storage bins, and an empty elevator shaft on the opposite wall. No sign of a terrorist cell, no trace of the Long Tooth missile launchers.

Finally Jack reached the sixth floor and the top of the stairs. Only a ladder climbed higher, leading up to a hatch in the ceiling. As he approached the steel door, Jack wondered if he was on a wild goose chase, if he'd trapped himself inside a burning building for nothing.

1:06:15 P.M. EDT
Sixth floor, Wexler Business Storage
Houston Street, Lower Manhattan

When the fire alarms began to sound, Tarik dropped his hammer, barked instructions in Pashto for the others to stay where they were and to keep working. They had to pack up the precious cargo in wooden crates, for transport to the airports, no matter what else was going on around them.

Tarik opened his cell, dialed up Taj. He cursed

when his call was rerouted to a voice mail system. He left his leader a warning in Pashto, then ended the call.

He turned, found the men struggling under the weight of the missiles; the launchers had not yet been sealed in their boxes. He wanted to curse these men, goad them into action with kicks and insults. But he did not. These men were old, some with missing eyes, hands, limbs—their legacies of the war against the Soviets.

Tarik reminded himself that these men were all that remained of Taj Ali Kahlil's once-mighty clan, heroes of the Afghan war, men who boldly risked their lives against the Russian infidels who'd invaded their homeland. They had shed blood and limbs and eyes for the cause of Muslim freedom—only to be betrayed by the American intelligence services that aided them.

Instead of berating these men, Tarik felt only respect. He was about to pitch in to help when Tarik saw movement through the window of the fire exit. Someone was lurking on the stairwell.

Tarik drew his Uzi and approached the steel door.

1:09:04 P.M. EDT
Green Dragon Computers
Queens Boulevard, Forest Hills

It took Liam a long time to cross the ten lanes of traffic on Queens Boulevard. Finally he was on the sidewalk, just a few storefronts away from Green Dragon Computers, when a black BMW squealed to a stop in front of the shop. The driver double-parked, blocking Shamus's car, then leaped out.

Liam halted when he saw Taj Ali Kahlil. The Afghani man wore an unadorned white skullcap over a lightweight suit. He strode into the Green Dragon store, an angry scowl darkening his long, narrow face.

Liam ducked into the exterior doorway of a dry cleaner's. An Asian woman inside the shop eyed him warily through the plate-glass window. Breathing hard, he shifted the metal case in his sweaty hands. He'd been dragging that attaché around so long, it felt like a bleedin' anchor.

His mind was in turmoil. He never wanted trouble, just a bit of money. Now trouble found him in the shape of a shiny metal attaché case and the piece of plastic and silicone it contained. Liam recalled the violence the FBI had used to smash their way into the Brooklyn store and decided Taj must be some kind of crook.

Now Liam didn't know what to do. He thought of his sister, and the world of hurt he was bringing down on her. *Maybe if I talk to her*, he thought, *warn Caitlin that trouble was coming*. The last thing Liam wanted to do was jeopardize the only person he had in all the world.

And the next to the last thing Liam wanted to do was face Taj and the Lynch brothers—he knew they were crooks now. Who knew what they would do to him?

So Liam turned and hurried away from the computer store as fast as he could. A few blocks away, he spied a pay phone and dug into his pocket for some coins, dialed The Last Celt. The pub was open now and Caitlin should have been working lunch duty. But it was a stranger who answered on the second ring.

"Can I speak to Caitlin, please?"

"Who's Caitlin?" the voice growled in reply.

"There's an apartment upstairs. Is that where this Caitlin lives?"

Liam heard other voices in the background, none he recognized. He stopped talking, but did not hang up.

"Listen, son," the voice said. "My name is Detective McKinney of the New York Police Department. If you know something about the murder of Donnie Murphy you'd better turn yourself in right now."

Liam hung up the receiver down, letting it go like a poisonous snake. Sick with anxiety, he didn't know where to turn. All he wanted to do was lose the attaché case and go home. Now it looked like he was stuck with the bloody case, and he had no home to go back to.

1:10:01 P.M. EDT
Sixth floor, Wexler Business Storage
Houston Street, Lower Manhattan

The fire alarm continued to ring throughout the massive brick building. On the sixth-floor landing, Jack peered through the wire-meshed glass, spied a group of elderly men in turbans and skullcaps frantically trying to load two Long Tooth shoulder-fired missile launchers and a dozen missiles into two large, unmarked wooden crates. A dolly waited near the open doors to the freight elevator to carry the deadly weapons away.

One of the men, younger than the rest, with an Uzi tucked into his sash, turned his head in Jack's direction. Jack ducked behind the door, but not quick enough—he was certain the man had spotted him. Slowly Jack drew the Mark 23 USP from its shoulder holster. A moment later, over the wail of the fire alarms, he heard the handle click, and the metal door opened outward. Jack immediately thrust the barrel of his gun through the narrow opening and fired. The blast was deafening. It continued to echo inside the confines of the stairwell as Jack ripped open the door and jumped over the corpse of the man he'd just killed.

Jack fired as he moved. Another man's head exploded, and a third pitched backward, clutching the fountain of blood that gushed from the wound in his throat.

Another young Afghani appeared out of nowhere, to let fly with a volley from an assault rifle. Jack rolled behind a steel storage bin as the chattering AK–47 tore up the floorboards where he'd stood only a split second before. With a shooter pinning him down, two of the old men stumbled toward the Long Tooth missile launchers, rolled them off the rack and onto the dolly. Jack managed to shoot one of the men, who had a stump for a right hand. But even though the Afghani was wounded, he stubbornly helped his colleague wheel the dolly into the freight elevator.

Jack knew he had to stop these missiles from arriving at their destination, but whenever he tried to move out of cover, the young Afghani with the assault rifle would open up on him. Suddenly the fire door opened again. Jack whirled, figuring he'd been flanked. When he saw a blue uniform, Jack tried to warn the newcomer of the danger. But the AK–47 barked first, and the New York City policeman who'd been sitting in the squad car was ripped in half in a hail of bullets.

Taking advantage of the momentary distraction,

Jack squeezed off four shots. They slammed the shooter backward, into a wall.

Jack was on his feet in time to see the metal grate close and the freight elevator begin its descent. Crossing the floor, he scooped up the AK–47. The banana magazine was nearly full—the shooter must have reloaded just before he shot the cop. Jack reached the elevator, thrust the muzzle through the grate, and opened fire.

But instead of firing down, into the cage, Jack shot the cables. Sparks flew, a pulley wheel broke and tumbled down the shaft. Then he heard a ripping sound as the cable snapped.

Howls echoed up the shaft as the freight elevator plunged to the basement. The screams ended abruptly when the elevator car was dashed to pieces. Smoke billowed out of the shaft, rolled over Jack until he had to shield his eyes. When the smoke cleared, Jack peeked down the shaft, saw two corpses and a pair of shattered missile launchers among the twisted debris.

Smoke began to rise up the elevator shaft from the fire raging on the ground floor. Jack decided it was time to go. He ran back to the fire door. But when he opened it, smoke and heat struck him. A bonfire roared at the bottom of the stairs. The roof was his only hope. Jack grabbed the first rung of the ladder and climbed up to the hatch in the ceiling, praying it wasn't locked.

1:21:13 P.M. EDT
Freight Terminal C
Atlanta Hartsfield Jackson International Airport

The hazardous material vehicles pulled away from the Boeing 727 and the ramp closed.

Dr. Colin Fife stood on the tarmac beside CDC Director Henry Johnston Garnett. They watched in silence as the jet taxied down the runway, then leaped into the sky.

Dr. Garnett sighed. "I only hope we've done enough to protect the public."

"Only an act of God, a totally unforeseen catastrophe like a plane crash could unleash the virus," said Dr. Fife with confidence. "And even then the explosion and fire would most likely destroy the cultures. Oh, perhaps if the aircraft broke apart, or it crashed without a fuel explosion there might be a danger, but the chances of such an event are simply astronomical."

1:46:44 P.M. EDT
Green Dragon Computers
Queens Boulevard, Forest Hills

Inside the Green Dragon store, Taj confronted Griffin Lynch.

"My brother is dead, the safe house in Brooklyn destroyed, and I still do not have the memory stick I require to shoot down the CDC aircraft," Taj complained.

"Don't panic," Griffin replied. "We sent Liam to deliver the stick. He's done it a dozen times. We don't know what went wrong this time."

"Do you think he went to the police?" Taj asked.

Griff exchanged an unhappy look with Shamus. "We don't know what happened, but our associates in Los Angeles know about the loss of the memory stick. Another missile launcher with a new stick has been dispatched from the Green Dragon factory in Los Angeles. It's scheduled to arrive at LaGuardia Airport in a little over an hour."

Taj face clouded. "That wasn't the plan."

"No, but it will get the job done," said Griff. "Me and Shamus will pick up the launcher and bring it to you ourselves. It'll mean changing our plans. We never wanted to come to the bridge. We should have been on a plane by now, but we'll do it to get the bloody job done."

"We won't have time to test it."

"We don't need to test it. We know from Dante Arete's trial run that the aircraft identification software works. Arete's men were able to target an approaching Boeing 727 in the busy skies over LAX without difficulty."

"Then the fool was captured and we lost the device," grumbled Taj. "And we lost another memory stick when your boy failed to deliver it to me."

"Liam will pay for that bloody fuck-up, I guarantee it," Griff swore.

Taj's eyes clouded as he thought of his murdered brother. "I have sacrificed much. This plan had better work."

"It's perfect," said Griff. "With the CDC aircraft nearly out of fuel, it's not likely to burn when you shoot it down. The aircraft will simply break apart— and it will be low enough to disperse the disease cultures over the city's population. Many of the cultures will be destroyed, but enough will survive to infect millions. New York City will become a ghost town within two or three weeks."

The Afghani's skeletal face split into a cruel grin. "Then I shall have my revenge, for my hand will be the Hammer of God that will smite millions."

The phone rang, it was Frank Hensley. Griff put the FBI agent on speakerphone.

"There's trouble at Wexler Storage," Hensley began. "Add that to the raid at the factory in Los Angeles, and it's obvious CTU is getting too close."

"We can't postpone the mission," Griff replied.

"The mission goes on as scheduled," Hensley agreed.

"The bridge has been secured," said Taj. "My men are in place.

"Before we can proceed I want all loose ends tied up."

"Your will be done, Mr. Hensley," said Taj. "I will send an assassin to kill them all."

"I've already taken care of my ex-wife in Los Angeles," the FBI agent replied, his voice flat and emotionless. "Dispatch your assassins, along with Omar Bayat, to handle everyone else. I want you to start with Felix Tanner."

Taj nodded. "Felix Tanner and everyone around him will be dead within the hour."

1 2 3 4 5 6 7 8 9
10 11 12 13 14 15 16 17
18 19 20 21 22 23 24

••

**THE FOLLOWING TAKES PLACE
BETWEEN THE HOURS OF
2 P.M. AND 3 P.M.
EASTERN DAYLIGHT TIME**

••

2:01:51 P.M. EDT
1234 Las Palmas Way
Brentwood, California

Mrs. Katherine Elizabeth Hensley was a California bottled-blond with platinum highlights, a tanning bed complexion, and a wealthy father who was an esteemed Federal Court judge. She lived in a mock Tudor cottage separated from the road by a swath of lush green grass. Low trees hugged the stone walls, and dense, tall shrubs framed an arched doorway. A picture window with vertical blinds looked out on the quiet street, but most of the windows were hidden from the street in the back of the house.

Tony stopped the CTU van across the winding

boulevard, under a sprawling eucalyptus tree. Jessica Schneider displayed her cell phone. "Should I call Mrs. Hensley, let her know we're coming?"

Tony's eyes narrowed suspiciously. "Wait. Something's not right."

Jessica fished in her purse, pretended to brush her hair while she scoped the area. "I don't see anything."

"Look up the block. The jet-black '84 Mustang GT with the Cobra R chrome wheels and Pirelli tires. It's too crass and showy for this neighborhood. That's a gang-banger's car."

Jessica checked the rearview mirror. "That car behind us has a jacked suspension."

"That's a Nissan 300ZX Turbo. It doesn't belong here, either. This neighborhood has been invaded."

"What do we do?"

"We'll approach the house, but carefully. For all we know, we might be dealing with a burglary ring or—"

A woman's sudden scream was followed by shattering glass. Marine Captain Jessica Schneider bolted out the door and across the street before Tony could stop her.

"Christ, not again," he moaned, racing after her.

By the time she reached the path to the house, the Captain had her .45 drawn. When she reached the entrance, she flattened herself against the wooden door. Tony was still twenty yards away when a figure in black leather lunged at the Captain from the thick bushes flanking the arched entranceway.

The man smashed her against the door and dashed the weapon out of her hand. Still running, Tony spied a flash of steel, saw the eight-inch blade penetrate the Captain's shoulder to the hilt. Despite the horrific wound, she fought back.

Suddenly the door opened inward. Jessica Schneider and her attacker tumbled inside the house, and the door slammed. Without slowing, Tony veered to the right and ran toward the huge picture window. He drew his 9mm, snapped the safety off, and jumped.

Momentum carried him through the glass, but the vertical blinds entangled his feet and Tony landed on his side. He felt more than heard a supersonic crack as a bullet passed over his head, and Tony rolled behind a massive couch. He was in a living room, on a thick cream-colored rug. Near the fireplace, two young Asian men struggled with Mrs. Hensley. In the opposite corner Tony spied the shooter, fired twice. The double-tap splashed the man's brains onto the peach-colored walls.

Still on the floor, Tony twisted around, fired again. One of the men yelped and let go of the woman. He was a clear target now, and Tony pumped a shot into his heart. He flew back against the fireplace and dropped, scarlet staining the virgin carpet.

The last man gripped the woman's long blond hair, held a razor-sharp butterfly knife to her throat. He barked something in Cantonese. Tony's eyes narrowed as he aimed and fired again. The bullet struck the man's knee and he went down. Tony rose and fired a second round into the writhing, screaming man, and his cries abruptly ceased.

Tony bolted past the sobbing woman, kicked open a door. On the other side, Jessica Schneider was still struggling against one assassin. The other lay dead or unconscious in the marble entranceway. Tony grabbed the Asian man by his long black hair, yanked him backward. The assassin lunged. Tony kicked him in the throat. There was a crunch as the Asian's larynx was crushed. Choking, he fell backward, legs kicking as he gasped for air. Tony ignored the dying man, checked Jessica's wounds.

The knife was still buried in her shoulder. She gritted her teeth as he slid it out. There was a lot of blood, but no artery had been pierced. The Captain looked up at Tony through glassy eyes. Her face was pale and beaded with sweat, and Tony feared she was going to pass out.

"Stay with me!" he yelled.

Jessica opened her eyes, focused. Then she grinned sheepishly. "Guess I was too much of a Marine, huh?"

"You'll live. But I'm going to get you to a hospital."

She waved him off. "Take me to the CTU infirmary. This day isn't over yet. You still need me."

Tony offered her a faint smile while he tried to staunch the flow of blood. "Always the cowboy, right Captain?"

"I'm from Texas. It's in the blood."

Tony's eyebrows rose. "So I see."

Mrs. Hensley appeared in the doorway, her blouse ripped, jeans torn, clutching the jamb for support. She had a nasty bruise on the side of her face; otherwise she was nearly as colorless as Captain Schneider.

From the floor the Captain spoke. "Mrs. Hensley? Are you all right?"

Wide green eyes stared at the female Marine. The stunned woman nodded.

Tony stepped up to Mrs. Hensley. "My name is Tony Almeida. I'm an agent from the Counter Terrorist Unit. Do you have any idea why your ex-husband wants you dead?"

2:07:09 P.M. EDT
CTU Headquarters, Los Angeles

Ryan Chappelle called an emergency video conference with the other regional directors of Counter Terrorist Units across the nation.

"As you can see from the briefing material I've sent to all of you, we've determined beyond a reasonable doubt that unknown terrorists are targeting six airports in five major urban areas for multiple strikes scheduled to commence in less than two and a half hours.

"From the intelligence we've uncovered here in Los Angeles and with our agents in the field, we've concluded that the goal of these terrorists is to shoot down a large number of civilian airliners in an effort to bring air commerce to a halt and cripple the nation's economy.

"Fortunately, we were able to get a digital outline of the plot, down to the smallest detail. That is why I propose we assemble strike teams in each of these cities, place them in strategic locations around each of the airports. When zero hour comes, we'll be ready . . ."

"It's risky," said Phillip Keenan, RD of CTU, Seattle.

"It's an opportunity," countered Chappelle. "With all our tactical elements in place, we have the potential for a perfect storm, a sweep of terrorist suspects larger than any in history. This raid could be a real feather in all of our caps."

2:09:48 P.M. EDT
Los Angeles Freeway

"I met Frank Hensley after he returned from the Gulf War, at a party at UCLA. He was still in the Army, waiting to be discharged. I was majoring in art history; he was working toward his law degree. We got married the following June . . . Frank was in kind of a hurry."

Katherine Hensley seemed small and fragile after the attack. As Tony drove back to CTU, she sat next to him in the passenger seat up front. Eyes downcast, the bruises on her face, throat, and breasts livid against her tan, Mrs. Hensley answered questions posed to her in an emotionless monotone.

From the backseat, Captain Schneider strained to hear the woman's soft voice over the muted road noise. A blanket, bandages, and a painkilling shot from the first aid kit were all the medical care she would accept until they got back to CTU. Jessica was determined to interrogate Katherine Hensley herself.

"How was the marriage?"

"When we first met, I thought Frank was the strong, silent type. Too late I found out he was just a man who never talked—never to me, anyway. People . . . people who knew him before the war . . . they all said he'd changed."

"Changed? How?"

"Frank was captured by the Iraqis. He was a prisoner for several weeks. I guess he had a pretty rough time because Frank would never, ever talk about it. When the war ended he served out the rest of his enlistment, then quit the Army."

Captain Schneider, face pale and shiny with perspiration, fought hard to focus on the woman's stum bling replies, to ignore the throbbing pain from the stab wound, the dizziness from loss of blood. She leaned forward from the backseat. "You said Frank was in a hurry to get married?"

Mrs. Hensley nodded. "I thought it was because his parents both died while he was a teenager, that he wanted stability in his life. But after he joined the FBI, our lives were anything but stable."

"The job affected him?"

"Frank took on dangerous assignments. He worked undercover and things between us became . . . tense. Then I found out he'd been having an affair with a coworker and I filed for divorce. In the end, I think my father was more upset than I was. Dad had helped Frank get into the Bureau, treated him like a son."

Mrs. Hensley looked up. She met Jessica's eyes in the rearview mirror. "Maybe you should be having this conversation with Frank's girlfriend. She knows more about my husband's business than I do."

2:11:57 P.M. EDT
Houston Street, Lower Manhattan

Jack leaped from the bottom rung of the fire escape, landed in a narrow space between two buildings. He moved through a smoky haze to the sidewalk. Fire engines blocked Houston Street, hoses curled along the pavement like thick vines.

Jack slipped through the crowd, rejoined Caitlin.

"You did good," Jack told her.

Caitlin blinked. "I burned the bloody building down's what I did. I feel terrible about it, too. I was so stupid, so stupid—"

"It was a terrorist safe house. You may have saved hundreds of lives."

Caitlin slumped down on the curb. "I need a rest."

Jack leaned against a *Village Voice* stand. What he needed most right now was a CTU Crime Scene Unit, an "autopsy team" to work with local authorities and gather intelligence from the remains of the terrorist safe house on the sixth floor of the burning building and the shattered missile launchers in the ruined elevator. But the establishment of field offices in some cities was slow in coming, and often resisted by entrenched bureaucracies like the FBI, or local law enforcement agencies concerned with protecting their own turf. New York City was just one political hornets' nest since its police department had its own counter-terrorist team in place. Richard Walsh was lobbying hard to increase CTU's presence, but change was coming slowly.

Jack's cell chirped. He listened while Nina told him about CTU's massive tactical response to the terrorist threat. Jack told Nina what he'd discovered at Wexler Storage.

"They are going to have a tough time hitting the New York airports now. I've destroyed the missile launchers stored here and killed most of their operatives. Except for the leaders, Frank Hensley, the Lynch brothers, and Taj Ali Kahlil, the New York cell has been neutralized."

"We're not so sure about that, Jack," said Nina. "A missile launcher got away from us at Green Dragon, LA. It will turn up somewhere. And Omar Bayat has yet to turn up."

"What have you found out about Felix Tanner?"

"Tanner used to work for YankeeLife Insurance, a

firm that specialized in insurance for airline clients. Tanner has since moved over to the CEO's spot at Prolix Security. Day to day, he works out of his midtown Manhattan office.

"I'll need the personnel files from YankeeLife downloaded to my PDA and then I'm on my way," said Jack.

"Not so fast, Agent Bauer." It was Ryan Chappelle speaking. Jack was surprised Nina had not warned him the Administrative Director was on the line. "We need you to take down the rest of the New York cell, Jack. That's your first priority. You hurt them with the attack on the storage building, but they still have the resources to carry out the JFK attack. The FBI and local authorities are not cooperating with us, so it's up to you."

"Listen, I can't do it, Ryan, but I think I know someone who can."

Jack explained his plan. Ryan was—no surprise—highly skeptical.

"Trust me, Ryan," said Jack. "This will work. Finding Tanner is more important than anything else right now."

"Listen, Jack," said Nina. "There's more to deal with than Tanner. Tony Almeida and Captain Schneider interrogated Hensley's ex wife. Turns out Frank Hensley had an extramarital affair two years ago. The woman in question was Fiona Brice, an FBI stenographer working in the New York office—"

"Can we find her?"

"We found her, Jack. Fiona Brice is currently employed by Prolix Security. She's Felix Tanner's personal secretary."

2:22:43 P.M. EDT
Green Dragon Computers
Queens Boulevard, Forest Hills

Taj was gone but the Lynch brothers would see him soon, at the bridge. Griff glanced at his watch.

"The shipment arrives in ninety minutes. That gives us an hour and a half to clean up the mess before we can cut and run."

"Do you think Liam still has the case?" Shamus asked.

"I think we should determine that right now. If he does have the attaché case, this will solve our problem."

Griffin drew a black box remote control box from his jacket. On its featureless surface the device had one gray button and a tiny liquid crystal display. With his thumb, Griff pressed the button.

2:44:15 P.M. EDT
Houston Street, Lower Manhattan

Jack and Caitlin were making their way to a subway entrance when Jack's cell chirped again.

"This is Special Agent Carlos Ferrer, D.C. Division," said the stranger's voice. "Ryan Chappelle sent me to rendezvous with you and pick up an Irish national named Caitlin O'Connor. Is the woman with you now?"

"She's close," said Jack.

"Good. When can we link up?"

"I have to take care of something before I can meet you," Jack replied. "After I'm done, I will deliver

Caitlin to you in person. Let's establish a suitable place and time to meet."

They did, and the call ended.

"So now what?" Caitlin demanded. "Are you going to dump me on somebody else?"

"I don't want you to get hurt," Jack replied.

"I'm a big girl, Jack Bauer. I can take care of myself."

Jack stared intensely at Caitlin. Uncomfortable, she looked away. "What's the matter?"

"Is your last name O'Connor?"

Caitlin blinked. "Yes. What about it?"

Jack frowned. "How did Agent Ferrer know your last name, when I didn't?"

●●

THE FOLLOWING TAKES PLACE
BETWEEN THE HOURS OF
3 P.M. AND 4 P.M.
EASTERN DAYLIGHT TIME

●●

3:03:21 P.M. EDT
CTU Headquarters, Los Angeles

Doris Soo Min's neck itched. She hated it when someone stood behind her. Now three people hovered there—Milo and Jamey and that creepy Ryan Chappelle.

The intercom buzzed. "That's the call," said Jamey.

Doris hit the button. "Hello," she said tremulously.

"Good afternoon. My name is Georgi Timko. Our mutual friend Jack Bauer tells me you have information I require to play my role in today's drama."

"Ohmygodohmygod . . . Is that a Russian accent?"

"Ukrainian," Timko replied, "but I speak Russian

like a Muscovite, thanks to a wonderful KGB education."

Doris tapped her keyboard. "I'm about to send you the data we have on the JFK strike. Are you ready to receive?"

"Ready . . . Yes, the data is here. Now let us discuss this mission CTU wants me to perform."

Doris did. Excitedly. In Russian.

3:05:45 P.M. EDT
Green Dragon Computers
Queens Boulevard, Forest Hills

Griffin and Shamus watched the tiny screen, currently displaying a map of Queens. On a street not too far from the store, a blip flashed intermittently.

Griff frowned. "Someone has the attaché case, that's for certain."

"It's close," said Shamus. "Less than a mile away and moving. Maybe Liam's bringing it back to us like I told him to."

"No, it's moving in the opposite direction, toward Queens Center Mall."

Griffin handed the tracer to Shamus. "Take the Mercedes and finish this. I'll use the van to pick up the package at the airport and deliver it to Taj."

Shamus slipped a 9mm into his jacket. Griff faced him. "This is it, brother. You'll never see this place again. By midnight we're on a plane to the Cayman Islands. One more job and we leave America behind forever."

Shamus nodded, face grim. Griffin squeezed his

arm. "Take care of the boy. We'll meet at the bridge tonight."

3:33:58 P.M. EDT
CTU Headquarters, Los Angeles

Nina Myers burst into Ryan Chappelle's office without knocking.

"I just heard from the National Transportation Safety Board."

Ryan looked up from his computer screen. "What did they say?"

"There is not sufficient evidence to ground air traffic around these crucial airport hubs. Quote, unquote."

"Christ. How much evidence do they need?"

"More than we gave them, apparently. The head administrator cited the economic damage such a grounding could cause; the public's reaction might send ripples through the travel and air shipping industries."

Ryan scowled. "They're not seeing the bigger picture. What kind of public relations disaster will they be facing if the terrorists succeed in just one of today's attacks!"

Nina shrugged. The point was moot. The NTSB had made their decision. "What are you going to do?"

"What choice is there? I have to go with the tactical solution."

"That's your call, Ryan. The other administrators will back you up, but this operation is under your command."

Nina knew that Ryan Chappelle was in middle-management hell. If he made the right choice, he might get a pat on the back, or perhaps even a departmental citation—mainly he would get to keep his job. If he made the wrong choice, his career would effectively be over.

Ryan slapped his palms on the desk and stood.

"We're going. Activate all tactical teams. Red Alert nationwide. I want both Crisis Management Teams to assemble in the situation room in five minutes."

3:47:18 P.M. EDT
Prolix Security, Fifth Avenue

Prolix Security was located inside one of the older skyscrapers above Forty-second Street along Fifth Avenue. According to the building directory, the Prolix offices occupied one half of the twenty-sixth floor. Jack and Caitlin entered the building hand-in-hand and walked right up to the first-floor security desk.

A bored guard looked up at their approach. "Can I help you?"

"Hi," said Jack. "My name is Norm Bender and this is my wife, Rita. I used to work for Felix Tanner at YankeeLife Insurance up in Boston before he moved over to Prolix. The wife and I were in the town and got to talking about old Felix, so we were wondering if we could pop in and pay him a visit?"

"One moment, sir. I'll see if Mr. Tanner is in the building."

The security guard lifted the receiver of his desk phone, dialed a four-digit extension, and spoke for a minute. When the guard hung up, he was all smiles. "Mr. Tanner's secretary told me to send you right up. Twenty-sixth floor, the elevator on the right."

"Thanks," said Jack, relieved the guard had not asked him for identification.

Jack and Caitlin were the only people on the elevator. When the doors closed she let out a breath. "Glad we freshened up at that restaurant. I want to look presentable. But what do I say?"

"You don't have to say anything. Let me do the talking. When Tanner sees me he's going to know I'm not Norm Bender." Jack's features darkened. "After that, it will be Tanner doing all the talking."

When the elevator doors opened on the twenty-sixth floor, a woman greeted them. "Mr. and Mrs. Bender? I'm Fiona Brice, Mr. Tanner's personal secretary."

Fiona Brice was a tall, poised, and elegant African-American woman, about thirty. She wore a scarlet Ann Taylor suit, her long straightened ebony hair in a French twist. A string of pearls circled her throat.

"Mr. Tanner is very pleased to hear from both of you. If you will please follow me."

She led them past a deserted reception desk and down a long, carpeted hallway. They passed by several offices, all furnished, yet strangely vacant. Jack saw no personal items of any kind on the desks, the walls, the shelves. The computers were idle, the chairs neatly tucked under the desks next to empty trash cans.

"As you can see, our staff is attending a special conference today. Only a skeleton crew is on hand."

Fiona paused to allow them to catch up. "Mr. Tanner's office is down this hall and around the bend. He occupies the corner office, with a view of Fifth Avenue."

Jack displayed a flashy grin. "That's Felix. He was always a corner office kind of guy."

As they approached the bend, Jack reached into his

jacket, clutched the .45's handle. He was ready to sub-
due Felix Tanner the moment the man recognized he
was a fraud.

At the corner, Fiona Brice paused again. She faced
them, opened her mouth to speak—and Jack heard a
muffled pop, followed by a supersonic crack.

"Get down!" Jack cried, pushing Caitlin to the carpeted floor.

Fiona Brice swayed on her high heels, startled.
Then she dropped limply to the floor. Caitlin
screamed when she saw the bloody hole in the back of
the woman's head.

Somewhere a door opened, then slammed.

"Move!" hissed Jack, pushing Caitlin into one of
the deserted offices, under a desk. Then he was gone,
into the hall or another office, she didn't know.

Sick with fright, Caitlin cowered in the empty office. She heard voices speaking in a language she
didn't recognize. A shadow appeared in the doorway.
Then came the pounding chatter of an automatic
weapon, filling the room. Caitlin whimpered as bullets chewed up the desk and shattered the plaster
above her head.

1 2 3 4 5 6 7 8 9
10 11 12 13 14 15 16 17
18 19 **20** 21 22 23 24

4:07:35 P.M. EDT
Queens Boulevard

Sweating and tired, Liam realized he was approaching Queens Center Mall. The place was a typical suburban-type enclosed mall in the heart of the city's second largest borough. It catered to a young crowd, including many of Liam's mates. It also had a food court and air conditioning, both of which sounded great to Liam. He could even visit his mate Ronnie—

That's it! thought Liam. *I'll find Ronnie. Ronnie will help me out.*

Though he was three years older than Liam—old enough to have a driver's license and work at the Captain Coffee kiosk at the mall—Ronnie was in the same grade as Liam at St. Sebastian's Catholic School. Ronnie had been held back twice because the nuns thought he had "disciplinary problems."

Liam knew Ronnie rented a garage from an elderly couple on Sixty-first Street. Last summer, when Conner Sullivan got in trouble with his da for stealing, Ronnie had let Con hole up with his motorcycle until things settled down. Conner slept in that garage for a week or more.

That's it, Liam decided. *Ronnie'll give me a place to crash until this all blows over and I can find Caitlin.*

Liam shifted the silver case from one hand to the other, wiped his sweaty, callused palm on his Levi's. He suddenly noticed a New York City police car rolling alongside him. Without glancing in the cop's direction, Liam sped up a bit. He noted with mounting panic that the car sped up a bit, too. *Could they be lookin' for me now?* he wondered.

The siren blared, sending a shudder through Liam. With watery knees he watched the car race ahead, to the next intersection, bubble lights flashing. Only then did Liam notice the word "TRAFFIC" emblazoned on the side of the squad car. The policeman had pulled over a driver for attempting an illegal turn onto Queens Boulevard.

It took a few minutes for Liam's heartbeat to return to normal, and the false alarm also forced Liam to make a decision. He was going to ditch the case. But he also wanted to hide it in a place where he could find it again—in case Shamus and Griff caught up with him and demanded it be returned.

Liam looked around. He knew he couldn't hide it in a public place, and the shrubbery surrounding the mall's parking garage was too thin to conceal much.

Up ahead, Liam spied an entrance to the parking garage. He left the sidewalk, trotted down the incline and into the concrete structure. The interior of the parking garage was at least ten degrees cooler than the hot June afternoon outside, though it took a moment for his sun-blinded eyes to grow accustomed to the dimness.

Finally, Liam spotted a huge steel Dumpster parked near one of the exit ramps. Raised on thick metal wheels, it allowed just enough room for Liam to shove the case underneath the bin, and then camouflage it with some of the free community newspapers blowing around the inside of the garage. It took Liam only a minute to get down on his knees, hide the case. Then he rose, dusted himself off, and stepped out of the shadows, moving toward the ramp.

Liam heard the squeal of tires behind him and turned—

4:10:27 P.M. EDT
Queens Center Mall, Parking Garage

Shamus had hardly used the tracer unit. When he'd first arrived at the mall a few minutes before, he'd spied the silver case among the crowd on the sidewalk, picked out Liam a moment later.

The lad still had the case, which would save Shamus time and trouble. He'd avoided using the detonator in his pocket, telling himself if he could retrieve the case unharmed, he would. The memory stick with its aircraft recognition system was still worth something on the underground arms market.

Shamus had steered the Mercedes off the Boulevard

and onto the side street that led to the mall. Trapped behind traffic at the corner, he'd watched Liam walk down the ramp and enter the parking garage, case in hand.

You stupid git. You stupid, stupid git. Why couldn't you have just delivered the bloody case?

The truth was . . . Shamus wasn't at all keen on killing Liam. He was an okay lad and one of his own countrymen, but the bruises Shamus had gotten from that fuckin' CTU agent were just fresh enough to make Griff's view of things right, and his brother's way of thinking had always been Shamus's way. Like Griff said . . .

"After all we've done, all that bloody water under the bridge, there really is no going back, only forward . . . It's business now, Shea, just business . . ."

When the clog ahead finally cleared, Shamus cut across two lanes of traffic and drove down the same ramp the boy had used. At the bottom, he tossed his sunglasses onto the seat next to him, next to the tracer. With sharp eyes Shamus thoroughly scanned the dimly lit parking garage.

He'd completely circled Level One before he saw Liam emerge from behind a line of cars on the opposite end of the garage. The boy was walking toward a ramp, a silhouette against the brilliant June sunlight. Shamus swerved the Mercedes and pointed the car up the center lane.

"Remember, Shea . . . no regrets, only opportunities."

Shamus stomped on the gas, too hard. The tires squealed on the oily pavement, warning the boy. Liam turned and saw the Mercedes as it bore down on him, but the boy seemed frozen in place. Shamus could see the shock in Liam's eyes, how young he was, how scared. Shamus felt his foot letting up on the pedal, his hands on the steering wheel readying to swerve.

Then he blinked and, suddenly, Shamus didn't see Liam in front of him anymore, just a needy little red-headed, freckle-faced child, planting explosives to please his older brother.

"No going back, only forward . . ."

Gritting his teeth, he pressed down mercilessly on the gas pedal with all his weight.

A Ford Explorer abruptly backed out of a parking space, into the path of the barreling Mercedes. Shamus tried to swerve out of the way but failed. The Mercedes clipped the SUV and spun out of control.

Instead of striking Liam, the careening car bounced off a concrete pole and skidded into the Dumpster Liam had just left, smashing into it hard enough to push the metal bin against the concrete wall.

The noise of the crash was followed by an eerie silence. The door to the SUV popped open, a young Hispanic woman stumbled out, clutching her head.

Liam raced over to the Mercedes, saw Shamus inside and halted abruptly.

Dazed, blood pouring from his nose and mouth, Shamus spotted the boy. He tried to exit the car, lunge at Liam, but the door was smashed. The Mercedes sat wedged between the concrete pole and the heavy Dumpster, where Shamus still had no idea Liam had hidden the attaché case.

Liam saw a chance to flee and took it. He vanished around a thick concrete pillar before Shamus could see that he was no longer carrying the case.

"Run, boy, but you won't get far." Shamus's voice

echoed hollowly in the confined space of the Mercedes as he fumbled in his pocket for the detonator. Then he pressed the button and listened expectantly for the blast.

Underneath the Dumpster, wedged next to the battered Mercedes, the twin blocks of plastic explosives in the silver case simultaneously detonated, rocking the entire Queens Center garage. Shamus died so suddenly, he failed to feel the superheated gases charring him or register the blast he'd been so intent on hearing.

4:21:01 P.M. EDT
Prolix Security, Fifth Avenue

The machine-gun fire was deadly, deafening. Caitlin whimpered, covered her face as plaster dust powdered her head and shoulders. Countless bullets chewed through the vacant office, shattering shelves, puncturing filing cabinets, splintering tables and chairs.

A curtain of silence abruptly descended. The shooter had paused. Despite the ringing in her ears, Caitlin could hear the shell casings rattle and ping on the linoleum floor as the man moved about. She held her breath, terrified he'd hear her frightened gasps from her hiding place beneath the steel desk.

The man reloaded as he moved—she knew because she could make out the hollow sound of the spent magazine hitting the floor among the brass shells, then the firm click of a new one being shoved into place. The silence continued for one minute, two. Unable to hold her breath any longer, she inhaled as quietly as she could. Finally, she moved a bit to peek around the corner. A shadow fell over her. Eyes wide, Catilin looked up, into the face of a boy.

Dark eyes stared at her. The young man had dusty brown skin and curly black hair topped by a pure white skullcap. His dark beard was thin, almost wispy. Caitlin could see he was just a teenager, not much older than Liam. She saw him swallow uneasily as he slowly raised the black Uzi, aimed it at her head.

Helpless, Caitlin whispered a prayer, but refused to look away, choosing to face death squarely. Her determination seemed to shake the youth. He hesitated, the gun wavering.

Powerful arms reached around the teen. One hand gripped his wrist, yanking the gun barrel to the ceiling. In the other hand, Caitlin saw something long and pointed. With a sickening crunch, Jack Bauer thrust a letter opener into the young man's throat, twisting the dull blade to rip through tissue, cartilage, bone. The teen tried to cry out. His mouth gaped, but no sound emerged.

Then the boy's eyes met Caitlin's. She watched in horror, her eyes filling with tears as life, awareness faded . . . until it was extinguished. Silently, Jack lowered the dying teen to the floor, slipping the Uzi from his grasp. Then Jack reached over the twitching assassin, grabbed Caitlin's wrist hard enough to bruise it. She winced as he jerked her to her feet. Jack's hand was wet and sticky.

"Let's go," he said.

4:45:46 P.M. EDT
Office of New York Senator William Cheever
Hart Senate Office Building, Washington, D.C.

The Honorable William Cheever appeared appropriately senatorial as he read his opening remarks. Sitting behind the shiny expanse of polished desk, framed by twin American flags, he spoke to the video camera in sober, sonorous tones. The Senator addressed six video monitors, each with the face of a different airline CEO or his representative.

Dennis Spain, out of camera range, ignored Senator Cheever's opening remarks. He'd heard enough of the man's banal platitudes to last a lifetime. Fortunately, he would not have to listen to any more of them.

While the Senator droned on, Spain used the Internet to check the balance of a secret numbered account at Banque Swiss in Zurich, Switzerland. He felt the hairs on the back of his neck prickle when he found that one hundred and fifty million dollars had suddenly appeared in the account, the amount transferred from another account with a Saudi bank in Riyadh.

Spain knew another payment of the same amount would also be his—all he had to do was type a code, reroute the videoconference to another server, where a different host would take control of the conference.

He glanced at the monitors. The airline CEOs all seemed to be listening intently, phony smiles plastered across their bland, corporate faces.

Well, they won't be smiling much longer.

Spain thought about all the things a man could do with three hundred million dollars as he carefully entered the prearranged code. Abruptly Senator

Cheever's face was replaced by another. The man's features were covered by a black ski mask; thick wraparound sunglasses obscured his eyes. A black curtain was the only backdrop. Seated on a stool, the man greeted the electronic assemblage.

"You don't need to know my name, though I know all of you."

His voice was an automated buzz, altered so much it no longer resembled a human sound.

"Unless you do as I say, each of your airlines will suffer a severe financial and public relations setback when, in the next two hours, a commercial aircraft from each carrier is shot down with heavy loss of life.

"Such a tragedy can be avoided. *If* my demands are met, your planes will be safe—for now. If you choose to disobey me, ignore my conditions, then the calamity that will soon unfold will serve as a powerful object lesson to your industry, and to America."

Dennis Spain could hardly contain his amusement. The esteemed Senator from New York was sputtering like the fool that he was. On the monitors, the CEOs registered shock, outrage, disbelief. The masked man continued to speak.

"The real question is whether you will learn from this attack, or suffer more grief in the future because you continue to ignore our cause . . ."

4:48:01 P.M. EDT
Prolix Security, Fifth Avenue

Leading with the Uzi, Jack pulled a shaking Caitlin into the hallway. The lighting was dimmer now. Many of the ceiling's recessed fluorescent bulbs had been shot out. Bits of plastic and glass shards lay everywhere. In the middle of the debris another man lay dead, his neck twisted to an unnatural angle, eyes wide and staring.

"There's one more shooter. Holed up in the corner office," Jack whispered.

He gestured for her to duck into a cubicle. She obeyed, then peered around the standing wall to watch Jack move cautiously down the hallway. Just before he reached the corner office, Jack ducked into another cubicle, came out wheeling a desk chair. Renewing his grip on the Uzi, Jack kicked the chair forward. The chair bounced off the closed office door with a loud crash. A burst of automatic weapon fire came from the other side, instantly shredding the wood. The top of the door fell to the floor.

Jack flattened himself against the wall, fired the Uzi through the opening until the magazine was spent. Then he cast the empty weapon aside, drew his .45 and kicked through the remains of the door, disappearing into the corner office.

For thirty long seconds, Caitlin waited, listened to the silence. Finally, she emerged from her hiding place and crept carefully down the hall. She peered through the bullet-riddled doorway. Another assassin lay sprawled on his back, arms outstretched. A line of ragged bloody holes had been stitched up his abdomen. The corpse's eyes were askew, dead lips curled back from yellow teeth. Then she saw Jack, hunched over a man in a thick leather chair. He wore a tailored suit, now ruined by powder burns and bloodstains. He was an elderly man. Silver hair framed a substantial hole in the top of his skull. Bifocals dangled from his ear.

"Mother of God. Who is he?"

"Felix Tanner." Jack tossed the dead man's open wallet onto the desk, but Caitlin focused her attention on the ragged hole in Jack's jacket, the blood seeping through the tear in the sleeve. She saw he was wincing.

"You're hurt!" She moved to help him, but Jack pulled away, searching the desktop.

"There's got to be a clue, something in this office that will tell me who's directing this terrorist cell. Whoever it is, he's covering his tracks. Felix Tanner probably knew the man's identity or he wouldn't have been murdered."

Caitlin watched Jack as he desperately tore through the office, scattering papers across the desk, over the dead body on the floor.

Her eyes drifted to a television monitor in the corner of the office. It was on, though there was no sound. The man on the screen wore bulky black clothes and a ski mask. He stared into the camera as his lips moved.

"Jack? Come here. I think you should see this."

Jack stared at the monitor, adjusted the sound. He and Caitlin both listened as the masked man explained that he would not shoot down any commercial aircraft if each major airline transferred five hundred million dollars to a numbered Swiss account in the next sixty minutes.

"This isn't terrorism," said Jack Bauer. "It's extortion."

4:58:25 P.M. EDT
CTU Headquarters, Los Angeles

A pall had descended over the Situation Room as the Threat Clock ran down to zero hour. The room was quiet, all eyes on the wall-sized HDTV monitor. The massive screen was broken up into five sections—each displayed live surveillance video feeds from locations inside the perimeters of Logan Airport in Boston, Ronald Reagan National Airport in Washington, D.C., O'Hare in Chicago, and Los Angeles International Airport just a few miles from CTU headquarters. One section in the middle of the screen was still dark.

"I don't see New York. Why don't I see New York?" Ryan Chappelle snapped, his voice betraying nervous tension.

"The satellite is almost in position," Nina replied. A moment later, crystal clear satellite imagery focused on a section of LaGuardia Airport.

"What about JFK?" Ryan asked.

"We're blind. Georgi Timko claimed he didn't have the resources to set up camera surveillance, and the NSA would only allow us access to one satellite."

"I don't like relying on some Russian mobster—"

"Ukrainian," Doris interrupted.

"Some *Ukrainian* mobster, just because Jack Bauer trusts him."

Nina frowned. "Face reality, Ryan. Without local resources, what choice did we have?"

"We're at fifty-nine seconds," Jamey Farrell announced.

Ryan stared at the huge screen as he spoke into a headset. "All CTU tactical units report. Is everyone in position?"

"Boston, ready," said Milo Pressman from a workstation. On his screen he watched a grid map of Logan Airport, where a blinking blip represented the CTU tactical team lying in ambush for the terrorists to arrive.

"D.C., ready," said a red-eyed Cindy Carlisle, the only survivor from Cyber Unit Team Alpha.

"O'Hare, ready," said Jamey Farrell.

"New York City, ready," said Doris. "Georgi says his teams are in place at both airports."

"LAX, ready," said the voice of Tony Almeida, speaking from the ambush site at the airport.

"Ten seconds," said Nina. "Nine . . . eight . . ."

"I see activity on the service road," said Jamey. "Positive contact at O'Hare . . ."

"Six . . . five . . ."

"Contact at JFK," Doris cried. "I hear gunfire."

On the HDTV screen, the satellite captured real-time images—flashes of gunfire, moving cars, an explosion. Eerily, there was no sound.

"Three . . . two . . ."

"Gunfire at Logan. The tactical team is already moving," yelled Milo.

"Zero . . ."

1 2 3 4 5 6 7 8 9
10 11 12 13 14 15 16 17
18 19 20 **21** 22 23 24

••

THE FOLLOWING TAKES PLACE
BETWEEN THE HOURS OF
5 P.M. AND 6 P.M.
EASTERN DAYLIGHT TIME

••

5:00:06 P.M. EDT
Los Angeles International Airport

A voice crackled over Tony Almeida's headset. "We
have contact. Two black Ford Explorers, coming in
from the south. You should be able to see them in
thirty seconds."

"Jamming?" Tony asked.

"Since they entered the perimeter their cell phones
and radios have been jammed," the voice replied.
"Not that they noticed."

Tony lowered the binoculars and stepped back into
hiding.

"I see them on the service road," he said softly.

Tony stood with Captain Schneider and a member of Blackburn's tactical assault team between two empty shipping containers the size of semitrucks. Other members of the CTU tactical team were also hidden—behind a cluster of aircraft signal lights, in a storm drain under the runway, inside a small concrete utility building. All wore black overalls and thick body armor and were heavily armed. Jessica Schneider's left arm was in a sling, wrapped tightly against her chest.

Captain Schneider squinted at the tiny screen on the PDA in her hand. "They're moving into position next to runway six, right where the data from the memory stick said they'd go."

"Get ready. We move as soon as they exit the vehicles. I want snipers to take out the drivers so no one gets away," Tony commanded.

"Roger," said Blackburn from inside the concrete building.

"Ready to go," said Special Agent Rosetti from his hiding place under the runway.

"Snipers in position, aiming at targets," reported the men at the signal lights.

Tony glanced at Captain Schneider. Under the harsh Southern California sun, her face was pale and drawn. Sweat beaded her upper lip, which trembled slightly. "Ready?" he asked.

"Maybe I should sit this one out," Jessica replied. "My arm . . ."

Tony grasped the problem immediately. Captain Schneider was gun-shy. Not frightened, exactly. Just rattled. She'd been wounded. Now she held back, hesitated to get back into the saddle.

"Come on," Tony said with a smile. "I brought you all the way to the ball. The least you can do is dance."

Jessica smiled back at him, and Tony saw some of her old spirit return. "You do go on, Special Agent Almeida. Why, I think you could turn a girl's head."

Tony fixed her with his gaze. "Don't go soft on me now, Captain. I was just starting to get back that old *semper fi* spirit. Anyway, you could take down these *cholos* with one hand tied behind your back."

Captain Schneider grinned. "Well, if you put it like that . . ."

Her voice trailed off as she drew her Marine-issue .45. Tony peered out from between the two metal containers. The terrorists for hire—members of the Manolos, a Mexican street gang Dante Arete recruited out of South Central—had exited their vehicles and were setting up the missile launcher.

Tony spoke into the microphone. "Snipers take aim. Tactical Team, move on my command . . ."

5:07:53 P.M. EDT
John F. Kennedy International Airport

Georgi Timko slung the AK–47 over his shoulder and stepped over to the bullet-riddled SUV. Safety glass lay scattered on the ground, sparkling like spilled jewels in the afternoon sun. Inside the SUV's open bay, a young Afghani's dead arms dangled over the edge of the truck bed. The Ukrainian dragged the man to the ground and sat down in the door of the truck with a satisfied sigh. Other armed men circled the perimeter, checking inside the vehicles, the contents of the dead men's pockets.

In the distance, beyond the shattered missile launcher, the airport shimmered in the June heat. No one had come, no one had even heard the shooting as Georgi's men ambushed the terrorists while jets roared overhead. Now the fight was over, the threat ended.

Timko felt a presence at his side. "Vodka, Comrade Georgi?"

His eyes went wide as he faced Yuri. "Yuri, do you know this is the first time you've spoken to me since the day I hired you two years ago. And this is the first time you addressed me by name, *ever*."

Old Yuri shrugged. His grin bared rotten teeth. "What is there to talk about. The job I have stinks. I sit around all day, wait for trouble. I bring you trays of food and brew hot tea. It's boring. I should make it more boring by speaking to you?"

Yuri handed his boss a metal flask. "Drink," he grunted.

Georgi took a deep gulp. Yuri sat next to him, gazing at the dead Afghanis.

"It was good this happened," said Yuri, nodding. "I was becoming complacent in my job. I needed a challenge."

5:11:59 P.M. EDT
CEO Felix Tanner's office
Prolix Security, Fifth Avenue

Jack and Caitlin watched the monitor. The man in the ski mask was issuing complicated instructions for the transfer of the ransom money.

Jack's cell chirped. He answered, heard Ryan Chappelle's exuberant voice. "We got them, Jack. Every cell. In Washington the tactical team took most of them alive, same in Boston. In Chicago and LAX we had to take them out. And your Russian friend—"

"Ukrainian," a young woman's voice cried out on Ryan's end.

"—they shot up the remains of the New York City cell at JFK. The threat is over Jack. We did it!"

"What about LaGuardia?" Jack demanded.

"Nothing, Jack. Timko's men were waiting but the terrorists were a no-show. Nina thinks you may have taken out that cell yourself, back at Wexler Business Storage."

Jack recalled the men he'd battled. Most of them were old. Some had missing limbs, eyes. "I don't think so, Ryan."

"Maybe they got cold feet, Jack. Whatever happened, the threat is over."

"Not quite." Jack told Ryan about the video conference, the masked man's blackmailing threat, which was continuing as he spoke. At the end of the conversation with Chappelle, Jack addressed Jamey Farrell. "Listen to me, you can trace the digital video feed to its source, just tap into Prolix Security's computer system."

"I'll need access to the computers in that office," Jamey replied.

Jack moved to the desktop PC, discovered Felix Tanner had logged on to his computer before he'd been murdered. Following Jamey's instructions, Jack opened a back-door channel for her to tap into the Prolix computer system.

"I've got the signal," said Jamey after a few minutes. "But it's going to take five or ten minutes to trace it back to a server, and then to the point of origin."

"I doubt he'll talk much longer," said Jack. "But try your best."

Less than a minute later, the masked man ceased speaking in the middle of a sentence. He touched his ear, as if he were wearing a headset under the mask. Then the screen went black.

"The signal is gone, Jack," said Jamey. "I didn't have enough time to run it down."

"Damn!" Jack cursed.

Ryan came on the line. "Why did the man's speech end so abruptly?"

"I think I know why," said Jack. "He was probably in contact with some or all of the airport missile teams. He knew they'd been neutralized, killed, or captured—and that we might try to trace his signal."

"Then we're out of luck. We'll never catch the ringleader," said Ryan.

"I have one more lead," Jack replied. "The man who contacted me claiming he was Agent Ferrer was a phony, I'm certain of it. I didn't let on I figured him out. I went ahead and set up a rendezvous. I'm going there now, with Caitlin for bait. Maybe if I capture this impostor I can make him talk, force him to reveal the leader's identity and location."

"That's your plan?" Ryan said, incredulous.

"I'm playing this by ear," Jack confessed. "I have no other choice."

Bauer checked his watch. "I wanted the rendezvous to happen somewhere nice and public, where the impostor would have a hard time making a move against me and escaping. The busiest place in New York City is Grand Central Station at rush hour, so that's where I'm going . . ."

5:29:52 P.M. EDT
Astoria, Queens

Griffin Lynch had driven from LaGuardia's freight terminal directly to his final destination. Taking the last exit on Grand Central Parkway, the unmarked van bounced along a multi-laned avenue of battered concrete. Directly ahead was the slowly rising entrance ramp to the Triboro Bridge. But Griff wasn't heading for that elevated toll plaza. Bearing right, he followed a branching road that angled down, all the way to the river's edge.

Before reaching the water, Griff came to Astoria Park, a sixty-five-acre stretch of greenery in the borough of Queens that bordered the East River. Griff turned right and followed a narrow street along the park. On his right was an unending line of modest row houses, on his left a wide lawn covered with trees and peppered with benches.

Near the middle of the park, Griff drove past a sprawling brick structure that served as the bath house for Astoria Pool, an Olympic-sized facility built by the WPA and the city's public works commission during the depths of the Great Depression. The pool attracted large crowds in the summer, but it wouldn't be opening for the season until the end of June. A good bit of luck, because crowds would not have been productive. At the moment, the park hosted no more than a handful of dog walkers, pick-up soccer players, and teenagers.

The grass sloped downward, toward the boulder-strewn shore. Across the river, the Manhattan skyline glimmered in the cloudless afternoon. Near the center of the park, the tall oak, elm, and beech trees—some of them more than a century old—were dwarfed by a mammoth structure built of beige granite blocks. Rising at the river's edge, the three-hundred-foot tower with its crowning parapets resembling a medieval fortress, served as the base for a high, arched railroad bridge that spanned the East River between Queens and the Bronx.

Constructed in 1916, Hell Gate Bridge took its name from the unusually turbulent area of water beneath the span—and the many men who'd plunged to their deaths in those waters while trying to erect it.

Griff continued to drive along the narrow road until he came to a break in the row houses. A chain-link fence stood unlocked. Inside, next to a massive supporting column for the Hell Gate Bridge above, a kelly-green New York City Parks Department truck was parked. Griff pulled his unmarked van next to the green truck and cut his engine.

Taj waited on the flatbed of the battered Parks Department vehicle, along with two other members of his cell. All wore Parks Department overalls, all carried valid IDs. More than two hundred feet above their heads, on the bridge's span of faded red steel, others waited beside a makeshift block and tackle. When Griff arrived, they lowered a rope. The light, saltwater breeze from the river knocked the rope back and forth against the massive support column until it reached the vehicles on the ground.

Griff hopped out of his van, opened the rear doors.

Taj climbed down to join him, and they both dragged the heavy box out of the cargo bay.

"One launcher with memory stick. Three missiles. You can't miss," said Griff.

Taj grabbed the lowered rope and secured the box to a steel hook, then stepped away. High above, the men hauled the rope, dragging the Long Tooth missile launcher to the top of the bridge.

After a long search, Griff had selected this location himself. Hell Gate lay directly in the flight path to La-Guardia Airport. The bridge was tall enough to afford Taj a clear shot, yet remote and inaccessible enough for them to act without detection. There was no pedestrian, car, or truck traffic on the railroad bridge, and any passing train would see only men in Parks Department uniforms. No one would suspect Griff or Taj or any of his men of anything sinister. No one would even fathom what FBI agent Frank Hensley had coordinated to unleash on America from the top of Hell Gate.

5:55:09 P.M. EDT
Boeing 727, CDC charter flight
35,000 feet over Trenton, New Jersey

Captain Stoddard activated the auto pilot, keyed the cockpit radio.

"This is Charter 939 calling LaGuardia tower, come in."

A crackling voice filled the cabin. "LaGuardia air traffic control responding. We read you nine-three-niner."

"We're on course and on schedule," Captain Stoddard replied. "Estimated time of arrival over New York City airspace, eight-three-eight P.M., Eastern Daylight Time. Over . . ."

```
 1  2  3  4  5  6  7  8  9
10 11 12 13 14 15 16 17
18 19 20 21 22 23 24
```

· ·

**THE FOLLOWING TAKES PLACE
BETWEEN THE HOURS OF
6 P.M. AND 7 P.M.
EASTERN DAYLIGHT TIME**

· ·

6:07:12 P.M. EDT
Grand Central Station, Main Concourse

Jack Bauer and Caitlin O'Connor stood on the mezzanine inside Grand Central Station. Though Grand Central serviced only commuter trains these days, the marble-lined interior of the imposing Beaux Arts structure evoked the romance of railroad travel at the dawn of the twentieth century. Below the raised balcony where they stood, the expanse of the main concourse spread out before them. High above their heads a vaulted ceiling was adorned with murals depicting the twelve signs of the Zodiac.

As Jack predicted, the terminus was packed with commuters, the human tide swirling around the massive clock that topped the information stand in the center of the main concourse, and the sculptural groupings executed by artist Jules Coutan back in 1913 when the building was constructed. But Jack hardly noticed the impressive interior space. He was studying faces in the crowd.

"I'm supposed to meet the man calling himself Agent Ferrer under the big clock at six P.M. sharp," Jack said, peering into the mob.

Caitlin looked, too, though she didn't know what to search for. The phony CTU agent could be any one of the thousands of businessmen who thronged Grand Central at rush hour. How was she to know who the impostor was? More importantly, how was Jack to know? Caitlin sighed, glanced at Jack's digital watch now on her own wrist.

"If you're to meet him at six, then you're late," she said.

"That's the point. I'm going to wait a few more minutes, scope out a couple of likely suspects from the people lingering near the clock. Then I'll call Agent Ferrer on my cell, explain how I'm running late. If one of the people we're watching answers his phone, I'll know he's the impostor."

Jack's cell chirped in his hand, interrupting them.

"Is it—?"

"It's CTU," Jack told her. He answered, listened to Nina Myers for a moment. Finally he spoke. "I'll tell her," Jack said, ending the conversation.

"Tell me what?" Caitlin demanded.

"Back at CTU, Jamey Farrell is monitoring all New York City police frequencies and emergency channels. A few moments ago she intercepted a Police Department accident report."

Jack paused. Caitlin's knees turned to water. "Tell me, Jack," she said.

"Shamus Lynch is dead. He was killed by an explosion inside a parking garage in Queens. At the scene of the accident, your brother, Liam, turned himself in. The police have him now. They're holding him in protective custody."

Caitlin covered her mouth, shut her green eyes to stop the flow of tears that flooded them. "Ohgod-thankgod," she cried, throwing her arms around Jack's neck.

He held her for a moment, then pulled away to look into her face.

"Listen to me very carefully. This whole thing is over for you now. Shamus is dead, Griffin is too busy running from CTU to chase after you. You don't have to do this anymore. You can go to a policeman right now, any policeman, and ask him to put you in protective custody, too. In a few hours this will blow over. In the meantime, you'll be safe . . ."

Caitlin pushed her hair back and shook her head. "No, Jack. I'm going to see this through . . . Look, me and my brother were a party to this bloody mess out of the gate. We didn't mean to be, but now that I know we are, I want to help clean it up . . . If there are any charges against me and my brother, then maybe at the end of the day my helping you will help a judge see his way clear to goin' easy on us. You understand?"

Jack nodded and they went back to watching the crowd. It was Caitlin who spotted the most likely candidate.

"How about that one, Jack?" she said, pointing.

Bauer scoped the man through miniature tourist binoculars he'd bought at a newstand. The man was in his mid-thirties, physically fit, broad-shouldered, with either a dark complexion or a serious tan topped by golden, sun-bleached hair.

"He's the right age, and time is running out," said Jack. "Let's give it a try."

But just as Jack made the call, the blond man stepped behind the clock and out of sight. Meanwhile a voice answered on the second ring.

"Agent Ferrer here."

"Jack Bauer. Look, I'm running a little late. Could you stay on the cell phone until I reach you. I'm with Caitlin, just outside Grand Central now. We're on Forty-second Street . . ."

While Jack talked, Caitlin waited for the blond man to reappear. When he finally showed, he clutched a cell phone to his ear. She slapped Jack's arm; he nodded. Jack had seen it, too. While Agent Ferrer continued to speak, Jack hit the mute button so the caller could not hear them.

"Stay here," Jack whispered. "I'm going to keep him on the line while I sneak up behind him, take him prisoner . . ."

She watched as Jack hurried down the massive marble stairs to the main concourse. Within a few seconds, he'd vanished in the dense, fast-moving crowd.

At the bottom of the stairs, Jack opened a hidden compartment on the cell phone case, extracted a tiny, single-wire headset. He slipped the wire over his head, the button-sized phones into his ear canal, the dot microphone under his chin without missing a beat in the conversation. Then he dropped the phone into his jacket, closed his right hand around the handle of his Mark 23.

With the headset, Jack was able to shut out the ambient noise from the people around him—to concentrate on "Agent Ferrer's" words and the noises around *him*.

Immediately Jack heard the hollow sounds of the terminal as background to Ferrer's voice, and he knew the impostor really was somewhere inside the terminus.

While moving toward the central clock, Jack decided to see how much the impostor really knew.

"Have you heard how the airport raids have gone?" asked Jack. "Did they stop the attacks in D.C., LA, Chicago . . . here in New York?"

Ferrer was silent for a moment, then he dodged the question.

"I'm not sure we should be discussing this on an unsecured line."

"Perhaps you're right."

"How close are you, Special Agent Bauer?"

Jack could hear impatience—and perhaps suspicion—in the man's tone. Meanwhile Jack slipped between knots of people until he saw the blond man's back. The impostor was only a few yards away now, still talking on his cell. In his Brooks Brothers suit, an attaché case in his hand, the impostor looked more like a stockbroker than an assassin, but Jack knew looks could be deceptive.

"I'm almost there," said Jack, stepping behind the man and slipping his weapon out of its holster. With the gun still behind his jacket, he shoved the barrel of the .45 into the blond man's ribs. "In fact, I'm right behind you," said Jack.

The blond man lowered the cell, whirled to face Jack. "Hey, dude," he cried. "At least say excuse me when you bump into—"

The man saw the gun in Jack's hands, only partially hidden in the folds of the jacket. He backed away.

"Good try, Bauer," the voice said in his ear. "But apparently you were stalking the wrong man."

"Where are you?"

"Look up. Check on your friend."

On the mezzanine Jack saw Caitlin, face pale. Beside her, a tall man with dark skin and bleached blond hair clutched her arm. Despite his Western clothes, Jack recognized him from the files on his PDA.

"Omar Bayat," Jack whispered.

"You recognize me," Bayat replied. "I should be flattered."

"Let her go. Take *me* hostage, instead," Jack insisted.

"I'm not looking for a hostage, Mr. Bauer. I just want to get out of here without you following me."

"That's fine. What do you want me to do?"

"There's a mailbox about fifty feet away. Do you see it?" Bayat asked.

"I see it."

"I want you to walk over to that box and drop your cell phone and weapon into it."

"If I do that, what do I get in return?"

"I'll let this woman go, after I'm out of the station. Otherwise I'll kill her on the spot with my bare hands, and no one in the crowd will be the wiser."

Jack hesitated.

"You know I can do it, Bauer. Move to the mailbox now or she dies."

"I'm going," said Jack. He was ten feet from the mailbox when the blond man Jack had accosted by mistake returned—with two New York City policemen in tow.

"He's the one!" The blond man pointed out Jack. "He pulled a gun on me!"

Members of the crowd around Jack heard the blond man's statement and moved to get out of the way. Jack used the crowd to shield himself as he turned and ran in the opposite direction. As he raced through the mob of commuters, Jack heard Omar Bayat laughing over his headset.

"Wait, Bayat. Let her go," Jack cried. "She can't hurt you now and neither can I."

"She goes with me, Bauer," Bayat replied. "A man named Griffin Lynch is anxious to meet her."

Jack heard the hiss of dead air. "Son of a bitch!"

"Halt!" a voice barked. Jack heard screams and glanced over his shoulder. The policemen were still chasing him. One of them had his weapon out. Luckily, the man couldn't get a clear shot because so many civilians were in the way. Jack continued to weave in and out of the crowd until he burst onto Forty-second Street.

Traffic was heavy, but moving. Along Forty-second Street, there were cars and trucks as far as the eye could see. Jack looked around, looking for a way out. At any moment, the policemen were going to emerge on the street, where they might just get a shot at him.

Then, across the street, Jack spied a burly man sitting astride an idling Harley-Davidson motorcycle, an American flag waving on a short staff above the rear wheel. The bike was all chrome and rumbling engine.

Perfect, thought Jack. Despite the traffic, he ran into the street, darting between moving cars. A taxicab driver refused to brake for him, so he rolled across the yellow hood. Landing on his feet beside the biker, Jack caught the man's long ponytail, yanked him off the motorcycle.

Before the man could stumble to his feet, Jack gunned the engine and sped away, racing down the sidewalk. Pedestrians scattered as he shot down the pavement for more than a block. Finally, confronted by a knot of tourists gathering under the awning of a hotel, Jack swerved back onto the street.

Using his headset, Jack made contact with CTU. Chappelle answered the call. "Let me put you on speakerphone, Jack."

"The man who assumed Agent Ferrer's identity is really Omar Bayat, Taj Ali Kahlil's associate and the leading exporter of terrorism for the Taliban government in Afghanistan."

"How do you know, Jack?" Ryan asked. "Did you capture him? Neutralize him?"

"No," Jack replied. "Bayat managed to get past me and grab Caitlin. He's holding her now. Is the tracer inside my watch working?"

"Perfectly," said Jamey Farrell. "I'm tracking Caitlin's every move. Good thing you gave her your watch in case anything went wrong."

"Where is she right now?" Jack asked.

"In a van, moving uptown on Third Avenue. The van's at Fifty-seventh Street, moving into the right lane. I think it's probably going to cross the Fifty-ninth Street Bridge, into Queens . . ."

"We'd better not lose track of Caitlin," said Jack. "Right now, she's our only connection to the terrorists. Without her we don't know where they're hiding or what they're up to."

••

**THE FOLLOWING TAKES PLACE
BETWEEN THE HOURS OF
7 P.M. AND 8 P.M.
EASTERN DAYLIGHT TIME**

••

7:19:43 P.M. EDT
CTU Headquarters, Los Angeles

The speakerphone at Ryan Chappelle's workstation buzzed, interrupting him. Tired and cranky, Ryan punched the button. "Yes?"

"It's Nina. I just spoke with Roger Tyson, Deputy Director of the National Transportation Safety Board."

Ryan snickered. "Don't tell me the airport raids hit the news? Does he want to apologize for doubting our intelligence?"

"News of the raids has been suppressed so far, but Deputy Director Tyson did hear about them through bureaucratic channels. He called us with a warning."

Chappelle sat up. "A what?"

"This afternoon a chartered CDC flight took off from Atlanta. It's carrying bio-hazardous materials—samples of the deadly 1918 influenza strain—"

"Why the hell weren't we told? CTU should have received the same security report as the other agencies!"

"The flight was mentioned in the daily DSA security alert, but no one here at CTU made the connection. We should have received a second alert when the aircraft left the ground, but we were shut out."

Ryan frowned. "What do you mean shut out?"

"It was Hensley," Nina replied. "According to Tyson, the alert was issued directly to the FBI. Apparently Hensley convinced his superiors to keep CTU out of the loop on alerts until Jack Bauer is apprehended and interrogated. He's convinced them that until that happens, the entire unit is compromised."

"I can't believe this!"

"Ryan, listen. It's worse than we thought. The CDC plane is a Boeing 727, the same type of aircraft Dante Arete was targeting at LAX. Its destination is LaGuardia Airport in Queens. It's due to land at approximately 8:45 P.M., Eastern Daylight—"

"Son of a bitch," Ryan exploded. "That has to be the final target. No wonder nothing happened at five P.M.! The CDC plane isn't landing until quarter to nine. They want to shoot down that aircraft, spread influenza virus over the entire city—and they just might be able to pull it off."

"We have to warn Jack—"

"First the NTSB has to order that aircraft to land at the next airport."

"It's too late for that, Ryan. The NTSB already tried without success."

"But they certainly have the authority to order it down."

"It's not a question of authority. Due to security concerns, the CDC aircraft is maintaining strict radio silence. The pilot reports in once every hour, and we just missed the last window. The next time they establish radio contact, the plane will be over New York City."

7:23:13 P.M. EDT
Fifty-ninth Street, Manhattan

"Where are they now?" Jack raced toward the Queensboro Bridge ramp, an ancient structure of dirty steel girders rising up from Second Avenue and flanked by multimillion-dollar apartment buildings overlooking the East River.

Jack had kept his cell phone connection to CTU, Los Angeles, open while Jamey Farrell followed Caitlin's blip on a grid map of Queens. The thirty-three-second coast-to-coast delay had caused a few tense moments, but so far they were tracking the kidnapped woman with accuracy.

"The vehicle Caitlin is in is still moving along Thirty-first Street in Queens," said Jamey. "It looks like they're heading for the Triboro Bridge, which means they could be going to Harlem, or even the South Bronx."

The Queens-bound traffic on the bridge's lower level was moving in a start-stop fashion. New York was a late city—late to work in the morning, later leaving in the evening—so rush-hour traffic had not yet lightened. Jack's years of youthful dirt bike racing served him well as he darted between cars and trucks with ease.

As Jack twisted the throttle to slalom around a lumbering tow truck, he heard Nina Myers's voice in his ears. "Jack, we've received some disturbing intelligence . . ."

She told him about the CDC aircraft and its deadly cargo, how the aircraft would be entering New York airspace in less than seventy-five minutes.

"That's their target." Jack was certain. It all added up.

"That's our feeling here, too," said Nina. "But Ryan is concerned that you're on a wild goose chase. That Omar Bayat isn't heading for Taj's location at all."

"No, that can't be right. Taj and Bayat are a team. They've worked together since the Ali Kahlil clan was wiped out in Afghanistan. After downing the Belgian airliner over North Africa two years ago, they escaped across the border to Libya together. I'm betting that's what they plan to do here, too."

For a moment there was silence on both sides of the phone connection. Then Jack spoke. "Let's assume Omar Bayat is leading us to Taj and another terrorist cell. Where would they launch an attack from? They need someplace close to the airport, above the city skyline, yet remote—a launch from a rooftop or a building would be seen."

"How about the Triboro Bridge?" said Nina. "It's the tallest structure in the area."

"It's high enough, but too public. Thousands of cars pass over that bridge every hour. The terrorists could be spotted, reported by anyone with a cell phone—"

"Jack!" It was Milo Pressman's voice. "About a quarter of a mile upriver from the Triboro there's railroad bridge called the Hell Gate. The bridge goes right over Astoria Park, and across the East River to Randalls Island, then on to the South Bronx."

"He's right," said Nina. "Hell Gate is actually a little closer to LaGuardia than the Triboro, though both bridges are right under the flight path to the airport."

"Jamey, what's happening to Caitlin now?" Jack asked.

"The vehicle is turning onto the Triboro Bridge . . . No. Wait. It's on Hoyt Avenue, a road that runs parallel to the Triboro, maybe under it . . ."

Over the snarl of the Harley's engine, Jack heard the analyst exclaim something unintelligible.

"Jamey? What is it?"

"Hoyt Avenue, Jack. It leads right to the shore of the East River. To Astoria Park—"

Three thousand miles away, Jack Bauer knew where he was headed. "Hell Gate Bridge . . ."

7:36:09 P.M. EDT
Astoria Park, Queens

On a quiet residential street bordering Astoria Park, Omar Bayat stopped the van in front of a locked gate of an eight-foot chain-link fence. The sun was a hot orange ball shining between the tall oak and elm trees, but the van was shaded by the steel span of a railroad bridge a hundred feet over its roof.

The Afghani looked over his shoulder at the woman, bound and gagged on the floor of the cargo bay. "I will be right back."

Bayat exited the vehicle, unbolted the padlock, and drove through the gate. He backed the van into a small wooden garage that butted up against one of the bridge's ivy-covered, concrete support columns. It was cool and shady under the span, with abundant greenery bordering the fenced-in area.

Hidden from view inside the garage and behind the concrete arch, Bayat changed into green New York City Parks Department overalls. Then he opened the back door and dragged Caitlin out by her red hair. She squealed, but the sound was muffled by the gag over her mouth.

Bayat cuffed her. "Shut up or I will slit your throat."

Caitlin whimpered, rocked unsteadily on her feet while Bayat untied her wrists. He left the gag in place. Then the Afghani pushed her to the back of the garage, where a hole had been cut in the ceiling. A twelve-foot ladder poked through that hole and up the side of the concrete support column.

"Climb," barked Bayat.

Caitlin looked up. On top of the portable ladder, rungs had been embedded in the concrete to form a permanent ladder that ran all the way to the top of the bridge. Caitlin's eyes went wide and she shook her head wildly, trying to tell Omar Bayat she was too afraid. He struck her again, so hard it drove Caitlin to her knees. He reached down and yanked her to her feet by her hair.

"Climb or die," he hissed, his hot breath on her cheek. Hands shaking, limbs weak, Caitlin reluctantly reached for the first rung.

"Where is Caitlin now?" Jack yelled over the roar of the cycle.

"She's still on Nineteenth Street, between Twenty-first and Twenty-second Drives," said Jamey. "Maybe it's a safe house, or a staging area."

Jack gunned the engine and ran a yellow light. "How far away?"

"Maybe twenty minutes. Less if traffic is light," Jamey replied.

Jack cursed. "Too far."

"Jack, Caitlin is moving again. Across the park. She's following the span of the bridge, moving under it."

Jack frowned, increased speed. "Caitlin isn't under the bridge, Jamie. I'm betting she's *on* it."

Caitlin thought the climb up the ladder was difficult until she reached the top of the span. High above the park, the gentle breeze became a gusting wind that tangled her long red-gold hair and tore at her ripped and dirty skirt. Caitlin saw four sets of railroad tracks, silver trails that led over the water and across Randalls Island. A narrow steel mesh catwalk ran along the edge of the span, paralleling the tracks.

"That way," Omar Bayat said, pointing toward the catwalk.

Behind the gag, Caitlin whimpered and hesitated. She wasn't overly afraid of heights, but the steel mesh in front of her looked like nothing more than a gossamer web, too fragile to hold her weight. Bayat pushed her and she stumbled onto the steel grating, yelping behind the gag. She grabbed the handrail, steadying herself.

Far below, she could see children playing in the green grass of Astoria Park. They looked so tiny to her, like scurrying mice . . . and then it struck her. *That's all they are to this man,* she realized. *That's all I am.* Closing her eyes, Caitlin swallowed, then squared her shoulders and continued on.

Movement became easier with time, as she became accustomed to the height, and the uneven feel of the catwalk's grating. Under other circumstances, Caitlin would have enjoyed the view. The setting sun dropped lower over the horizon, illuminating the city with a golden glow.

Still over the park, they passed through a beige stone tower with a high stone roof. Over her head, parapets overlooked the East River and Manhattan beyond. When she emerged from the tower a few minutes later, Caitlin was struck once again by the view.

A quarter mile or so south, the arch of the Triboro Bridge also spanned the river, its roadway clogged with traffic. Beyond the long highway bridge, the skyline of the Upper East Side peeked over the tip of Roosevelt Island. Caitlin could see the Empire State Building, the spire of the Chrysler Building, the slanted roof of the Citicorp Center, and in the distance, the gleaming twin towers of Lower Manhattan's World Trade Center.

By now, Caitlin had passed over the entire length of the park. Far beneath her, a narrow road paralleled the Queens bank of the East River. Rap and hip-hop music wafted up from hot rods. An ice cream truck's jingle and the snarl of a passing motorcycle lifted on the breeze to Caitlin's ears. It seemed strange to her how normal, everyday life was simply continuing . . . how people could be so oblivious to the terrible thing about to happen just over their heads.

Suddenly, the faded red steel began to vibrate under her feet. Omar Bayat pushed her into a recessed area, then stood between her and the tracks. A moment later, an Amtrak train roared past them, shaking the bridge so hard, Caitlin thought she would be shaken off, plunging to her death far below.

Finally the train passed and they resumed their hike, leaving the boulder-strewn shore behind them. Now, beneath her feet, Caitlin could see only the gray-green waters of the East River, swirling and roiling with dangerous riptides and whirlpools. Here, nearly three hundred feet above the water, the wind increased until it whistled through the high-tension electrical wires strung over the bridge, its powerful gusts threatening to sweep her slender form over the edge.

Ahead, in the glare of the setting sun, Caitlin spied activity. She counted three men in green overalls, circling a strange device mounted on a tripod. The object looked like a telescope with two optical cylinders instead of one.

Omar Bayat put a boot to her rump, pushing her forward. As Caitlin approached the men, someone stepped out of the shadows beside her.

"Take off the gag," growled Griffin Lynch. "She can scream her bloody head off and nobody will hear her up here."

Omar Bayat ripped the gag away, Caitlin rubbed her bruised lips. "What do you want with me, you bleedin' sod? Why don't you just kill me and be done with it?"

Griff grabbed Caitlin's chin, gripped it in his scarred but still bruising hand. "Never fear, lass. You'll die soon enough. When it's good and dark out here, I'm gonna toss you off this bridge. With luck your corpse won't wash ashore for a week, and by then Shamus and me will be long gone, while you join your dead brother in hell."

Caitlin's jaw dropped.

"That's right, girl. I sent Shamus to kill your brother and he agreed to do it. Serves your boy right for messing up the delivery to Taj. His fuck up forced me out to this bloody bridge when me and Shamus should have been halfway to the Islands by now. At least it's good to know Liam's probably been blasted into dust already."

For a moment, Caitlin's heart stopped. But then she realized that Griff's words were all wrong. *Shamus* was the one who'd died in the explosion. Her own Liam had escaped and turned himself in. He was in police protective custody now. She was about to tell Griff as much, but quickly choked back the words. It was better if Griff thought her brother was already dead. Then Liam could go on living his life, safe and sound and hopefully happy . . . even without his big sister to kick his ass and trim his bangs. *Yes*, Caitlin thought, *Liam is alive. He's all right. He's protected*. That realization alone gave her the strength she needed to face her own death.

Her eyes flashed defiantly. She pushed Griff's hand away from her face. "Ya talk big, Griffin Lynch. But like all the Provos, you're good for pushing violence and nothing more."

A brief, disgusted smile flashed across Griff's stone cold expression. "I can't wait to kill you, girl. But at least your death will be fast and clean—more than I can say for the rest of the folks in this city."

Caitlin choked back her fears. Over Griff's shoulder, the blazing rays of the setting sun were now touching every particle in the air, spreading their red-orange tinge until the entire horizon appeared as if someone had set it on fire. That's when she realized what Griff and his associates had been erecting—a missile launcher, its ominous silhouette pointed at the sky.

1 2 3 4 5 6 7 8 9
10 11 12 13 14 15 16 17
18 19 20 21 22 23 **24**

....

**THE FOLLOWING TAKES PLACE
BETWEEN THE HOURS OF
8 P.M. AND 9 P.M.
EASTERN DAYLIGHT TIME**

....

8:05:53 P.M. EDT
Hell Gate Bridge

Thanks to the GPS beacon in the watch Caitlin wore, Jack knew where to go. He found the fenced-off area on Nineteenth Street. He found the garage, the van, and the ladder.

"Where is she now?" Jack said into his headset.

"In the middle of the bridge, Jack, facing south. The blip hasn't moved for several minutes." Jamey's voice was tense. Jack knew what she was thinking— were they going to throw Caitlin off the bridge?

"I'm going up right now," said Jack. "I'm taking the earphones out but I'm leaving this channel open. You'll be able to hear me, but I won't be able to hear you."

"Is that a good idea, Jack?" Ryan asked.

Nina answered for him. "Jack will need all his senses on that bridge."

Ryan frowned. "Well, good luck, Bauer."

Jack did not reply.

Crouching low, he reached under the van, rubbed road dirt and oil on his hands, then on his face. It wasn't exactly camouflage but it would help him fade into the darkness on the bridge—he hoped.

Jack drew the Mark 23 USP, checked the magazine, his extra ammunition. Then he tucked the weapon in the holster under his arm, yanked the earphones out and began to climb.

It took him more than five minutes of climbing to get to the top. By the time he reached the span it was twilight; the sun had dropped below the horizon. The park beneath him was shrouded in purple shadows, broken by tiny islands of light under glowing lampposts.

Without a watch, Jack used his PDA to check the time. He had less than thirty minutes to find the terrorists and stop the missile from launching. He took off at a run on the narrow catwalk.

Under normal circumstances, Jack would be charging into this situation with aerial intelligence and support in place, a backup team there for him at every turn. He would be wearing sound-absorbing chukkas and Kevlar body armor, a helmet with night vision goggles. He'd have tactical support, too, on both sides of the bridge.

But for this, Jack was alone. Despite his throbbing muscles, aching arm wound, his hunger, thirst, and near-exhaustion, he pressed on. Jack knew if he wavered now, Caitlin would die and the terrorists would unleash a terrible pandemic, the likes of which America had not experienced in nearly a century.

8:23:25 P.M. EDT
Switching booth, Hell Gate Bridge

Caitlin had been shoved next to a metal shed set flush against the support beam on the very edge of the span. She had very little room on the ledge. Below, the river's black water spun in a dozen violent whirpools, each one appearing to yawn open and closed, like living monsters demanding to be fed.

Omar Bayat had used duct tape to bind her hands behind her back, but Caitlin had already managed to free them. Now she bided her time, clinging to a slim chance that Griff would change his mind about throwing her over—or she'd find a way to escape.

Omar Bayat returned to loom over her with an Uzi in hand. Nearby, the men manning the missile launcher had activated something. The Afghanis appeared to be fixated on a tiny green screen on a black box attached to the side of the launch tubes.

Griff stood on top of the metal shed, scanning the twilight sky with binoculars. Occasionally he would shift his search, peering down the tracks toward Astoria Park. His features were taut, worried. Caitlin suspected he was waiting for his brother, Shamus. She knew he would never arrive.

Inside the shed, Taj sat beside Frank Hensley on a wooden box. Caitlin knew the stranger was the FBI agent Jack had spoken about because Taj had addressed the man by name. It was Hensley who issued instructions to the Afghanis, Taj who translated them into some foreign tongue she was not familiar with.

Caitlin continued to watch these men come and go, heard every word they spoke. Some of what they said surprised her.

"Still no signal from the 727," Taj reported.

"It's too soon. If anything, the CDC airplane will be late." As he spoke, Frank Hensley glanced at his Rolex. "I have a call to make. Let them know how the mission is progressing."

Taj smiled, revealing yellow teeth. "This operation has gone well. Baghdad will be satisfied."

Hensley's features darkened. "Baghdad will be satisfied when America suffers the way Iraq has suffered." He tapped out a number on a bulky satellite phone. A moment later he was speaking another foreign language Caitlin had never heard before.

8:31:13 P.M. EDT
Hell Gate Bridge

Knowing Caitlin was somewhere on the south side of the bridge, Jack crossed over four sets of train tracks to the northern edge, hoping to move close enough to surprise the terrorists before he was discovered. On the north catwalk, Jack had an upriver view dominated by a sprawling Department of Environmental Protection facility on Randalls Island.

The twilight sky was bright purple, twinkling lights from the Triboro Bridge a quarter mile away and the Manhattan skyline beyond the only illumination. There were no lights on Hell Gate and the railroad bridge was cast in deep shadow. Through the steel mesh under his feet, Jack saw black rippling water far below.

As he approached the center of the span, Jack became more wary. He drew the .45, released the safety as he moved cautiously along the rickety catwalk, aware of every sound. Suddenly Jack spied a silhouette framed against the purple sky—a man was standing on the roof of a shed, watching the sky through binoculars. Jack was forced to duck behind the railroad tracks, sprawl flat on his belly across the catwalk.

Jack held his breath, listened. A barge chugged under the bridge, Jack stared down at its decks and the rippling, white-topped wake. Over the howl of the wind through the wires, the rush of the tide far below, Jack heard voices. Cautiously, he lifted his head over the tracks. The man on the shed still watched the horizon, his back turned. A few yards away, Jack saw three other men clustered around a Long Tooth missile launcher mounted on a tripod. It was too dark to make out their features, but Jack was certain Taj was one of them. Jack hoped the renegade FBI agent was among them, too. Jack had a score to settle with Frank Hensley.

Jack weighed his options, deciding he would have to crawl along the catwalk for the last fifty yards if he wanted to take his enemies by surprise. If he stood or even crouched, Jack would be exposed—the man with the binoculars or the men at the tripod would spot him, cut him down before he got close.

Before he could move, Jack felt the catwalk vibrate under him, heard the distant rumble of a train crossing the long span. He glanced over his shoulders to see a locomotive was rolling over the park, barreling toward him.

Jack was pleased. He could use the train as a shield to mask his progress, cover the noise of his feet on the mesh grating. He could run alongside the train until he reached a point opposite the terrorists—*if* he moved fast enough.

Rising to a sprinter's crouch, Jack waited until the engine reached him. The bridge shook like a Los Angeles earthquake under his feet; the noise became a shrill, pounding roar that battered his ears. Finally the train reached him, and Jack took off in a run.

Feet pounding, Jack thundered down the catwalk, the sound of his footsteps mingling with the thunder of the rolling Amtrak cars. Quickly—too quickly— the final car rolled by him and down the tracks. Jack dropped flat on the catwalk as the roar receded, poked his head up a moment later. The man with the binoculars was directly across from him, separated only by the train tracks.

He shifted the weapon in his grip, wiped the sweat from his palm. Still on his belly, Jack crawled to the side of the tracks, over the first rail—still hot from the friction of the train's passing. Jack crawled quickly across the wooden ties, then over the second rail. He slipped into a shallow depression between the tracks, then moved to the next set of rails.

Jack heard excited voices. The men at the tripod jumped to their feet, and Jack spied Taj as he raced from the shed to the Long Tooth missile launcher. With the others, Taj stared at the green glowing screen affixed to the launcher. From his vantage point, Jack could see a single blip on the screen.

The CDC aircraft had arrived. Time had run out.

Caitlin watched as Taj bolted from the shed, ran to the missile launcher. Omar Bayat followed his leader to join the others. The Afghanis clustered around the tripod, talking excitedly.

Caitlin looked up to find Griff still perched on the roof of the shed. But he was not watching the others. Griff squinted into the darkness, staring across the tracks.

Hensley emerged from the shed a moment later. He saw Griff peering into the darkness. "What's the matter?"

Griff frowned. "I saw movement on the tracks. Someone is out there."

"Maybe it's your brother?"

Griff shook his head, still staring at the tracks. "He wouldn't be sneaking up on us."

Hensley followed Griff's gaze. "I don't see anything—"

A shot rang out. An Afghani next to Taj clutched his throat and tumbled over the edge of the bridge. The others scattered, diving for cover. Another shot was followed by a howl. A third shot silenced the wounded man.

"He's over there, across the tracks!" Griff cried, pointing. He was crouching now, but remained on the roof of the shed. Hensley reached into his jacket, drew his FBI-issue handgun.

"It's Jack Bauer. I'm sure of it. I'm going to flank him, finish him off."

"Go," said Griff, dragging an Uzi from his belt. "I'll keep the bastard pinned until you clip him."

Still crouching, Griff aimed the Uzi into the darkness and squeezed off a burst. Sparks erupted as the bullets bounced off the steel rails.

"It's Bauer!" Hensley cried from somewhere out of sight. "He's pinned between the tracks. Pour it on!"

Griff fired away, the noise deafening. Caitlin thought of Jack out there on the tracks, pinned down and waiting to be ambushed, and she did not hesitate.

With a shrill cry she jumped to her feet and threw herself against Griffin Lynch. She slammed against his legs with her full weight. Surprised by her sudden move, Lynch dropped the Uzi as he reached for a steel cable—and missed.

With an expression of shocked surprise, he tumbled over the edge of the bridge.

Her own momentum carried Caitlin across the shed's roof. Now she dangled precariously over the black water. Gunfire rattled around her as Caitlin tried desperately to crawl to safety. Someone jumped onto the roof, grabbed her. Caitlin rolled onto her back, looked up—into the murderous eyes of Omar Bayat. The man pointed his Uzi at her breast—then his head exploded, showering Caitlin with hot blood, brains, and bone shrapnel. The headless corpse spilled over the edge to vanish in the yawning black currents below.

Caitlin whimpered, tried to wipe the gore from her face. Then strong hands grabbed her, pulled her back from the brink. A moment later, she was clutching Jack Bauer.

"We have to move!" he cried.

More gunfire spattered the metal support beams around them. Jack pushed Caitlin along the catwalk, toward Astoria Park.

"We can't leave, Jack!" Caitlin cried. "Those men are going to shoot an airplane down."

"No they won't!"

To Caitlin's surprise, Jack pushed her onto the train tracks, forced her down on the wooden ties between the rails. "Stay here," he hissed. "And no matter what you hear, don't move."

She opened her mouth to protest, but Jack was already gone.

Jack ran back toward the missile launcher and the men clustered around it. He was stopped by a sustained stream of automatic weapon fire. Bullets twanged off the steel beams, eliciting sparks. Jack saw Taj at the tripod, aiming the missile launcher at the fast-darkening sky. The Afghani was mere seconds away from pulling the trigger.

He knew he had no hope of reaching the terrorists before the missile was fired. Nor could he get a clear shot—every time Jack tried to aim, his movements were met with a hail of bullets. Jack looked up, at the bridge supports rising over his head. He was searching for a way to get around the shooters, to flank them. Then he spied the electrical wires strung along the tracks.

Of course!

The trains that ran across Hell Gate Bridge were electric, not diesel-powered. Thousands of volts moved through those live wires. A second peek told Jack that the Afghanis were all standing on the steel catwalk. He jumped up, rolled across the railroad tracks to land on his back. Lying across the wooden ties, Jack aimed the .45 at the wires and emptied the magazine.

The wires didn't snap until he'd fired his last shot. Jack watched as the live wire dropped onto the catwalk. The blue flash was so bright, Jack had to shield his eyes. He smelled ozone and heard screams as thousands of volts coursed through the Afghanis, causing their bodies to jerk convulsively before they burst into flames. The tripod was also electrified, and carried the current to the Long Tooth missile launcher. One of the two missiles exploded in its tube, adding to the fiery chaos.

A moment later, the noise died away as safety breakers cut the power to the cables, and the span was once again plunged into darkness. Jack rose, ran along the tracks to Caitlin. The woman sat up at his approach, rubbed her eyes. Jack helped Caitlin to her feet.

"Oh god, Jack. Is it over?"

Jack opened his mouth to speak, then his eyes went wide. He pushed Caitlin to the side, and she heard two shots. She saw Jack fall, his gun discharging once as he went down. She whirled to find Frank Hensley behind her. The man's legs were braced, he clutched a weapon in his hand, but his eyes were clouded, and he seemed to sway in the wind.

Then Caitlin saw a hole in the center of Hensley's chest, the spreading stain. The man opened his mouth and black blood oozed out. Slowly, he sank to his knees, then pitched forward, sprawling across the tracks.

Caitlin heard a moan, saw Jack stumbling to his feet.

"Jack, are you hurt?"

"He clipped me, but I'm not dead yet."

Caitlin ran to him, draped Jack's good arm over her shoulder and wrapped her own arms around him.

"Let's get you to a doctor," she said.

"Don't need a doctor," grunted Jack. "What I need is a good night's sleep."

Arm in arm, they limped across the bridge, toward the distant shore.

EPILOGUE

After Jack Bauer wound up his part of the debriefing, the conference room was quiet for a long moment. Finally, Richard Walsh spoke. "Talk about Frank Hensley. Has your team come up with anything?"

Jack leaned back in his chair, finally relaxing now that the whole of this mission was out of him. "Hensley was a mole."

"Can't be, Jack. No mole could get past the FBI's screening process; their background checks are legendary."

Jack shook his head. "I had Nina contact the Pentagon, retrieve Hensley's military records. Tony went over it all, discovered that Hensley's pre-Iraqi records, including his fingerprints, had been tampered with— probably by another mole somewhere in the Pentagon. We went back even further, discovered that when Hensley was a teenager, he was fingerprinted for a security assistant's job at a local department store in Morgantown, West Virginia. We accessed those old prints and compared them with the fingerprints on file in the FBI's personnel office."

Jack met Walsh's incredulous stare. "The prints didn't match. The man who went to war in Desert Storm and the man who came back to America were not the same."

"999?" Walsh guessed.

Jack nodded. "The real Frank Hensley was a true war hero. He was captured by the Iraqi forces during Desert Storm and taken to Baghdad. We know that for a fact. What happened after that is speculation, but we suspect he was tortured and murdered by 999, Iraqi's secret special operations service. They likely extracted enough personal information from Hensley to replace him with one of their own. His parents were no longer living. Some plastic surgery and a standoffish attitude after the war would have helped him make the transition back into civilian life."

"But he had a wife?"

"Not until after the war. He met and married a woman whose father was a Federal judge. That alliance would have helped him into the FBI. Over the years, Hensley forged more alliances, and not with more judges. He began to make deals with the criminals he supposedly investigating. But the big payoff he promised Felix Tanner and Fiona Brice, the Lynch brothers and Dante Arete, it was all a lie. The plot to blow up airliners to extort money was really just a mask for Hensley's real mission to down the CDC airplane and unleash a pandemic on New York City and most likely the entire Northeastern seaboard. From what Caitlin told us about what she overheard, Taj and the Afghanis were in on the real plot, and were willing accomplices."

"And Dennis Spain, Senator Cheever's aide?"

"He disappeared. The FBI is looking for him,

but . . ." Jack turned his palms to the ceiling. "Nothing so far."

"And the Senator's in the clear?"

Jack frowned. "Not with me."

Walsh nodded. With thumb and forefinger he smoothed his walrus mustache. "And what about that anonymous tipster? The one who triggered this whole mission with the events at LAX? Ever get an ID?"

"That one was easy. A voice analysis of the tape message proved the man's identity conclusively—it was Georgi Timko. It seems Georgi's brother was a HIND helicopter pilot in Afghanistan during the Soviet occupation. His chopper was shot down by insurgents; Georgi's brother died in Afghan captivity. I guess Timko felt he had some unfinished business with Taj and his followers . . ."

"So it's over now?"

Jack shrugged. "Maybe. Maybe not. Time will tell."

Walsh switched the tape recorder off, signaling the end of the official debriefing. Jack rose, gathered the papers spread out across the table.

"One more thing," said Walsh. "The crap hit the fan so fast, we never came up with a name for this operation. Any thoughts?"

Jack nodded. "Call it Operation Hell Gate."

"Why?"

"The police never recovered the body of Griffin Lynch. A detective told me it was because of the unnatural turbulence under that railroad bridge."

Walsh blinked. "Excuse me?"

"There's a nexus beneath the bridge, a spot where the Harlem and East rivers merge with Long Island Sound to create riptides and deadly whirlpools powerful enough to swallow even the strongest swimmer. One urban legend says a World War Two Air Force bomber ditched under the bridge and vanished without a trace."

"Your point?"

Jack shrugged. "Arete's gang, the Afghanis, Griffin and Shamus Lynch, they were like those waters under the bridge, all had their own directions. It took Frank Hensley to bring the factions together into something devastatingly deadly. To bring them to one place."

"Hell Gate?" Walsh chewed on it for a minute. "Okay . . . good name." He pushed back from the table and unfolded his large frame to its full height. "Jack, I have to be straight with you. Nobody in Washington's gonna buy the connection to 999 . . . that Frank Hensley was a mole planted by Iraqi special ops."

"Why not?"

"Most likely reason . . . it'll make them look bad."

Jack swallowed his frustration.

"Either way," said Walsh, "the threat's been neutralized." He checked his watch then extended his hand. "Thanks, Jack."

Still distracted, Jack shook. "Sure. If you need any more information—"

"No, son. You misunderstood me." Walsh smiled. "*Thanks*, Jack."

THE GAME

INTERROGATE ENEMIES, USE MODERN DAY CTU TECHNOLOGY AND BEAT THE CLOCK TO SAVE THE DAY!

XPERIENCE "ONE OF THOSE DAYS" AS JACK BAUER

T INTEL AND ASSISTANCE FROM THE ENTIRE CTU TEAM

  PlayStation.2